Shifted

Shifted

The Changers Series

Kati Ward

Library of Congress Control Number: 2011909851
ISBN: Hardcover   978-1-4628-8803-0
              Softcover   978-1-4628-8804-7
              Ebook   978-1-4628-8805-4

To order additional copies of this book, contact:
Xlibris Corporation
1-888-795-4274
www.Xlibris.com
Orders@Xlibris.com
87451

DEDICATION

I would like to say a special thanks to Stephanie Legendre who held my hand through the entire writing process. I could always count on her to tell me exactly what she thought. I can remember numerous nights where she stayed up with me until 6am. Steph you were my rock. Also to Shanna Pierson, Candice Gibson, Jennifer Cuthbertson, Jaime Pierson and my Parents Margo and Andy Millar for there never ending support. Of course this book wouldn't be what it is if it hadn't been for the patience of my son Dawson and encouragement from the love of my life Ken Given. Thank you to anyone that was there for me. You all mean so much.

CONTENTS

PROLOGUE

I LOOKED AT THE clock on the bottom of my screen and realized, for the third time this week, I was working overtime. I clicked Save on all my open documents and collected my purse, keys, and coat to head home.

I passed the vending machine on the way out of the thirty-fourth-floor building I've come to think of as my second home and fed two dollars into the machine. As my Twix bar dropped into the bucket, I bent and grabbed it. I had the odd feeling I was being watched and quickly turned around to check my surroundings.

Alone on the floor as usual. My paranoia seemed to be getting worse in my old age. I recently turned twenty-five, and it dawned on me that I was a quarter of a century old. Not the best thing to realize when you are single and living in a one-bedroom apartment with a less than satisfying job.

I waved my "good nights" to the security guard manning the main floor; he gave me a curt nod and a half smile. Unfortunately, since I didn't own my own car, I had to walk to my building, which was fifteen blocks from the office. Twice a day, I had to make the horrible journey to and from home.

As I rounded Railway Avenue, I got the feeling I was being watched again. All the hairs on my arm and neck stood up. Strange, I walked this route every evening in the dark; it normally didn't faze me. Another quick glance around revealed once again that I was being a paranoid basket case.

I forged on, trying to concentrate on my upcoming holidays and plan what I was going to do when I didn't have to be at the office. Most people probably couldn't wait to get on holidays and go to the beach or camping or whatever it is that normal people did on their time off. Me, however, I didn't have much to look forward to.

I was raised in a foster home and bounced around until I was sixteen. At which time I landed a full-time job working in the evenings at a Starbucks for minimum wage, which was surprisingly enough to put me up in a very small, very dirty apartment until I graduated. So I didn't really have anyone to call family, and I worked too much to make many friends. The friends that I did have, I would call them more of acquaintances anyway.

The hairs on my neck rose again, and as I went to turn around for another quick glance, I ran face-first into a very large, very muscular chest. I let out an embarrassing shriek as the man looked down at me and smiled. "I'm so sorry, you scared me, I didn't realize there was anyone behind me," I apologized.

The man just looked at me, continuing to smile, not saying one word. Creepy. Again all of my hairs stood at attention.

"Well, have a good night, sir," I squeaked and turned to make a break for it, when I felt him grab the back of my shirt and toss me into the alley. My world faded to black.

CHAPTER 1

LILY

I STRUGGLED TO OPEN my eyes, but the pain shooting through my body made even that mundane task seem impossible. Lying there while the rain pounded down on my broken body was no better, so I tried once again to open my eyes.

I got a quick flash of the dark sky up ahead and realized that I must have been still lying in the alley where I was attacked. My mind was running crazy, trying to assess what parts of my body were injured and to what extent. However, it was the oddest feeling I have ever had. It wasn't a bruised-and-broken-bone feeling; it was more of a blood-burning-from-my-insides-out feeling.

After about twenty minutes of persistent trying, I got my eyes open. I stared at the sky for a few minutes before deciding that I had better try and move. The odds of someone finding me in the black alley and taking me to a hospital were slim. If I could just crawl to the street, surely someone would help me.

I started with trying to wiggle my fingers and toes to see if either arm or either leg were broken. It appeared I had nothing broken because I could move my extremities; it just caused agonizing pain. I tried for a good hour to move my body even an inch, but the pain was too much. I finally gave up and accepted my fate of dying alone in an alleyway. I closed my eyes again and let the unconsciousness take over.

When I awoke for the second time, it was daylight; however, the alley still seemed dark and taunting. I tried to call for help, but my throat didn't seem to be working. Had he crushed something vital in my throat? What else had he done to me? The pain in my body seemed to be fading slightly; however, I couldn't figure out how to work my voice box.

I tried to push myself up into a sitting position so I could get a better look around. Apparently, the pain ebbed enough to allow me to push up. I was left feeling completely exhausted from that small task and wanted nothing more than to lie down again. I glanced at the alleyway opening. It was so weird; I swear I could smell the people as they walked through the streets of Banff. Strange, I must have hit my head—extremely hard.

I tried again to call for help, but all that escaped was a strangled moaning sound, not even loud enough for someone to hear if they were ten feet from me.

I guess my only option was to attempt to stand up. It took what seemed like an hour to finally get myself in a semistanding position. Once achieved, I leaned on the building wall and struggled to catch my breath. Just as I began to feel like I had a small bit of energy and was convinced I would make it to the alley opening, the weirdest thing started to happen.

My hands began to feel as if they wanted to turn inside out. Stretching and bulging and tingling; it was almost a good feeling. When I looked down at them, they seemed to be contorting. Wow, I really was losing my mind. As I continued to watch, I saw my fingers begin to disappear. Or reform. Or shrivel? Brain damage was the only explanation that I could come up with.

Eventually, the weird contorting feeling spread throughout my whole body. Was that fur? What in god's name was happening to me? The best solution I could find was to close my eyes and hope someone found me before I lost my mind completely. Or had I already?

Somewhere between all the weird tingling and contorting, I dropped to the ground. Finally, everything stopped. I felt completely fine. I could feel my body lying on the cold ground, but there was no pain coursing through me anymore. Was I healed? Was it all a weird dream from hitting my head too hard? Was I dead?

I opened my eyes, and to my surprise, it was once again night. I glanced down at my body for a quick check to make sure everything was in physical order, but what I saw sucked the air from my lungs.

This wasn't my body. I realized I must still be dreaming, a weird dream where I was a dog or some other four-legged furry animal. This had to be the strangest dream I have ever had. I could feel my nose start to twitch and a hunger burn in my stomach. Did that happen in dreams? I pondered whether I had ever had a dream where I felt hungry before but came up with nothing.

I lay there stunned for a good while, hoping I would wake up. When I didn't, I decided I should get up and go exploring. I mean it's not every day I get to walk around like a dog.

I struggled to walk on four legs; the mechanics were all different, and my brain was having a heck of a time trying to organize which leg to move first. I finally caught the rhythm and headed toward the alley opening. I poked my head around the corner to see if anyone was nearby. I saw nobody, so I darted across the road into an alleyway that ran through to an open park.

Once in the park, my strange instincts took over, and I leapt into a full-out run. I even chased my own tail. I played for quite some time in this park, smelling, jumping, even trying out a pee.

Out of the corner of my eye, I saw a furry white blob dart past me. I could smell it. The thought revolted me, but at the same time, somewhere deep down, I wanted nothing more than to chase the rabbit and devour it. Gross.

So I did. I chased the rabbit for a while, playing really, until I tired of the game and pounced. My brain was telling me that what I was eating was a cute little bunny and how wrong it was, but at the same time, I had never tasted anything more delicious in my entire life.

Hours passed, and I was reluctant to leave the sanctuary of my park. I guess I was just trying to wait out the dream. Daytime came and daytime left, and my dream still continued. This had to be the longest dream I have ever had.

I was even beginning to consider reincarnation. Perhaps I died and I became an animal, and that was why I was not waking up.

As night fell again, I found a patch of trees and bushes and squeezed into the center trying to hide myself from anyone who may pass through the park during the night. I was now beginning to worry that whatever happened to me was permanent. I laid in thought for quite some time, trying to understand what exactly happened and what reasonable excuse there was that could explain how I got attacked in an alley and turned into a dog. What a strange predicament.

Eventually, I dozed off but not for long. I could smell someone, someone very close by, very, very close by. I peeked open my eyes and saw a shadow just to my right. Leaning up against a tree trunk was a man. He slowly opened his eyes and stared at me. I returned his stare but did not make a move.

"Hello, I'm Jack. I know you can understand me, and I'm here to help you," the man said in an almost whisper.

I tried to respond but let out a strangled gurgling growl noise. Instead, laughter filled my ears. Not mocking laughter but playful laughter, like you would laugh at your new puppy. That was exactly how it felt.

I glared at the man, or what I thought was glared. It probably just looked ridiculous.

"I know that none of this makes any sense to you, but if you would allow me to take you some place safe, then I could explain what is happening," he said.

My mind raced. Who was this man, and how did he know what was happening to me? Did he see what happened in the alley? I needed answers, and right now he was the closest thing to answers I was going to get. So I got to my feet.

He rose slowly as if not to startle me then turned and walked out of the tree sanctuary. I hesitated only for a few moments before catching up. We walked out of the park and straight to a parked car. I was getting more nervous by the second.

Was I making the right decision following this stranger into his vehicle?

At the moment, it seemed my only option. I certainly couldn't continue hiding out in the park for the rest of my life.

He opened the backdoor and waved me in. I jumped into the backseat and curled up. I could feel myself shaking but could get no control over it. He closed the door and walked around to the driver's side. We drove for so long that we were outside of Banff. I couldn't tell where we were, just that it was a very rural setting. He drove down a long driveway and up to a beautiful large old Victorian home. When he opened the backdoor to let me out, my nerves flared again and I couldn't find the courage to leave the vehicle.

After numerous minutes of coaxing me out like a stray dog, I finally gave in and followed the man. We entered the house, which strangely was a very abnormal feeling. Somehow I felt like a house was a completely suffocating and uncomfortable idea. The man led me into a large parlor filled with the warmth from the burning fireplace.

"Please lie down anywhere you feel comfortable. What I'm about to ask of you is going to be very difficult, but the more relaxed you are, the easier it will be," Jack said.

I lay down next to the fireplace and looked straight at the man.

"I know that you are probably wondering why you are a wolf and not yourself. However, I will explain that later. First thing I need you to do is change back. You need to listen to me and try to do exactly as I say. Relax all the muscles in your body, inhale and exhale deeply, and try not to worry about anything at the moment. I know that is hard, but I need you to do it."

I was so confused. What did he mean "change back"? And "wolf," not quite what I expected, but I went with it. I tried to do as he said but found the more I tried to clear my mind, the more I thought.

Finally, his soothing voice coaxed me into a relaxed state. Like being hypnotized I guess.

"Perfect, now I need you to concentrate on your human form, think about your paws turning into hands and feet. Think about what it felt like when you changed into a wolf, and imagine it changing back. The first change back is always the hardest. Keep focusing. I know that this sounds crazy, but you need to put all your energy and concentration into this," Jack said.

I tried to remember that strange feeling when I saw my fingers changing and tried to imagine it happening in reverse.

This went on for hours. I lay on the floor while Jack walked me through the "changing" process, but nothing seemed to happen. He was extremely persistent though and kept trying.

Something finally started to happen. I felt that tingle creep into my fingers for real and slowly make its way up my arms. I started to breath heavily. I could feel the breath rushing out of me. I could feel Jack grab my head to cushion it. When the feeling stopped and everything seemed to be normal, I opened my eyes.

I was lying with my head on Jack's lap, and I was human—and very naked. I jumped up in surprise, covering myself, and for the second time, Jack laughed at me. I stood there unsure of what to say or do.

"I'll go grab you something to wear, and then we can talk. I'll be right back." Jack left the parlor and returned in seconds with a fluffy white robe. I quickly wrapped it around myself and sat on the armchair nearest the fire.

I finally found my voice. "Where am I?" Of all the questions I had, that was the first to pop out of my mouth?

Jack sat on the couch opposite me. For minutes he just looked at me, then he said, "You were attacked four nights ago. The man that attacked you was what we call a shape-shifter. I realize that this is hard for you to believe, but you have seen the proof."

"How do you know?" Another stupid question fell out of me.

"I know because I am also a shifter. My name is Jack Cameron, and I am a member of a pack of wolf shifters.

I just stared. Did this guy think I was an idiot? More like some sort of weird cult. However, I did spend the last couple of days as a furry four-legged mammal, so was he really that far-fetched? I couldn't come up with a better explanation than his.

"So you're telling me that I got bit by a wolf and then turned into a wolf, and you know this because you are a wolf?" I asked.

"Yes, and I know that sounds crazy, but it is the truth. I realize in the human world this would be some sort of spooky myth told to children . . . for whatever reason. But most of the myths you are told have much truth to them." He looked at me with a concerned look and waited for my reply.

"Okay, so if what you're telling me is true, then what does that mean for me?" I asked. "I'm gonna turn into this 'wolf' all the time?"

Jack's concerned look turned to pity, and my heart dropped into my stomach.

"It means that the life you had as a human is over. I'm sorry." He looked down at the floor.

I snapped. I leapt from the chair so fast it startled him. I grabbed him by the throat and growled. "What do you mean my human life is over?" I realized what I was doing and released his throat.

Where did that come from? I was not a big woman, and I definitely was not a strong woman. Standing 5'9" and about 130 pounds didn't really give you much strength. But somehow I managed to pick up a grown man who stood at least 6'2" and hold him in the air by his neck. If turning into a wolf and back wasn't proof that something was different with me, then that definitely was.

"I'm sorry. I'm so confused right now. I don't understand what is going on." It was my turn to look at the floor. I could feel my eyes start to burn and then the hot tears start to stream down my face.

Jack just sat there and let me cry until I was finished. I looked up at him, and for the first time I realized how beautiful he was. He had the blackest hair I had ever seen. And his eyes. Oh, those eyes, one as blue as the ocean and the other as brown as chocolate.

His body was nicely toned, not overly ripply like a body builder's but chiseled like a surfer's. I realized I was staring and quickly looked away.

"I never got your name," he prompted.

"Lily. Lily Madsen," I quietly replied.

"Well, Lily, it's nice to meet you," Jack said

Jack spent the hour explaining that a wolf shifter had bitten me and that one of his pack members was tracking the rogue shifter when they saw me get attacked.

I wasn't the first person this shifter had attacked, and the other victims never survived; that is why the pack member, whose name I found out was Reagan, didn't stay to help me. Although when he returned to "clean up the evidence" so the human police wouldn't suspect anything, he saw me changing. Jack explained that they had to let the change fully happen before they could approach me because I may have reacted violently like any animal in pain.

Once they returned for me, they realized I was gone. That is when Jack tracked me to the park. Jack later explained that his pack members lived together sort of like living in a real pack and that they spent most of their time in human form.

"There are all sorts of different shape-shifters in the world. We are not like werewolves. We don't turn into half-animal, half-human form and terrorize people. We honestly don't know where we came from, just that we have been around as long as the human race, if not longer."

The grumble of my stomach stopped Jack in the middle of his explanation. Once again, I heard that laughter rumble from him.

"Someone sounds hungry. Shall we go to the kitchen and find something to eat?"

Jack put together a couple of sandwiches and grabbed a fruit tray from the fridge. I followed him back to the parlor carrying two cans of soda.

"So, Lily, how are you feeling?" Jack asked.

"I don't really know, Jack, this is a lot to take in. A week ago if you had told me there were such things as shape-shifters, I would have laughed in your face, but the more we talk, the more I realize I have no choice but to believe it. There must be some sort of explanation . . . like an experiment gone wrong . . . or some sort of genetic mutation brought on by some sort of chemical reaction—" Jack cut her off in midsentence.

"Lily, we are not some sort of science experiment. This is something that most of us were born with. We didn't take bad medication or eat the wrong foods. We are a race, just as humans are. That means it goes beyond the realms of normal and explainable. You need to accept that there are others in this world that don't necessarily live the same as humans." There was an underlying tone of irritation, but his face remained passive.

"If you say so, Jack. I just think that there may be an explanation. I'm sorry if I offended you," I apologized.

Jack looked at me with those heart-stopping eyes and replied, "Well then, how do you explain all the others?"

"Others?" I asked.

"Yes, Lil, the others . . . cougars, bears, coyotes, leopards, lynx, rabbit shifters, do you think they are all some sort of science experiment gone wrong too? I know that as a human, your mind automatically tries to explain away everything, which is actually a trait that helps our world go undetected.

"Humans only see what they want to see, and if they see something they don't understand, then they explain it away with simple science. There is a whole world out there that humans are completely oblivious to."

I had no reply. I mean, what could I say? Oh, okay, neato, lots of freaks out there, good times.

Clearly, that would not go over well, so I settled for giving him my stink eye.

"Look, you've had a long couple of days. Why don't I get you set up in a room, and you can get some rest," Jack offered.

"I want to go home, Jack. I've missed work, I have responsibilities. I need to get back to my life."

Jacks face filled with sorrow. "I wish I could take you home, but you're not ready. I can't send you home when you don't know how to control yourself. You have no choice but to give it up, Lil. Besides, you are a wolf shifter now, you should be with a pack.

"You're going to have to stay here. Don't worry about money, we will take care of you. You are one of us now," Jack said.

"So what, I have to quit my job? Get rid of my apartment? Move in with you? This is all happening a little fast for me. This isn't what I want, Jack. I need my life. I need to be normal again," I begged.

"Lil, I completely understand, but you just don't get it. You can't go to work. How do you think you would explain away spontaneously puffing into a not-so-cuddly one-hundred-pound wolf while talking on the phone at work?"

Well, I guess I never really thought about that. Hmm. "So you're telling me that I'm just gonna go through that at all times of the day? How am I ever supposed to do anything . . . ever?" I placed my face between my hands and sobbed.

I didn't want to talk anymore. I'm sure Jack could sense that because he looked away from me, remained that way for a few minutes, then left me alone in the parlor.

I lay by the fire in my soft white robe and thought. I thought about everything that Jack said. I thought about everything that I saw and felt. I thought about my job and my apartment and everything that I have worked so hard to get in my life.

I didn't know this man for more than a day, and he was telling me that I had to leave my life behind. That I had to move in with him? How was I supposed to react? What was I supposed to say? For the first time in my life, I had absolutely no idea what to do. All I could do was lie there and cry. Think and cry.

Then it began. I was alone sobbing uncontrollably when I felt the beginning tingles. Shit, where was Jack? I didn't want to be alone through this. I tried to call him, but just like the first time I changed, my voice box was empty.

Maybe if I thrashed and knocked something over, it would alert him. But I couldn't. I had no control, and this one was going fast. So much faster than my first change. Before I knew it, I was lying on the floor in my 'wolf' form panting heavily.

Great, now what? Should I bark? Did wolves bark? Maybe howl. Yes, I would attempt a howl.

I opened my mouth and attempted it; however, it is not working. I couldn't figure out how to make a howl. I felt like a baby trying to talk for the first time. I knew that I should be able to form a howl, but I just couldn't put my finger on the exact sequence.

As time passed, I started to get agitated. I never did well in confined spaces, and being a wolf in a confined space was even worse.

As my agitation grew, so did my temper. I couldn't lie there anymore. I needed to get out. The more I thought about it, the worse it got. All I could think of was getting out, *now*. My temper flared, and I began digging at the floor, knocking tables and lamps over; before I knew it, the entire parlor was destroyed. It didn't help. I frantically loped around the room.

The door creaked. I bolted for it. As it opened, I saw Jack, but only for a second as I blew past him and smashed through the entranceway window. Glass shards penetrated my skin and clung to my fur, but I didn't care. I was free.

Run, my brain told me, *and don't look back.* I ran until I couldn't run anymore and then finally collapsed of exhaustion.

CHAPTER 2

JACK

I T TOOK ME a few minutes to realize what had happened. I sat on the floor stunned. The force of Lily blowing past me knocked me over. She was way stronger than I initially realized. My mind started racing. *Get up and find her.* I couldn't understand why she was so important to me. I mean I realized that she was important to me because I needed to protect our secrecy; therefore, I needed to be concerned over her actions. However, those were not the feelings I was feeling the strongest. Honestly, I felt betrayed, hurt, and a bit rejected. Which was strange. I should not have had such emotional feelings toward someone I barely knew. I mean I would admit, Lily was a very beautiful woman with an explosive personality, but I was a mated man. I had been with Mayla as long as I could remember. That was how it was supposed to be. Or so I always thought, until now.

I quickly got to my feet and shook myself off just in time to realize that Duke, Mayla, and Reagan were all standing there staring between me and the broken entranceway window.

"What happened, Jack? Are you all right?" Mayla asked, genuinely concerned.

"Yes, I'm fine but Lily took off, I have to find her. Get this window fixed. Don't wait up for me," I screeched, not quite realizing why I was using such a rude tone with Mayla.

"Just let her go, Jack, she can learn the hard way like most of us did. It's not up to you to babysit her and make sure she behaves," she snapped back.

"Are you serious, Mayla? That's exactly what my job is. I'm going," I swore.

"I would have to agree with Jack on this one, Mayla, he is right. We can't let her run around by herself, try to jump right back into her old life. She will blow our cover, and it will ruin everything. There is no explaining how a woman pops into wolf form midworkday," Reagan said

"Ever since she was changed, that is all I hear about, Lily this, Lily that, and frankly, I'm getting sick of it. It's not like she is the only shifter in the world. You're acting like she is one of a kind and has to be absolutely babied. We all learned how to adapt. I've barely seen my mate in four days," Mayla snarked.

"Mayla, this is hardly the time for your insecurities. We are adults, let's start acting like it." I regretted it as soon as it was out of my mouth.

I couldn't quite explain it, but ever since the first time I laid eyes on Lily, it had not been the same between Mayla and me. I found myself avoiding her, snapping at her for no good reason. The thing was, Mayla and I met, and it just seemed the right thing to do was mate. I never took the time to fall in love with her; it always seemed it was something that would grow with time. I was not saying I didn't love her; I just was not sure if I was in love with her—or if I ever was.

It never seemed to bother me before. I never really was the love-seeking family man. My pack was all the family I would ever need. Babies were a far, far-off thought. I guess I was just comfortable with Mayla, and that always worked well for us. I've always known that Mayla was much more committed to this relationship than I was; however, leaving her was never really something that I considered either. Wolves often mated for life.

Mayla just stared at me with an expression I knew all too well—pure anger. Not the type of anger where your spouse wanted to throw some choice words your way or make you sleep on the couch, more like she wanted to kill you in your sleep or at least cut off a choice appendage. She did always have a horrible temper. Neither sounded overly fun to me. I knew an apology would be the right thing to do, but the truth was that I was enjoying this fight. It sounds stupid, but while we were fighting, I felt less guilty about having these strange thoughts and feelings about Lily.

Just thinking about Lily there brought me back to reality.

"Look, Mayla, like I said, don't wait up. I have to find her. I can't sit here fighting with you all night. Reagan, can you make sure the window gets fixed?" I asked.

"Consider it done, boss." Reagan had always referred to me as boss even though I was not a boss and more of a brother; it has always stuck.

I grabbed my shoes and took off out the door. I fully trusted my tracking skills even though several minutes had passed since Lily blew through the window and took off into the forest.

I picked up her wonderful sent instantly and stood there absorbing it for much longer than necessary. It veered off in the southwest direction, so I took off that way. It would be much faster for me to track her in my shifter form; however, if I shifted, I would lose my clothes. And something told me that being naked when I found her may not have been the best idea. My mind began to wander—her beautiful body and sensual lips. What I would do for one night inside of her.

I felt my pants get tight in the groin area. I knew I had to think about something else or I'd never find her. I couldn't get the picture of her perfect naked sweating body out of my mind. Maybe shifting would be in order after all; at least if I was in wolf form, I would be more focused on the hunt and not sex.

I quickly unrobed and piled my clothes next to a tree. I don't know why I always felt it necessary to fold my clothes. I rarely returned to collect them after a shift. Once I was completely naked, I got down on all fours and prepared for the shift. It was a lot more controlled for me than it was for Lily. I quickly induced the burn sensation and immediately felt the familiar oncoming change. It took about thirty seconds for the full shift to happen.

Once changed, I stood on all fours and shook out my forest-coated fur. It was an extremely liberating feeling to be in animal form.

My nose filled with her beautigul scent, and I took off in its direction. It took a good two hours for me to find her, completely naked, asleep beneath a tree. My heart started racing. I hid behind a tree and quickly shifted back to human. I slowly approached Lily. I was no fool; I realized she was not going to be overly excited to see me. As I got within five feet, she heard me and quickly sat up.

"What are you doing here? Why are you following me? Just leave me alone, Jack," she ordered.

"Lily, I can't do that, and you know it. The best place for you to be is with me." There was much more meaning in that sentence than she realized.

She looked at me with her beautiful eyes and flushed cheeks. I could tell that she was exhausted. Everything that she had been through in the last few days alone was tiring, not to mention the stress of her first few changes. I had an overpowering urge to touch her. I wasn't positive if I could stop myself. I wanted nothing more at that moment than to have her warm naked body pressed up against mine. I instantly felt myself get hard.

She began to tremble, clearly seeing my arousal. I slowly closed the distance between us and dropped down beside her. My heart started racing as I braced myself for rejection, but it never came.

I saw her nipples pebble, and I literally came undone, crushing my mouth to hers. My body swelled with desire, and gooseflesh spread across my skin as she trailed her fingers up and down my spine. Sexual tension was never a good thing for a shifter. Our animal side wanted to come out. I could feel that I was losing control, but in that moment I didn't care.

After what seemed like a lifetime, I pulled away from the kiss. She tasted so amazing; I needed more. I wanted to taste all of her. I had to. I looked into her beautiful eyes, sitting at half-mast, and her lips swollen from my kiss. I gently laid her back against the ground and dropped my face to her neck, inhaling the scent that was purely hers. My hand traced up her side until I found purchase on her left breast. It was a perfect fit. As if it was made for my hand.

"Jack," she whispered.

I slowly trailed my lips down her body and kissed the inside of her thigh. Her legs trembled, and she began to pant.

Being so close to her center was amazing. There was no denying that she was ready for me.

I slowly brought my mouth to her but didn't touch her. I wanted nothing more than to take her in my mouth and fully taste what she had to offer, but I wanted this moment to last forever. I opened my mouth millimeters from her beautiful skin and let the hot air touch her. She moaned again, and I loved it. I placed my tongue just barely on her swollen nub and licked gently. I needed more. I put my whole mouth on her and devoured her. My fingers prodded at her entrance, begging for acceptance, and just as they entered, I felt her clench as she threw back her head in climax.

I crawled up her trembling body and placed the head of my pulsing manhood at her opening. She was still clenching in aftershock. I pushed inside her and felt her folds invite me. She was tight. So tight and warm. I buried myself as deep as I could go and remained in that spot for a full minute until she lifted her hips in anticipation. I knew she'd be an animal in bed. I pulled all the way out and pushed back inside her. Her moaning was beyond sexy, but I wanted her to scream. I wanted to hear her scream. I rammed all the way in and continued a quick pace. Her breasts bounced beautifully, and I brought my face down to taste them. I could feel her muscles begin to clench around me, and I knew she was going to cum again, and I knew the minute she did I would too.

"Jack, I'm gonna—," she screamed, but her words were cut short as her body was sent into spasms of pleasure.

I buried myself as far as I could inside her and let out a growl as I filled her.

I heard someone clear her throat behind us.

Lily was staring behind me with a confused look on her face. I followed her line of vision to see no one other than Mayla staring at us. She must have followed me. She saw everything. I could see the red in her face. I knew this was not going to be pretty.

"What the fuck is going on here?" Mayla asked.

"Mayla, I'm sorry." It was the only response I could come up with.

"You're sorry? My mate just fucks some whore in the woods and he's sorry? And what do you have to say for yourself, you little tramp?" she yelled at Lily.

"Excuse me? Don't speak to me like that. You don't even know me. You know nothing about me . . . How dare you?" Lily said in defense.

Mayla raced toward Lily. She grabbed her by the throat and began to throttle her. Lily flailed. She was tough but nowhere near as tough as Mayla. Mayla had been a shifter her whole life and was well trained in combat. Lily clearly was not. I pounced on Mayla and tried to haul her off Lily. As I finally got a good grip on Mayla, she twisted and pulled a knife from her belt loop and slammed it into Lily's chest.

"You've ruined my life, you whore! You have taken everything from me!" Mayla yelled.

Lily screamed as the knife went hilt-deep into her flesh. I ripped Mayla off Lily and threw her into a nearby tree. She hit the ground and lay still.

I raced to Lily's side to assess the damage. Thankfully, she was stabbed close to her left shoulder. No permanent damage. She should begin to heal in no time. I turned around to see if Mayla was moving, and to my surprise, she was gone. I placed my body in front of Lily's and surveyed the area. I didn't see her anywhere.

I quickly realized that I had nothing to tie around her stab wound to stop the bleeding. I lifted her into my arms and began the hike back to the house. Thankfully, the trip would be quicker without trying to track someone!

We were about halfway home when I noticed the wound had finally sealed itself over. Thank god for our fast healing, or I feared Lily may have had lost too much blood on our travel home.

Lily had passed out in my arms, which was a blessing because everyone, human or shifter, healed best when they were asleep. I tried to carry her as smoothly as possible as not to disturb her.

We finally approached the house, and the dread of informing my pack what I did and what Mayla did set in. Would they blame me for Mayla's actions? Would they exile me for disrespecting my mate? These people had been my family my whole life, and I would have liked to hope they would understand; however, they had been Mayla's family as well. I guess the only way to find out was to find out.

I entered the house through the back door, which led into the kitchen and quietly passed through to the stairwell, where I carried Lily up to my bedroom and placed her on my bed. I raced back down to the kitchen to find the first aid kit.

Thankfully, as we were not human, we had all become very skilled at first aid. Some shifters had so much knowledge in the medical field that we could self-treat almost anything. I gratefully learned how to stitch at a very young age.

I cleaned the wound on Lily's chest and put nine stitches into it. Once it was stitched, I cleaned the area again and put a double layer of gauze over the top and left her to rest in my bed.

Now came the time to explain what happened to my pack. I straightened my shoulders and walked downstairs to the theater room where everyone usually hung out.

I was surprised to find everyone in there sitting patiently. They must have sensed that something was wrong and were waiting for our meeting.

I told them everything that happened. Leaving out nothing. As a pack, we were always honest with one another and accepted whatever consequence our actions may have lead to.

CHAPTER 3

LILY

I WOKE UP WITH the worst headache I've had in years. I thought about the events of last night, and for some odd reason, being stabbed wasn't the first picture in my head. It was Jack, naked. I felt my face blush and my blood boil.

I crawled out of bed and went into the en suite bathroom. My chest was bandaged where Mayla stabbed me; however, it did not hurt. I peeled back the bandage to see nothing but a slight red mark and counted nine pointless stitches. They clearly did not need to be there as the wound was clearly mended together and mostly healed over. Wow, talk about quick healing. Now if I could just shake this headache, I would be good as new.

After throwing my bandage in the garbage, I turned on the shower and let the water get hot. I couldn't remember ever needing a shower more in my life. I still had nothing to change into, so I crept back into the bedroom and rooted through Jack's closet. I found numerous pairs of female clothing and remembered what Mayla said just before she stabbed me. "My mate." Oh my god, it dawned on me for the first time why she stabbed me. She watched me screw her mate. That's just as bad as sleeping with somebody's husband. I couldn't believe I never thought about it before. I guess everything happened so fast that it didn't have time to really sink in. All of a sudden, I felt completely uneasy. I wasn't sure what to say to Jack when I would see him again.

Would he be mad at me because of the outcome of our encounter? I guess I should have been the one mad as he never told me he was mated to another woman. Although I was not sure if that would have stopped me.

I didn't think anything could have stopped what happened. It was as if it wasn't me controlling myself. Like something took over me.

Again I found myself remembering Jack and what he did to me. That was by far the most exhilarating sexual encounter I have ever had. And I prayed it would happen again. I could only hope that Jack felt the same way.

I wondered if he spoke to his pack yet—well, I guess our pack—about what happened. In a way I hoped he told them so that we could get this mess out of the way, but in another, it would have been completely embarrassing to meet them all after they knew what happened.

I pulled a blue T-shirt and a pair of grey sweatpants from the closet and took them to the bathroom with me. I let the hot water wash away my sins from the night before. It was so scalding hot; I could see my skin turning a slight shade of red.

As I dried myself off, I noticed my headache was gone. Thank God. I slipped into the sweatpants and Jack's T-shirt. If this situation was going to be permanent, then I was definitely going to need to get my clothes and necessities. Perhaps I would have Jack take me to my house today.

For the first time, my stomach didn't travel to my throat when I thought about staying. It actually quite appealed to me now. I mean, how bad could it be living in a house with the sexiest man alive? I could feel my anticipation to see him rising.

After brushing my teeth with my finger and pulling my hands through my hair, I opened the door to find my Jack. That was how I was planning on thinking of him from now on. My Jack. Screw Mayla; she was clearly psychotic. Jack clearly was attracted to me after the way he acted last night.

I searched the main floor and saw nobody. Where could everybody have been? I glanced outside in the backyard and saw a group of men sitting around an oversized deck table. Slowly I opened the door, hoping that Jack would be the first to notice me. He wasn't.

"Well, hello, little missy," said a blond-haired beefcake.

"Oh, Lily . . . morning. How are you feeling?" Jack stood up from his chair, looking completely awkward. Great.

"I actually feel great. I can't believe that I healed overnight," I replied just as awkwardly. Then instantly regretted it in case Jack had not told the pack what happened and they would be wondering what I had to heal from. Thankfully, nobody seemed to notice the remark other than Jack.

"That's great, so let me introduce you to the guys. This to the left is Duke Cline." Jack waved toward a rather large brunette with bulging muscles. He actually looked like he could crush me in one squeeze, but I guess most of the boys at that table appeared to be abnormally large.

"Hello." I nodded toward Duke. He smiled politely and followed through with a wink. Well, this was going to be fun. I didn't miss that fact that there were no females at the table, and I began to worry that Mayla had been the only female pack member.

"This is Reagan Smelt. He was the one who initially found you," Jack supplied. I glanced at Reagan, who appeared to be one of the more normal-sized males. I'd have put him no taller than six feet and 180 pounds. He was handsome in a strange way, with his brown hair and striking hazel eyes. His features on their own were sharp and angry looking, but when you looked at his face as a whole, it was strangely sweet. Well, that would have taken some getting used to. I smiled at Reagan, and he returned the gesture.

"This is Mike Mitchell." I glanced at Mike and took what felt like a lifetime to remove my eyes. He was beautiful. His body looked as if it had been chiseled in stone by a god. He had to be either 6'3" or 6'4"; it was hard to tell as he was sitting down, but the thing I couldn't take my eyes off was his white-blond hair and sea green eyes. I felt awkward when I realized that Jack was staring at me with intense eyes. I quickly nodded toward Mike and glanced away. I didn't even notice if he nodded back or not.

"And this is P. J. Ryker, but we all call him Jay." Now this man was strange; he definitely wasn't the biggest in the bunch, perhaps 6'2" at most and maybe 205 pounds, but he definitely was intimidating. He struck me as the tough guy in the crowd. Which was strange because Duke definitely had at least two inches on him, but just the way he carried himself warned you not to mess with him.

"This is Luke Blair, but we all call him Shorty. I'm sure you can see why." Luke's cheeks turned as red as his hair. He looked young, no more than eighteen, but I knew that wasn't the case. I didn't think any of these men were boys. Luke threw me a nervous smile and looked away. He seemed so different than the rest. He couldn't have been more than 5'11" and 160 pounds soaking wet. His hair was as red as a fire truck and eyes as brown as chocolate. This was a strange combination in and of itself. His eyes somewhat clashed with the color of his hair. It was akin to wearing orange and red together or something of the sort. "Hello, Luke," I said, hoping to ease some of his unnecessary unease.

"Hi" was all I got back.

"This here is Flynn Bell or 'Tank' if you wish," Jack continued. My eyes travelled to whom he was now introducing. I could see why they called him Tank. He was a little on the chubby side. But not the jiggly kind of chub, but the solid kind of chub. Like a giant beer belly. He looked as if he belonged in the mafia or perhaps the Hells Angels. It was definitely going to be difficult to live in the same house as all these giant intimidating men.

"And last but not least, this is Johnny Pierce." Wow, Johnny was also quite the looker. He had a head full of dusty blond hair and orange eyes. That may have sounded strange, but orange was the only color that came close to describing them. At first glance, you may have said light brown, but upon further inspection, you would notice they were not brown at all but a rustic orange color. They may have been the most interesting color of eyes I had ever seen.

"Hey there, cubby. Pleasure is mine." Johnny threw me a flash grin and glanced from my ankles all the way to my face in a slow and painful sweep of his head. It took me a minute to understand the nickname that he dropped on me. Cubby. He was clearly referring to me as a child of their species. I knew he was just trying to be friendly, but I couldn't help feeling a little insulted.

"Hello, it's nice to meet all of you," I offered in my sweet and innocent voice. Still not sure if they knew the whole story from the night before or not. I wasn't positive if Jack would tell them about our impromptu romp in the forest.

"Hear you had and interesting and tiresome evening, you must be exhausted." Johnny winked at me as he said it, and I instantly knew that Jack had told them everything. I felt my cheeks heat up as the embarrassment hit me like a ton of bricks. My god! I hoped they got the short version of the tale. I really didn't think that Jack would have gone far into detail with these men when he knew that I would have to face them at some point. But then again, I really didn't know anything about Jack at all. Just that he was a fantastic lover. I would actually have liked to learn that all over again. I felt my face get even hotter, but not from embarrassment this time.

"Lil, are you hungry? Why don't I help you fix something to eat in the kitchen?" Jack pushed himself out from around the table and slowly walked toward me. His eyes remained on mine the whole time, and I wondered if he was thinking what I was thinking.

Once we were alone in the kitchen, I anxiously waited for him to start the conversation. However, he remained completely silent as he rummaged through the refrigerator.

"So I take it you explained what happened to everyone?" It was left to me to start the conversation.

"Yes, I have explained the whole situation, and they have decided on a punishment for our actions," he offered.

"Our actions? We are being punished because I got stabbed. That hardly seems fair!" I felt instantly defensive. I didn't know what Jack ever saw in Mayla; she struck me as a chemically imbalanced nut job.

"Lily, we are not being punished because Mayla stabbed you and ran off. We are being punished for what we did together to set Mayla off."

Again I felt my cheeks flush but felt instantly better when I noticed the red tinge in his cheeks as well.

"Oh" was all I could muster.

"They have decided that since Mayla took off because of us, it is now our problem to find her and make sure she is not causing 'trouble,'" Jack said.

"Why do we need to find her? What kind of problems can she cause? Can't she take care of herself? I mean seriously, Jack. She stabbed me. She could have killed me. And now I have to chase after her and assuage her ego and calm her hissy fit. This is ridiculous. She is a grown-ass woman and she can take care of herself. And to be completely honest, if trouble does come her way, perhaps she deserves it. I mean really, just because she saw us . . . doing what we were doing does not give her the right to try to kill me. I didn't even know that you had a girlfriend." I could feel the anger in my voice. When I was pissed off, I could go on and on and on, but the grin on his face made me stop where I did.

"What about this is funny?" I snapped.

Jack let out an audible giggle that he tried to cover up with a cough.

"You are just extremely cute when you are mad. I'm sorry, I didn't mean to laugh, I just couldn't help it."

"Jack, this is serious. You want me to go chase after a lady whom I don't know at all except for the fact that she tried to kill me. And once we find her, then what? Am I supposed to hug her and tell her that I am sorry and to please come home? I will keep my paws—no pun intended—to myself? And that I pinkie swear that I won't have sex with her boyfriend ever again? It's complete bullshit, Jack." That goddamn grin was creeping back onto his face.

"Ahhhhh! You're impossible, Jack."

I turned out of the kitchen and stormed off to his bedroom. I wished that I had my own bedroom to storm off to as I couldn't exactly lock him out of his own room. But to my chagrin, he didn't follow me.

Now I felt like a complete idiot. Was I just gonna sit up here in his room all day? Like an idiot? This did not go as planned. He was supposed to follow me and apologize for being a jackass then take me back downstairs to eat. Damn, I was starving. I felt like my stomach was eating me from the inside out. I had never felt that hungry in my whole life.

Hours passed, and finally I couldn't stand it anymore, so I decided to sneak down to the kitchen and find some food. Unfortunately, all the guys were in the kitchen. I stood at the doorway and felt my face heat. Had Jack told them all that I had a hissy fit and stormed off? God, I hoped not.

"Hey there, lassie, hunger get the best of you?" asked Johnny.

My face got even hotter than before, and I stuttered over what to say that wouldn't make me sound like a pouty baby. Jack didn't even glance in my direction.

"I, uh, I just fell asleep. I guess I'm still tired from these last few days. I figured I should probably eat something."

"Well, make yourself at home. We aren't the most gracious of hosts. You will probably starve before you find us fussing over you. I mean, we may be shifters, but we are still just a bunch of men living in a big house together. Don't be shy." Johnny waved toward the fridge.

I felt completely awkward. Now that they were all watching and I had to go peek through the fridge. I had never felt more awkward in my life. I was also a little more than pissed that Jack would not even look at me. What the hell was his problem? I was the one who was supposed to be mad. Or did he think I was acting like a complete girl? Now I felt even more embarrassed. I hoped all the boys didn't know that he was now apparently mad at me. Whatever! I would just have to find something to eat and then retreat again. That started me wondering.

"So if I'm going to be staying here, is there a room or something that I will be able to use?" I asked anyone in general. I definitely didn't want to lock myself up in Jack's room again; I wanted to get far away from him.

Again, Johnny was the one to speak. "You bet we got a couple spare rooms upstairs, you can choose which one you want. Why don't you figure out what you want to eat, and when you are done, I will give you the grand tour." He winked at me.

"No. I will do it," Jack finally spoke and even looked in my direction. His voice did not seem mad but hesitant as if I may object.

"Fine!" was my only reply. I opened the fridge and grabbed some sandwich meat and some mustard. On the counter I found a loaf of bread and made a couple of sandwiches then grabbed an apple from the fruit bowl. Now what? I glanced at the table and noticed that there was a chair empty right beside Jack. Perfect, so I either had to go sit and eat beside him or retreat to his room looking like a complete idiot. I opted for the first option.

Jack stood as I walked to the empty spot. He pulled the chair out for me and then waited till I was sitting before he sat back down. Now I was beginning to feel like an ass for getting pissed at him. Jack had done nothing but try to help me since we met, and I jumped down his throat every chance that I got.

I scarfed down my food in record time then stood to wash my dish in the sink. The boys babbled and bickered the whole time that I ate about nothing in particular, just boy talk. Strangely, it was not as uncomfortable as I had thought it would be. They talked just as if I was not the new girl, more like they had known me forever.

As I dried off my dishes and put them back where I found them, Jack stood from his chair. I glanced back at him.

"I suppose we should get you a bedroom of your own. We should probable take a ride into town and get you some clothes as well." Jack eyed me from feet then back to face, and I remembered that I was wearing his clothes. My face heated again. How stupid did I look today? I show up downstairs wearing his clothing, screech at him, then lock myself in his bedroom all day.

"Yeah, sorry, my clothes were ruined, and I didn't know what else to do, so I borrowed these from you. Hope you don't mind," I apologized.

"Yeah, it's no problem, they look better on you anyway. I just figured you would like to have some choices and perhaps there are other things that you will need. We can get whatever would make you comfortable," he said.

"Look, Jack, about earlier, I'm really sorry, this is just all a little much for me. I mean a week ago, I had the plainest life ever. Now, I know nothing about myself and I have nobody. I guess I'm used to that part, but everything is completely unfamiliar to me, including myself. You'll have to forgive me when I snap like that. I just get so mad and you just always happen to be near, so I guess I take it out on you." I looked down at the floor.

"Lily, you don t have to apologize, I understand completely. I was being insensitive, and I'm sorry for that. It's just that there are so many things that you need to understand about our race before I can expect you to understand the urgency of finding Mayla. It has nothing to do with any of us trying to get her to come back. Unfortunately, with our race, things become much more complicated."

I looked at him as if to say "obviously," but he just continued talking.

"Mayla has betrayed her pack. Even though you don't really know Mayla, you are still a member of this pack whether she liked it or not. And she tried to kill you. No matter her reasons, the pack has agreed that she is a threat. Mayla has always struggled with her emotions. She is not the type of female that you can just apologize to and expect everything to go back to normal. She will never forgive us for what we did. I can't blame her for being angry. I mean I never should have done what I did, but . . ."

He stopped talking there, just let that word hang in the air. I felt strangely hurt. He regretted what happened between us. Well obviously, I mean I ruined his life. I show up, play damsel in distress, screw him in front of his mate, inducing her to attack me and therefore chase her from the pack and Jack, and now we had to find her. I was such an idiot to think that anything good could have come from this. Jack would never see me that way. I was nothing but a distraction to his life.

"Jack, let's just try and forget that ever happened. I will help you find Mayla and do whatever we need to do, but in the meantime, I am going to need to get clothes and personal effects. Let's just try to figure that out." I said it in a ruder voice than I intended.

"Sure" was all he said.

He led me down the hall and showed me three bedrooms that I had a choice from. I picked the biggest, clearly. It was actually quite cozy considering it was a house mainly filled with guys before I arrived. I didn't see Mayla as the cozy homemaker, so it must have been someone else's decorating skills that turned this house into what it was. Perhaps they had it professionally decorated, who knew.

We decided to head into town to get me clothes and personal products.

After filling in the guys as to where we were going, we headed out to the garage. Inside, Jack opened the passenger door for me on a fancy silver car. I wasn't sure what the make or model was, but it was a sporty little number, which told me these boys clearly had money. Big house, fancy cars, fridge filled with food. I figured it would have taken a couple thousand to feed the men in the house every month. The thought of food had my stomach growling.

Jack glanced over at me and smiled.

"Don't worry, supper should be cooked by the time we get home. Breakfast and lunch are kind of a free for all, but we always eat dinner as a group. Tonight, PJ is cooking. Lucky you, he is probably the best cook out of us all." Jack glanced back at the road.

"Oh, that sounds great," I replied.

I lead him up the front steps of my apartment building. As we were heading to my suite, I realized that I didn't have anything. I lost it all the night that I got attacked.

"Crap, we are gonna have to go to the front, I don't have any keys. Hopefully the doorman can get us a spare," I told Jack

"That's not a good idea, Lily. You shouldn't be talking to anyone. How about we just break the door and get what you need. I would feel better about that," he said.

"I'm pretty sure that we would draw a ton more attention to ourselves if we break down my door," I claimed.

"You are probably right. Well, let's try and make it quick. You haven't changed yet today, and I'm concerned just being out in public. I would prefer to grab your essentials then send the boys back to get everything else."

"Everything else? Do you mean like everything?" I asked

"Yeah, well, there is no point in leaving it here. They will ask you to clean it out when you tell them that you are moving. I thought I explained this all to you, Lily. You can't keep this apartment." He looked sad.

"I know that I can't keep the apartment, but what are we going to do with all of my stuff? I don't think it will all fit in that bedroom. Well, I guess most of it will, except for my couches and stuff," I said.

"Well, we could have the boys bring it all to the house, and then what you don't find necessary, we can have them take to the Goodwill," Jack suggested.

I can't believe we were talking about this so causally. It's not that I was overly attached to my apartment; it wasn't even that nice. It was simply that I felt like I was kissing away all of my independence.

I had had to work hard for everything that I had, and I guess it felt like it was all for nothing.

I and Jack rounded up all of my necessities using the new luggage that I bought myself two years ago at Christmas and had never used. I grabbed all of my clothing, which wasn't an overly excessive amount, my bathroom products, and the few pictures that I had around the apartment to take with me. Jack assured me that the guys would be by soon to pack up the rest of it. I wanted to tell Jack that it was pointless for them to load up all of my furniture as I would have nowhere to put it, but I couldn't bring myself to say get rid of it. I guess I would deal with that later.

Once we returned to the house and Jack opened the door, my senses were overwhelmed by the delicious smell wafting from the kitchen. My mouth instantly watered, and my stomach growled profusely. Jack glanced down at me with that little smirk that he always gave me, and for some reason, I instantly got butterflies. Crap, this was going to be difficult, living under the same roof as he was.

"Sounds as if you are a little hungry? Let's see how close supper is to being done."

"Yeah, I have been so hungry lately. I just can't seem to fill myself up."

"It's because of the change, your metabolism is a lot faster now than it used to be. You will get used to it."

"Well, at least it is because my metabolism is high, I don't have to worry about gaining too much weight from all the food I'm eating." My face strangely blushed as he glanced at me with a condescending look on his face.

"I don't think that is anything that you have ever had to worry about." His eyes traveled up and down my body until he realized that I was watching him and quickly turned away.

After that, the walk to the kitchen was quiet, neither one of us knowing quite what to say.

We walked into the kitchen to find supper was made and all the boys were gathering around the table to get started. Perfect timing. I decided to help set the table, feeling much more like I was attending a family dinner than eating with a group of males I never knew. Their personalities, while all very different, were all very welcoming and comforting, brother-like.

We sat around the table eating our meal of pot roast, mashed potatoes with gravy, and steamed vegetables. There was such an outrageous amount of food that you would think they were feeding a spread of thirty people, not nine of us. I was surprised to see that there was almost no food left once we were all finished. For the first time in days, I actually felt full.

I spent the next twenty minutes helping Reagan clean the kitchen and then retreated to the front door to haul my luggage up to my bedroom. Jack was already hauling everything up for me.

"Oh, Jack, you didn't have to do that, I could have gotten it," I said.

"No problem. It's all up there now. Why don't you make yourself at home and get some rest. Perhaps tomorrow we can talk about . . . uh, well, we will talk tomorrow." He quickly passed by me on the staircase and continued into the parlor.

I walked up to my room and began unpacking my belongings into the cherrywood wardrobe and matching dresser. I then opened what I thought was a closet to hang more articles of clothing and realized it was not a closet after all but a bathroom. Wow, I had never had an en suite in my life. It made me ponder just how big this house really was. I mean clearly, the master suite wouldn't be unclaimed; therefore, that meant that this was not the only bedroom with its own bathroom. I wondered how many of the boys had their own bathrooms. I knew that Jack did, but I guess I just presumed that that was the master suite.

I went into the bathroom and unpacked all my feminine products. The bath looked so inviting; I decided to soak in the tub. A nice book would have been a good way to take my mind off everything that had transpired in the last few days. I decided to go downstairs to the parlor and ask Jack if I could browse through the bookshelves.

I found him lying on the couch in the parlor reading a book himself.

"Hey, sorry to bust in on you, but I was just wondering if I could take a quick look through the bookshelf and perhaps borrow a book or two to keep myself occupied?" I asked from behind Jack.

"Absolutely, help yourself. Hopefully, you can find something you will enjoy. I'm really the only reader in the house, and my taste is someone directed more to the classics than anything new and exciting." He waved me toward the bookshelf.

I nodded my thanks and walked over to the wall with the massive built-in bookshelf.

"Wow, have you read all of these books? There are hundreds here."

"Yeah, well over the course of my life. I grew up in this house, so there has been years for the collection to grow. Not all of them are mine, a few have come from the others, but I think I have read all of them." He flashed me that sexy smile, making my stomach do flip-flops.

Wow, my butterflies just wouldn't seem to go away. It felt as if they were flowing into the rest of my body. I glanced away from Jack and back at the bookshelf. I figured that would help, but the tingling feeling just appeared to get worse. Uh-oh! Those were not butterflies. Oh my god, I knew that feeling. I started to panic and whipped toward Jack.

"Lily, what's wrong? You look like you have seen a ghost," Jack asked concerned.

"Jack" was all I could say.

He glanced down toward my hands and realized that I was going through another change. He leapt off the couch and ran to my side.

"Lily, it's okay. Don't panic, it is completely natural. You will tend to go through this quite often in the first year. Can you walk? Let's try and get you up to your room so you can change in private."

He took me by the hand and led me out of the parlor. We got halfway up the stairs when I had to stop because my legs were not working properly. The contorting was beginning, and I wasn't sure I was going to make it. Before I could say anything to Jack, he had me in his arms and was quickly walking the rest of the way to my room. I prayed the whole time that no one was in the hallway to see this.

Once we were inside my room, Jack laid me on my bed and began to retreat.

"Where are you going?" I asked with more urgency than necessary.

"I was going to give you some privacy, I know it can be a hard thing to try and change in front of someone. I just thought you might want to be alone," he said.

"Please don't leave me, Jack, I'm scared. I hate being alone when I change. Please stay with me till I change back. Don't leave me," I whined.

"I'll stay if you want me to," he replied.

I lay on my bed and let the change take over. The whole time, Jack lay beside me, rubbing my back then switching to behind my ears once I was fully changed. Some might have said it was a little strange lying on a bed with a man while he scratched behind your ears; however, I didn't ever remember feeling more relaxed. I fell asleep with Jack "petting" me.

When I awoke in the morning, Jack was gone and I was fully human again. I couldn't believe the change back never woke me. Strange. I crawled off my bed and began the day the same as yesterday, except I had my own clothes plus all my feminine necessities to make myself presentable. And that was my plan. I wanted to look great for Jack. He had never seen me the way I normally looked. From the day we met, I had been a complete mess. Well, not today.

CHAPTER 4

JACK

I BUSIED MYSELF IN the kitchen making breakfast for the boys and Lily, trying to keep my mind off her. What we shared last night felt so intimate. Mayla never wanted me around her during a change, and Lily wanted me there more than anything. Lying beside her last night did nothing to curb my feelings for her, which seemed to be getting stronger and stronger every day. I never knew these kinds of feelings actually existed. I mean, you read about love and romance in books and see it on TV, but it all seemed so made up, so blasé. You didn't ever expect that someone would walk into your life and literally consume it. I mean, I couldn't stop thinking about her, dreaming about her. I couldn't get enough of her.

Just thinking of her now made my mouth water. I had turned into an obsessed seventeen-year-old boy.

I added another pound of bacon to the frying pan and continued with the smorgasbord that would be consumed in ten seconds or less. I saw Johnny walk into the kitchen out of the corner of my eye.

"Smells good in here, Jack."

"Yeah, you look hungry," I replied.

"I noticed you weren't in your room last night," he said and followed it with a wink.

"Oh." was all I replied.

"I came by to see if you wanted to shoot a game of pool, noticed you weren't in your room. Had a good night, did ya?" He chuckled.

"Ya." I wanted to tell him how amazing my night actually was, but at the same time, he would take it wrong. He would never believe me if I told him I just lay beside Lily until we both fell asleep. Plus, to admit that just sleeping beside Lily made my night so great would make me sound like a complete tool. I used to make fun of the men in books and movies that seemed so controlled by how they felt for a woman. Now I was one of them. Great!

The conversation ended with Johnny flashing his boyish grin and yet another wink my way. I used to feel like me and Johnny had the most in common. I mean I always had Mayla, but I didn't necessarily spend that much time with her. I was content hanging with the boys drinking beer and playing pool. I guess I acted a lot more like a bachelor than a mated man, but Mayla never gave me too hard a time over it. Only when I looked at another woman or spoke to one would her temper flare, a temper that I knew all too well. She really did fit in with a bunch of males with high testosterone. There was not much feminine about her. Perhaps that's why I was never overly attracted to her.

"Morning," Duke mumbled in his sleepy stupor.

"Morning," I called back.

I noticed now that all the guys were sitting around the large table graciously awaiting the meal I was preparing.

"Just a few more minutes, guys," I said.

"Morning, guys." The voice made my heart pick up pace, and I could feel my palms get sweaty. I turned around to wish her good morning, but when I saw her, I felt like my breath was sucked out of my lungs. All I could do was stare.

She must have noticed my astonishment. "Jack, are you all right?" she asked with a smirk on her face.

"Oh . . . uh, yeah, great. How are you? Did you sleep well?" I quickly spat out and turned back to the stove to move the bacon from the pan to a bowl lined with paper towel.

I quickly snuck another glance at her when I took the platters full of food to the table. She was wearing a pink sundress that clung to her beautiful curves. I couldn't tear my eyes off her lower section. I never noticed before how amazing her legs were. They went on for days. Her hair hung in golden curls to the middle of her back. She had makeup on but not an overbearing amount; it really brought out the deep blue of her eyes. She looked absolutely beautiful. I wanted to comment on how great she looked, but I didn't want to make her feel uncomfortable in front of the guys.

Perhaps I could get some alone time with her later to run over "plans" for our hunt for Mayla. That would give me a good excuse to spend time with her.

I finished loading all the food onto the table and took a seat next to Lily in our spot.

I was beginning to feel completely natural to have her in the house. I should have felt a little out of sorts considering that the life I had known for the last few years came to an abrupt halt when Mayla took off and the regular routine flew out the window. But I wouldn't trade this new routine for anything. I woke up this morning with a whole new need for existence.

I was also going to have to try and work on change control with Lily sometime as well. She needed to learn to control her changes a lot better and find her triggers. At this rate, I would come up with an excuse to spend the entire day with her and perhaps the entire week.

We all ate in relative silence. I noticed every single one of the guys staring at Lily at one point or another. She seemed completely oblivious. I excused myself from the table when I finished eating and put my dish in the sink. There was no way I was doing dishes after cooking all morning. Someone else could take care of it.

I noticed Lily start a conversation with Johnny. He was going to be a problem. He always was good with the ladies, a real smooth talker.

"Lily, uh, when you're done, I thought we could run over some ideas for locating Mayla and perhaps spend some time on your control?" I asked feeling abnormally self-conscious.

"All right, Jack, I'll come find you when I'm ready," she said, clearly dismissing me to continue her conversation with Johnny. Crap.

I would have to have a talk with Johnny. I couldn't believe how much it bothered me to walk out of the kitchen and leave her there. I felt like I was handing her over to Johnny and all his charm.

I went into the study to busy myself with a book until Lily was ready to grace me with her presence. I really needed to get a handle on myself. This jealousy thing was not working out so great for me. It's also completely bizarre. I mean, I hardly know her.

My thoughts were distracted when the phone rang. I quickly crossed the room to answer it as we didn't associate with many people outside of our own pack, so when we got a phone call, it was usually important.

"Hi, Jack here," I answered.

"Jack, just the person I was looking for. It's Leo," the man replied.

"Leo, it's been a long time. How are you? How is the, uh . . . family?" I asked.

"They are all well, but, Jack, the reason I'm calling is because we have been concerned over some activity that your pack has been engaging in," he said in a solemn voice.

"I can assure you, Leo, we have been keeping very much to ourselves, we haven't so much as run in your territory. You know how we feel about your family, and we wish to remain close friends," I apologized, not really knowing what for but trying to keep the peace regardless.

"Well, we have been having some trouble in our area lately. Dead animals being left all over the place, and yesterday my niece came home saying that she saw a large wolf not five miles from my home. Also, Jack, I have to tell you we can smell your kind all over the place. So sent out my two brother to try and see what they could find, and do you know what they found, Jack?" he asked.

"No, Leo, I don't know," I responded, genuinely concerned.

"They saw that mate of yours, Megan or Mia or whatever, and she was not alone. She was sitting in the forest maybe three miles from my home, talking to a beast of a man. It was a pretty heated conversation too, Jack. I was concerned when the boys brought this news back to me because your name came up a few times, and apparently it was not good. Jack, I really need you to take care of this. I can't have hostile shifters running close to my home, not with Hunter. I worry about him and what could happen. We still aren't completely sure of his comprehension," he pled.

"Leo, I promise I will take care of this. Mayla has abandoned the pack, and she did not leave on good terms. We have made it a full-time job to find her and eliminate the issue. As for whom she is with, that is news to me. Did your brothers give you a description of the man other than that he was tall?" I asked.

"Well, they never gave me much to go on, just said he was a beast of a man with a nasty-looking scar stretching from his right eye to his left jaw. I hope that'll help, Jack. We will keep our eyes out, and if I spot them again, I will contact you immediately now that I know you are looking for them. Thanks again for your quick attention to this, you know how I worry about my son," he said in a sad voice.

"I completely understand, Leo. I will do everything in my power to fix this. Thanks again for the information, you have no idea how helpful you have been," I thanked.

"Take care, Jack," he said then disconnected.

This was not good. This was worse than I thought. I needed to speak to the pack right away.

I walked back into the kitchen hoping all the boys hadn't disappeared just yet. PJ, Luke, and Flynn loitered around the counter glancing at the newspaper. Johnny and Lily still sat at the table talking. I felt the jealousy rising in my throat and had to turn to focus back on the three boys by the counter to calm myself.

"Where did the rest of the guys go? I just got a call from Leo, and there is something we should all discuss as soon as possible."

"Uh, I think the boys went downstairs to shoot some pool. I will run down and get them up here. Why don't you throw another pot of coffee on Flynn?" PJ said then headed toward the basement.

"Everything all right?" Johnny asked with genuine concern on his face. I had to take two deep breaths before answering. Completely juvenile, I knew, but I couldn't help feeling completely irritated that he was sitting at the table with Lily, clearly trying to swoon her when he knew damn well I had my eye on her.

"I'll explain when everyone is here," I answered, trying to keep the irritation in my voice down to a minimal.

All the boys started piling into the kitchen and sitting back down in the chairs they were just sitting in eating breakfast.

Once everyone was sitting, I grabbed a cup of coffee, threw in a package of Sweet'n Low and a shot of milk, and then took a seat in my chair next to Lily.

"I just got off the phone with Leo," I said.

"Who is Leo?" Lily asked.

"Leo is a cougar shifter. He and his family live fifty miles south of us. Normally, we don't associate with other, uh, 'species,' but we have built a strong alliance with the cougars over the last twenty years. They live a little different than us in the sense that we have a pack. The size of our pack changes over time based on death and birth. Mayla was the only female werewolf that had been a part of our pack for a very, very long time. That is why there are no children. Most of us grew up together, and as such, we will always remain together as a pack until we die. That is the way of our kind." I stopped to take a drink of my coffee. All eyes remained on me, engrossed by my story.

"The cougars live as an actual family. There are eleven of them that all live in the same house. Leo and his wife, Cher, have three grown children—Trey, Luca, and Hunter. Leo's two brothers along with their wives and their two children live with them as well."

"Wow, eleven people in one house," Lily responded

"Well, it's not so different than here. I mean there are nine of us living here," I replied, holding her eyes longer than necessary.

"True. I guess I forget sometimes how many of us there are in this house. It surprisingly is so comfortable to live here with all of you." She blushed and looked down at the table.

"Not quite as comfortable as living here . . . I mean considering their oldest child hunter," Johnny threw in.

Lily glanced at him wonderingly.

"What's wrong with their oldest son?" she asked

"Hunter was born with a strange birth defect. Well, I guess it would be a defect," I answered.

"What kind of defect?"

"Well, it's sort of a long story, but the short of it is that he remains in his cougar form. He was not born human and has never shifted to human in his twenty-odd years of life."

"Oh my god, that is terrible. Is he purely an animal? I don't quite understand." Lily looked astonished.

"Well, when a female of our kind gives birth, she must be in her human form. It has always been that way as we mainly live as humans and think, as humans, it is only natural for us to be in our human form while giving birth. It's much easier to communicate that way. It had never been tested as far back as we can remember being done while a shifter was in their animal form. It just seemed very unnatural. As such, pregnant females try to refrain from shifting in their third trimester. Cher was pregnant with her first child. I don't know all the details, just that for some reason, she was in her cougar form when she gave birth to Hunter. When a child is born of our kind, they are born human, and as they hit puberty, the change happens. But while they are growing, they are taught what to expect and how to embrace the change. Everyone thought that Hunter would just be the opposite. Remain in his cougar form until he went into puberty, at which time he would be able to shift into a human. It never happened that way. Leo thinks it is because it is hard to communicate with Hunter. They were never able to teach him to shift or what to expect. Also, the aging cycles of a cougar are much different than that of a human. As they have no distinct age at which they hit 'puberty,' Leo thinks that there may be no real way for him to change."

"Does he think like a human? I mean, when I am in my wolf form, I still think as if I was me. I fully understand everything that is happening around me, I just have added urges," Lily said, face blushing while she stole a glance at me. A glance that set off a weird fluttering in my stomach.

"We can't be sure. He does seem to respond to them in an advanced manner. Like for instance, they will say 'Hunter, jump on the couch if you understand what we are saying,' and he will jump on the couch, but it is hard to be sure if he just associates words such as *couch* like a dog would *sit*. I personally believe that he is fully human on the inside, just unable to change," I answered.

"So they raise him like a pet?" Lily asked, disgusted.

"No, no, they fully try to incorporate him into the family, but I mean at the end of the day, he is a cougar. He can't necessarily eat dinner at the table with them and take his turn doing the dishes if you know what I mean," I said, feeling more defensive for my friend Leo than necessary.

"Oh" was her only reply

"They love him very much. It is very hard on Cher. She cries all the time from what Leo tells me. She feels like she let him down, like it was her fault for not shifting back in time to ensure his proper birth. They worry about him all the time. This brings me back to why I need to speak to everyone. Lily, do you have any more questions before I move on?" I asked before rudely dismissing her curiosity.

"No, go ahead Jack," she encouraged.

"Well, Leo phoned because they are having some trouble their way. Apparently, there have been numerous animals killed and left lying around without being properly disposed of." I ran them through what Leo's brothers and niece saw in there surrounding area.

"There is only one person we know that has a scar stretching across his face," Reagan responded once I was finished.

The look on Lily's face was enough to tell me she also knew who I was talking about.

"His name is Tony McKenna."

"Are you telling me that Mayla has hooked up with the man that attacked me? That turned me into this?" She motioned to her body with her hand. My gaze lingered on that body too long. Noticeably long. I felt that longing to be alone with her stir in my stomach. Finally, I tore my gaze away to answer her question.

"It appears that way. I have no idea how that happened or why she would associate herself with him. I don't even understand how she found him. We have been searching for him for months now, trying to eliminate the threat that he is," I answered.

"Who is he? Do you know much about him?" she asked, her eyes filled with horror. Obviously remembering the events from the night she saw him.

"Well, actually, that is also a very long story. Perhaps we have had enough for one day on that topic. I can understand if perhaps you would rather discuss something else right now, Lil," I offered.

"Jack, seriously. Don't you think that this is something that I should know considering we are looking for Mayla? Who just so happens to be associating with the person who ruined my life," she spat.

I tried to hide the hurt from my face. I knew that Lily would be upset for a while. I mean, she was ripped out of the only life that she knew and forced to live in our world. A world that hadn't been overly kind to her so far. I understand fully how she felt, and she had every reason to treat me that way, but a part of me always hoped that she would forget all that. Just enjoy her life here with us—with me. I had to try and accept the fact that she was not here of her own free will. No matter how bad I needed her or wanted her around, at the end of the day, she was only here because she had nowhere else to go. I had absolutely no idea what to say.

"Jack, I didn't mean it like that. I am completely grateful for everything that you all have done for me, and I am actually adapting pretty well. I just meant that I really thought that this was something I should know," she apologized.

Clearly, I didn't hide the hurt from my face fast enough. I knew she was easily guilted , and I felt bad for guilting her into an apology.

"No sweat, Lily, I completely understand," I quickly answered then stood to walk to the coffee pot to fill my cup again. I felt insanely uncomfortable with seven pairs of eyes burning a hole in the back of my head, waiting for me to continue. The real reason why I didn't want t explain to Lily about Tony was because I wasn't sure how she would react.

Tony also started out human just like Lily. The story surrounding his first change was not necessarily a story that I liked to tell. Our pack did what was necessary to protect ourselves. Unfortunately, we made a mistake, and now numerous people including Lily had paid for it. I knew that she had a right to know, but selfishly, I didn't want to give her a reason to think less of me.

"Well?" she prompted.

I slowly turned with my coffee in my hand and leaned on the counter, not ready to return to the table.

"Lily, the thing is . . . it's not exactly the most pleasant story. And I just feel like there are certain things about us that you will need to understand before I tell you about Tony," I said hesitantly.

"I'm listening. What is it that I need to understand?" she asked.

Johnny snorted, and I knew he was glad I was the one doing all the talking. The rest of the guys sat there in silence, clearly looking as uncomfortable as I was. We screwed up, and we all knew it. It wasn't exactly the easiest thing to confess.

"Look, Lil, the most important thing in our world is our secrecy. Above all else, we cannot let the human world find out about us. They are threatened by what they don't understand. If they ever found out that we existed, we would be eliminated just like any other threat to them. As such, we must do the same. We remain anonyms, but every now and again, someone gets nosy, they catch on to the weird group of people that live in the giant house in the middle of nowhere. They see weird things. You understand, I'm sure, that we cannot let that happen. Most things can be explained away, but Tony McKenna became a huge threat to our pack some years ago, and we were unable to avoid 'dealing' with him." It all came out in a rush. I felt my eyes drop to the floor, unwilling to see the look on her face.

"When you say 'couldn't avoid dealing with him,' you mean what exactly?" she asked, not seeming mad at all.

"Well, Tony was a human. He and his wife were ethologists. Meaning they studied animal behavior. They began their research not far from our house, which was a huge problem considering these are the forests we run in while in our animal form. We did our best to avoid them, but they came back day after day, month after month. It was as if they were specifically watching us. We began noticing human footprints around our house, in our yard. It was clear they knew more about us than was acceptable. Still, we did not want to take action unless absolutely necessary. It was about four months after they started watching us when they came across one of the pack members midchange. As humans, they couldn't believe what their eyes saw. To them it was an abomination. They wanted to destroy what they saw. I mean yes, they had their suspicions about us, but until they saw that, they had no proof. Now they could collect hairs, take them back to their lab, expose us completely. That was not something that we could let happen. The pack member that they walked up on completed his change and dealt with the humans posing the threat in the way that we were taught. They had to be destroyed to keep our family safe. There was nothing else that we could do." I glanced back up to Lily just in time to see her raise her hands to cover her mouth in horror.

I guessed I had better just get it all out. She was already disgusted with us. How much worse could it have gotten?

"It is not something that any of us like to think about. These were the first humans that we had to kill, and we did not take it lightly. No matter what you may think about us right now, we really are not heartless. It was a horrible thing that we will have to live with. Unfortunately, since we do not kill many humans, we screwed up. We thought they were both dead. We left the bodies in the forest, hoping that if the authorities found them, they would just assume they were attacked by wild animals. We found out more recently that Tony survived the attack but however, like you, became a shifter." I finished the story and turned to look out the kitchen window.

"Oh, Jack, that is horrible!" was her reply.

"I know. But there was nothing else we could do. So many lives would be at risk if they outed us. We couldn't risk it. I mean, it's not just us Lily. There are more families and packs and groups of shifters out there, and we all depend on one another to keep our secrets. Our mistake was not being

100 percent sure they were dead. We should have been more thorough. It was a lesson that we have been paying for months now."

Lily just looked at me as if waiting for me to continue. So I did.

"Tony has now been spending his time attacking humans within the city limits. Trying to make it look like there is a wolf problem. He is hoping that the humans will find it enough of a problem to come hunting for us. To destroy us or ones we love as we did to him. He knows that he would not stand a chance taking us on by himself, so he feels this is the only way to seek his revenge for what we did to him. The fact is, we don't blame him. Of course he would try to seek revenge on us. We killed his wife, left him for dead, and went on with our lives. But no matter how much we empathize with him, doesn't change the fact that he is attacking humans, killing them, or in your case, changing them. This is a big problem that we have to deal with. He will need to be destroyed. That is why we have been looking for him for the past few months. So we can kill him." There, I laid it all out for her. She could never fault me for not being honest with her. Brutally honest.

"Wow," she responded.

That was completely not the response that I had prepared myself for. The guys all looked at her as if she had ten heads.

"Sorry, I didn't know what else to say. It was a terribly sad story. I just need to absorb it for a while perhaps," she continued.

"Lily, you don't look so good. Maybe you should go lie down. You're a little pale." Johnny was looking at her with his concerned face. Douche. I was supposed to be the one comforting her. Telling her she needs to lie down.

"Yeah, that might be a good idea. It was a lot to take in. Jack, do you mind if we reschedule our discussions until tomorrow. I think I have heard all that I can for today. I'm going to go lie down. I'll see ya all around supper time maybe." And with that, she headed for the stairs to retire to her bedroom.

I knew what she must have been thinking about me. I knew that any chance I had with her just went out the window. I wanted to break something. I could feel the anger bubbling up my spine. It was time for me to change and perhaps go for a run in the forest to burn off some steam.

"Hey, I'm gonna go for a run. I haven't changed in a while. Now seems like a good time. I'll catch up with you all later, and we will finish this discussion." I didn't wait for any of them to respond. I pushed open the backdoor, flew off the deck, and fled into the sanctuary of the forest.

CHAPTER 5

LILY

I GLANCED OUT THE window to my bedroom just in time to see Jack rush into the trees of the surrounding forest.

My heart was racing after the information that Jack just dumped on me. I was having conflicting feelings toward this Tony McKenna. After Jack's story, I knew that I should have had enough compassion to feel sorry for the man. I knew all too well how terrible it was to wake up in the middle of the change and not know what was happening to you. To feel completely alone in the world and terrified as to what was happening. I could only imagine how much more horrible it would have been to wake up in the midst of that, only to find my spouse dead beside me. At any rate, I couldn't bring myself to feel sorry for the person that brutally attacked me in an alley and left me for dead.

I had to get out of that kitchen before the guys realized that I didn't share their guilt. I harbored way too much hatred for this Tony. I couldn't feel sorry for him, and I didn't want them to see my lack of compassion.

Jack would have thought I was such a terrible person if he knew that I was glad to hear they were still searching for Tony. I wanted him to be "destroyed" as Jack put it. I wanted to be the one to tear him apart.

I decided on a cold shower to calm my nerves before taking a rest or perhaps losing myself in a book.

I turned the water all the way to the right and let it run while I tossed a glance at the mirror. Crap, I forgot how long I spent doing my makeup and getting ready today. Maybe a shower was not the best idea. I walked back to the shower and turned the tap off, deciding to skip the shower and go right to my book.

I pulled the copy of *Pride and Prejudice* off my nightstand and flipped it open to where I dog-eared it.

As hard as I tried to get lost in the words, I couldn't. I kept thinking about Jack. The way he looked at me this morning when I walked into the kitchen. I had to put effort into making myself "presentable" every morning just so I could see that look on his face.

I instantly regretted throwing away our day together. I had the perfect reason to be with him, and what did I do? Panicked like a baby and ran to my room. I was just so unsure if I could hide how I really felt. Letting him know just how heartless I really was wouldn't help me get him. I could see the pain in Jack's eyes and hear it in his voice when he spoke about Tony. That pain would never be in my eyes for that man. I could never feel sorry for him like my pack did, and I was not sure if Jack would understand that. Retreating to my room was the best choice.

Finally, I felt like I was in better control of my emotions and prepared to face the guys again. If I couldn't put on my caring face, then I would just keep my mouth shut about the topic. Just let the boys hash it out. I would not risk letting Jack think of me as a monster.

I ran down the stairs, a little too eager to see Jack again. The kitchen was empty, and I figured I would check downstairs for the boys. Seven bodies filled the game room downstairs. My hungry eyes searched for the one face I wanted so badly to see, but it wasn't there.

"Hey."

"'Sup."

"Lily."

They greeted me in chorus.

"Hey, guys, have you seen Jack around? I was hoping we would work on my, uh, control before supper. I know how concerned about it he is." I felt my cheeks flame in embarrassment, hoping they didn't see right through my lame excuse.

"Uh, he went for a run a while ago. Hadn't shifted lately, thought he would get it in while you were resting," Reagan answered.

"Oh, all right. I guess I'll just go wait for him to come back," I answered feeling oddly shy.

"Why don't you hang down here with us? We are playing doubles, you can be with me. I've been sitting out since we had odd numbers. You're just in time to even them up," Johnny said with a wink.

I was beginning to feel a little uncomfortable with all the extra attention that Johnny was paying me. As harmless as it probably was, I just didn't like it. But not wanting to be rude, I smiled in agreement and took a seat in one of the plush lounge chairs to wait our turn.

"Hey, Lily, you want a beer?" Flynn asked.

I never was a beer drinker. Only could stand it if there was enough Clamato juice in it to cut the bitterness.

"No thanks, Flynn," I declined.

"Don't like beer, eh? How about something else? We got everything behind the bar. What do you drink?" he replied.

I glanced at the clock hanging on the wall. Whoa, it was quarter past five. I didn't know where the day went. It didn't feel like I spent it all in my room. Time flew when you're lost in your thoughts I guess. That meant Jack had been gone since this morning. It made me wonder if that was normal. Shifting and spending all day in animal form? Sounds too much like my first few days after I changed. Not something I wanted to repeat anytime soon. The least amount of time I could spend as a wolf, the better.

"Uh, do you have vodka?" I asked.

"Sure, like I said, we got everything. What do you want in it? 7-Up? Or straight?" he smirked at me.

"Ha, definitely with Seven. I don't drink much, so go easy on me." I smiled back.

"Oh, well then, I'll make it a double." He laughed.

Great! Not wanting to look like a total, um, girl, I accepted the drink and took a sip. Whew, it was definitely strong. I was going to get a good buzz off this drink for sure.

Finally, Johnny and I were up. We were playing against Duke and Mike. Apparently, they did not often leave the table. They were the reigning pool champions around here. It finally dawned on me that I was completely not good at pool and really wasn't even sure of the rules. Did I have to call all my shots? I didn't even know how to do that.

"I don't play pool much, maybe I should let someone else be your partner, Johnny, I'll just hold you back," I said.

"Nonsense, have you never heard of beginners' luck? Besides, nobody holds me back," he said following the comment again with a wink.

"Sure, uh . . . I'm not really sure how to call my shots though," I said, deciding to be completely honest.

"Don't worry about it, we will play flukes," he replied.

Luckily, we didn't do too bad on our first game. We only had two balls on the table when Mike sunk the winning ball. And so the next couple hours went. Before I knew it, I drank four double vodkas and was feeling pretty good. Well, pretty good might be putting it pretty lightly, but everyone seemed to be right there with me. Everyone except for Jack, who still hadn't returned from his run. None of the guys seemed concerned by this fact, so I didn't say anything.

Finally, I heard the backdoor open upstairs and knew it had to be Jack. I decided to wait downstairs and continue having fun with the guys until Jack came down to join us.

After ten minutes, the stairs finally creaked, letting me know that Jack was coming down. I quickly tried to smooth out my hair with my hand and run my fingers under my eyes, making sure there was no mascara lingering.

I was feeling pretty good until I saw the look on Jack's face. He looked miserable. We were all here having a great time, drinking, playing pool, and he was stressing about the new issues with Tony and Mayla. It seemed so unfair. I wanted him to relax, have fun with us.

"Hey, Jack," I said in my happiest voice, trying to lighten his mood.

He glanced at me, and the frown disappeared to make way for a smile.

"Hey, looks like you're all having fun," he said, all traces of angst gone from his face.

"Here, have a beer, Jack. Looks like you've had a long day. I'll sit out, you can partner with Lily. She's a terrible shot but pretty good at distracting the opposite team." Johnny tossed his pool cue to Jack, who seemed to glare at him.

I wondered about the relationship between Jack and Johnny. It seemed to me as if there were some issues between them. Perhaps they just got on each other's nerves the most. Well, to be honest, it only really seemed like Jack had a problem with Johnny, not so much the other way around.

"I'm not that bad," I said in defense, shooting Jack my sexy smile. Well, I hope it was my sexy smile. I guess I haven't really practiced my sexy smile in a while, not to mention I have had one too many drinks tonight. With my luck, it probably looked more like an impression of Quasimodo. I quickly looked away before any of them could see the heat filling my cheeks. I really needed to work on that.

"Yeah, sure . . . sounds good. Throw me a beer, Flynn," Jack said.

Jack was an amazing pool player, but from what the guys said, he didn't often play. It was nice to see him cut loose for a while.

Just after midnight, there were five of us left downstairs—Jack, Flynn, Reagan, Johnny, and myself. My stomach growled, reminding me that I hadn't eaten anything since breakfast.

"Sounds like you missed a few meals today," Jack said, glancing at my stomach.

"Yeah, I missed lunch, and I guess we kind of forgot about supper," I replied.

"What do you say we go raid the fridge," he offered.

"Sounds great to me!"

We said our "good nights" to the guys and headed up to the kitchen.

"How was your run today?" I asked him. Not really knowing if that was something you should ask another shifter. I was still so new to all of this.

"It was good. I just needed to clear my head. Just easier to think when I'm out running I guess," he answered, seeming a little uncomfortable.

"Good. My day was pretty uneventful until I joined the boys downstairs. They are definitely a bad influence on me. Especially Flynn. He made every one of my drinks a double." I laughed.

"Yeah, he can get a little excited when he gets to bartend for someone new. They all just love to have a good time. Never really did grow up I guess." He flashed me that sexy smile, and my knees went weak.

I pulled open the fridge, not feeling at all awkward. I really was beginning to feel at home here. I pushed a few things around in the fridge, looking for something to eat. I grabbed a package of Farmers sausage then hauled the freezer door open to pull out the bag of frozen perogies I noticed earlier.

"Perogies and sausage sound good?" I asked.

"Sounds great," he answered.

I cut eight of the sausages lengthwise and threw them into a large frying pan. Next I filled a pot with water, dumped some salt in it, and turned the burner on high. The whole while, I could feel Jack watching me. I stole a quick glance over my shoulder and saw him leaning against the counter nibbling on his bottom lip. He was beautiful.

I looked back to the pan and continued frying the sausages. Once the water was boiling, I threw in the whole bag of perogies.

We continued this way in complete silence while I waited for the perogies to float, telling me they were cooked. I rooted around for another frying pan to dump them into, finally finding one in the drawer under the stove. I flipped them into the pan and hauled an onion out of the pantry and began chopping it as quick as I could as not to let my eyes water.

"So did you shift today?" Jack asked out of nowhere.

"Uh, no, not since last night." It instantly brought back how wonderful last night seemed. I could get used to shifting if Jack would stay with me every time.

"Well, that is a good sign. Looks like you made it through twenty-four hours without shifting. That is great in your first year."

I spun so fast toward him that I almost dropped the plates I just pulled from the cupboard.

"Are you telling me that I'm going to shift every day of my life for at least a year?" I asked, irritated.

"Well, not necessarily, but most need to really concentrate in order to keep from shifting. Then again, I'm used to people going through the change due to puberty, not being bitten. I guess it could be different for you." He looked genuinely dumbfounded.

"I guess we will see," I said.

We filled our stomachs, not leaving a scrap of food uneaten. When we were finished, we both got up and took our dishes to the sink.

"Leave the dishes, I will do them. You must be exhausted, it's getting very late."

I wasn't tired at all, and I really didn't want this alone time with Jack to end.

"Actually, I slept most of the day," I lied.

"Oh, well, if you're not tired yet, I was going to head into the parlor and pop in a movie. Just relax a bit. You are more than welcome to join me."

My stomach filled with butterflies. The thought of watching a movie alone in the parlor with Jack was too much to pass up.

"I'd love to. Let me help you with the dishes, and we'll head in there," I said.

"Nah, I'll do the dishes in the morning. It won't hurt to leave them for one night." He looked me up and down then walked toward the door, motioning with his index finger for me to follow.

I stumbled after him, unable to contain my excitement. We walked into the parlor, and Jack closed the door behind us. The DVD rack was filled with so many movies that I didn't even know where to begin. To be completely honest, I didn't care if he put *The Little Mermaid* in as long as I got to spend more time with him.

"What do you want to watch?" he asked so casually, it made me wonder if my excitement over our alone time was misplaced. I really hoped he wasn't just being polite when he asked me to join him. Jack was so hard for me to read. Sometimes I felt like he was looking at me with longing in his eyes; other times he seemed so unfazed by my presence it was unnerving.

"It doesn't matter, I like everything. I'm a bit of an eclectic," I said just as casually as he asked.

"All right, well, why don't you just reach out and grab one, and whatever it is, we will watch." He smiled at me.

I reached toward the DVD rack not taking my eyes from his. He was staring deep into my baby blues and I back into his beautiful mismatched. I felt my heart rate accelerate. During our intense glare, I stopped paying attention to my reaching hand, which in turn knocked several movies off the rack, resulting in a shocking crash. Instantly we both looked away from each other toward the floor, where several DVDs now lay.

"I'm so sorry," I quickly apologized and bent to pick up the fallen DVDs. Jack bent at the same time as me to help me clean up the mess. Or so I thought until he grabbed my hand and lifted my chin with his other. I looked straight into those eyes again, our faces only inches apart. He slowly closed the distance and pressed his warm lips to mine.

His kiss started soft and warm but quickly got urgent and demanding. I needed more. It felt so right, like I was exactly where I was supposed to be. I let my hands trail up his muscular arms and rest behind his head. He pulled me closer until I was almost on top of him.

We sprawled across the floor making out like we were in tenth grade for about ten minutes before I started unbuttoning his deep-blue shirt. I could smell his musk, and it made my mind soar. I needed all of him. I wanted his clothes gone now, and mine.

I stumbled over the last few buttons, unable to get my fingers to work properly. I finally tore my mouth away from his, realizing I would need my eyes to get these dang buttons undone. Once free from his kiss and the spell he always seemed to hold over me, I quickly realized why I could not get his shirt open. My hands were changing, fingers no longer clearly there, instead receding into my hand, forming what I now knew as my paw. Yup, there was the distinct tingling feeling I never noticed while we were kissing. Could there have ever been worse timing? I looked up at Jack's face to see the horror I thought would be there. Instead he looked disappointed, about as disappointed as I felt.

"Jack, I . . . I'm sorry. I didn't realize . . . I didn't feel it start. I should have been paying more attention." My voice broke a little on the last word as my voice box began changing.

"Lily, don't worry. It's not something I expect you to control without practice." He threw me a half smile and moved a few feet away to give me room to change.

I had never been more irritated in my life or completely mortified. How embarrassing. Making out with a man you barely knew but had spent numerous hours dreaming of when your body starts morphing and growing hair. Sexy!

I lay there, no longer trying to talk as my voice box was no longer compatible with my voice.

"Looks like we definitely need to start working on your control . . . soon," he hissed, clearly disappointed.

He scooped my now wolf form up off the floor and carried me out of the parlor. I thought for sure he would take me to my room, which would end much like last night. He would stay with me until I fell asleep then leave. I would awake alone. But instead he carried me into his bedroom and laid me down on his bed then disappeared into his bathroom.

I spent the next few minutes trying to concentrate on shifting back, hoping to salvage some of this evening with Jack. The door to the bathroom opened, and Jack came out wearing a loose-fitting pair of gray sweats and no shirt.

It felt a little weird to be having these feelings while in animal form. He sauntered over to the bed and sprawled out beside me.

"Lil, I'm going to try and talk you out of this shift because I'm selfish and not ready for tonight to be over." He put his hand between my shoulder blades and scratched.

"All right, try to relax, try not to think about anything but your body. Remember the first time we did this? Try to do that."

It was hard to put everything out of my mind when Jack was sitting so close wearing no shirt. I tried anyway. The sooner I changed back, the sooner I could get on top of him. You would think that shifting into an animal would curb all romantic feelings, well, not for me. It made them worse.

After what felt like forever of Jack relaxing me and my intense concentration, I finally felt the now familiar tingle telling me the shift back had begun.

He continued caressing me between the shoulder blades while the change happened. It went quite quick this time.

As soon as I felt my human body again, I pounced. I pushed Jack flat on his back and crawled on top of him.

My animal instincts still raw, I needed to feel him and feel him now.

I pressed my mouth to the dip in his throat and rocked my hips, which were straddling him. A groan escaped his throat, and before I knew it, he had flipped me off him and onto my back. He wanted to be in control, and I wasn't going to argue. I had been waiting for this moment for days; ever since our romp in the forest, I couldn't wait for the next time.

He pressed himself between my legs. His rock-hard pleasure pressed into my inner thigh, making me squirm to align myself. Realizing he still had pants on and I was fully clothed, I whipped my dress over my head then yanked the bra from my chest, not caring if I ruined it. Jack grabbed my black lace panties and snapped them. Now all that was in the way were those damn grey sweats.

I couldn't even try to get them off; he was still braced over top of me. My arms would never reach to shove them down. Not wanting to break the mood by asking him kindly to take his pants off, I hooked both of my feet on the rim of his pants and shoved as far as I could. I think they made it to around his knees before he shifted and kicked them the rest of the way down.

His naked body knocked a strange growl from my throat. He looked at me with a hungry smirk then devoured my lips.

There was no foreplay this time. He went right for the kill, filling me as deep as he could. Over and over. There was nothing gentle or sweet about it.

I would have liked to say that we made love long into the night. However, that was just not the case. We were both too starved for it, too ready for it that it was over almost as fast as it began. Not to say it wasn't absolutely amazing.

"Lily, I can't seem to get enough of you," he whispered into my ear while we lay there.

I leaned in and kissed his forehead.

"I guess we know one of your triggers," he smirked.

"My triggers?" I asked, confused.

"Yeah, what sets you off," he said.

I felt my face heat. I guess I never had a guy talk dirty to me after sex. It seemed strange to hear him talking so casually about getting me off.

"Yeah, well I guess I know what gets you off too," I replied.

Understanding dawned on his face.

"Oh, Lil, I meant shifting. What triggers you to shift," he said looking as embarrassed as me.

Crap, how did I manage to keep humiliating myself in front of this man? Could I not act like a normal human being for more than ten consecutive seconds? The answer to that was easy. Of course not, I no longer was a normal human being.

"Oh, ha-ha, yeah, I knew that," I lied, trying to brush it off as a joke.

"Right, yeah. Well, we should get some sleep. We are gonna have a long day tomorrow, lots to discuss and work on."

"Okay," I reluctantly agreed.

"Well, good night, Lil." He leaned in, kissed me on the cheek, and then settled into the pillow.

"Night, Jack," I replied.

I prayed that when I woke up in the morning, Jack would be beside me. I didn't want to have another awkward day. I didn't know what any of this meant. Him sleeping in my bed one night, me sleeping in his bed the next. I wanted to think that this was an arrangement I should have gotten used to, but the truth was I wasn't sure. The kiss on the cheek threw me off. My parents used to kiss me on the cheek when I was a kid; it felt more like a kind gesture than a romantic one.

I quietly got up to go to the bathroom to clean myself up. I snagged my clothes off the floor on the way, not wanting Jack to think I was a slob, and headed into the bathroom.

I dropped my undergarments on the counter and quickly folded my dress into a square. I looked down and realized I must have grabbed one of Jack's shirts on the way. Oh god!

Those were my panties, stretched out like a frigging tent. I felt my face heat for the umpteenth time, realizing I had been lying on Jack's bed fully clothed like the big bad fucking wolf. Pink dress and all. How many more times was I going to humiliate myself in front of this man?

CHAPTER 6

JACK

I SNUCK A GLANCE back at the bed where Lily still lay sleeping. It was an intense feeling to see her lying there naked under my sheets, in my bed. I wanted nothing more than to wake up this way every morning.

I quickly finished grabbing my clothes from the closet and disappeared into the en suite for a quick shower. I planned to go downstairs and start breakfast as soon as I was out of the shower. The sooner breakfast was prepared, the sooner Lily could eat and then we could begin our day—together.

The hot water running down my face felt nice. It took everything I had not to stay in bed with Lily, but I wanted to get started as soon as possible.

I shut the taps off and quickly towel dried. Trying to be as quiet as possible so as not to wake her, I snuck a peek at myself in the mirror, ran my hands through my shaggy black hair, and brushed my teeth.

Coffee was the first priority on my list now that grooming was taken care of. It was quite late before Lily and I fell asleep last night. I really hoped that she didn't sleep too late.

I would have to remember to send a few of the guys into the city today to empty out her apartment. I guess Lily would need to take care of a few things as well before people started reporting her missing.

I whipped up a huge batch of pancake mix and started heating the pan. It seemed like I was the only person awake so far. Hopefully, the smell of coffee and breakfast would draw everyone to the kitchen.

The smell of bacon usually did the trick. I pulled open the freezer door and rooted around until I found four packs of bacon. They were frozen, so it would take a lot longer to fry than I cared for, but oh well.

Finally, there started to be some movement around the house. Duke was the first to enter the kitchen.

"You making breakfast again?" he asked.

"Yeah, I seem to be the first one up every morning lately," I replied.

"You have been up extra early every morning. What's that about? Can't sleep lately or what?" he asked seeming genuinely concerned.

I always liked Duke. He was the most levelheaded, relaxed one out of the whole bunch. The type that would never pry for gossip's sake but merely because he was truly concerned. If I didn't want to speak about something, he would be just fine with that.

"Eh, days just don't seem long enough anymore I guess," I sort of answered.

"Oh, I see. That wouldn't have anything to do with a certain female now, would it?" he asked with a smirk.

"It might." I winked at him

I knew he wouldn't ask anything further on the topic. Instead, he shot me a smile and walked right over to the frying pan to haul out a piece of bacon.

"You need some help? I'm feeling in the mood for some eggs. Why don't I whip them up while you finish with the pancakes?" he offered.

"Perfect."

Duke plugged in the electric frying pan and got to work on the eggs. The rest of the guys finally started to file into the kitchen. Letting their hunger get the best of them. A few grabbed coffees; others just sat right down at the table waiting for breakfast to be ready.

Duke and I started loading the table. I didn't know what to do about Lily. Would she be offended that we ate without her? Should I have woken her or let her sleep? Maybe I should have waited to eat until she woke up. Would that seem weird?

My pondering was futile as she walked into the kitchen just as I was heading to my chair.

"Morning, boys," she said.

They all stared at her. Hair tussled wildly about her face, clearly disheveled from the night before. She was wearing my white cotton bathrobe, who knew what underneath. She looked strangely beautiful. I mean she looked beautiful yesterday morning all dolled up and dressed up, but something about a woman wearing your bathrobe looking completely ravished was truly sexy. Clearly, the others thought so as well.

"Morning, Lil," I said, trying to break the strange silence. I guess they just weren't used to Lily acting so casual around them. She seemed to feel completely at ease this morning. Like she truly could give two craps what anyone thought of her. Like we were all just a great big family and she was just coming down for breakfast in her pajamas.

This thought conflicted with me for two reasons. One, did she not care what I thought of her? Was I merely just a play toy for her? Not that being Lily's play toy upset me, but it was clear that I was starting to develop feelings for her, and I guess I just hoped she felt the same way. Yesterday when she came down looking completely stunning, I thought that she had done it for my benefit. Perhaps I was wrong and she simply wanted to feel great after so long of not having her own things. Two, no part of me wanted to feel like I was Lily's family. Well, not in the brotherly way anyway.

I scooped food onto my plate, not really sure what all I was taking, completely lost in my thoughts.

"How'd ya sleep?" Johnny asked Lily. My blood boiled. I knew it was just a simple question, but why did he have to ask her with that smirk on his face. Like she was honored that he even spoke to her. Like he was some frigging gift to women. I realized I was glaring at him, so I quickly shoveled some food into my mouth and looked away.

"I had a wonderful sleep" was all she replied. It was strange. She didn't respond to him the way most females did. Then again, she wasn't most females.

My mind drifted off the thoughts of last night. Lily was the most beautiful I had ever seen. I didn't mean that she was the most beautiful woman in all of the world, but to me she was exactly right. Every person had their personal preference. Some liked big girls, some liked redheads, and some preferred brunettes with wooden legs. Well, every preference that I could have in a woman Lily possessed. I couldn't have handpicked a person more suited for me.

I hated the fact that Lily was ripped from her life and changed to what we were, especially considering the manner in which she was changed. It made me sick to think of what Tony did to her that night in the alley, but a small part of me was thankful to him for thrusting her into my life.

I brought the fork up to my mouth, noticing that it was empty, and glanced down at my plate. Hmm, not a trace of food left on it. Everyone at the table was staring at me like I was completely nuts. Made me ponder how long my food had been gone for. How many times did I put the fork in my mouth empty?

"Wow, don't know where my head is at today," I said trying to break the awkward silence.

"Yeah, earth to Jack," Reagan teased.

Lily shot me a half smile and continued eating. I excused myself from the table and dropped my plate into the sink, next to the dishes Lily and I used last night.

I had no intention of washing them. One of the guys could do it. It was someone else's turn.

"Hey, could a couple of you shot into town and unload Lily's apartment today? I would like to get all those loose ends tied up as soon as possible," I asked of no one in particular.

"Sure, me, Flynn, and Reagan were heading into town today anyway. We could shoot over there and pack it all," Duke offered.

"Great. Lily, when you're done eating, perhaps you should make some phone calls. Like to your landlord, tell him you're moving out. We will pay whatever required to break the lease, so no worries there. And I suppose you will also need to quit your job and call anyone else that would be otherwise worried over your disappearance," I said.

"Well, that should be easy enough. I don't really have anyone to call. Major lack of family and all. So I guess it's as simple as quitting my job and calling the landlord I guess."

"Perfect. I will feel much better when everything is dealt with," I said.

"Oh and, Duke, I really don't need most of the stuff in my apartment. Clearly, I will have no need for the furniture. I already have a bed here, and you guys clearly have enough furniture. Why not just donate all of the furniture and dishes and whatnot? Just bring back any personal items. That's all I need. Nothing I have has any sentimental value anyways," she said, despair written across her face.

"Oh, uh, you sure Lily? We got lots of room here for storage if you want to keep it all," Duke asked, clearly not feeling right about giving away all of her stuff.

"I'm sure. Seriously, if it's not something personal, I don't need it." she said, this time with a smile on her face clearly trying to reassure Duke that she really didn't mind.

"Well, all right. As long as you are sure," he said.

Finally, Lily got up from the table and dropped her dishes into the sink on top of mine, not showing any intention of doing the dishes. Sweet.

"So, Lil, once you are done with your phone calls, why don't you come find me, and we will get to work," I offered.

"Sounds great, Jack, this shouldn't take too long. Would you mind if I used the phone in the study? Just seems quieter there."

"Lily, you don't need to ask to do anything around here. What's ours is yours. This is your home now too. Please help yourself to anything."

"All right," she said simply.

She weaved between me and the counter heading toward the study. I was glad she was going to get these calls out of the way. One less thing to worry about.

I went back to my room and sprawled across the bed. Figured I would lose myself for a few minutes while she made her phone calls. Then as soon as she was done, we would get busy working on her shift control.

She seemed to already be doing quite well. I couldn't believe she already went twenty-four hours without shifting. I suppose it was closer to thirty hours when it finally happened, and I couldn't help but wonder if it would have happened at all if she had been alone.

A light rap at the door startled me out of my reverie.

I hopped off the bed and yanked open the door. There she stood now fully dressed and looking absolutely stunning. Her tight jeans hugged her legs in all the right places, and I could only imagine what it did for her ass. She had on a simple white T-shirt, but it also hugged her luscious curves.

Finally, I dragged my gaze back up to her face, where I noticed her flashing her coyest smile.

"Hey" was all I could muster.

"Hey," she shot back.

"How did the phone calls go?"

"They went all right. My office wasn't too impressed with the lack of notice, and not to mention the days that I have already missed without so much as a phone call. But it doesn't really matter, not like I'm going to be requiring a reference anytime soon."

"Yeah, I guess that is right. Still, I should have had you call days ago. I could have saved you the lecture if nothing else."

"Eh, it wasn't that bad. I also called the apartment and told the landlord that I would be moving out. He is leaving a key at the front desk for the boys. I gave him their names just to be safe. The bad part is that we will have to pay out my lease," she said.

"That's not a problem, Lil, whatever it is, we will take care of it. I'll let Duke know to deal with it while he is there."

"So am I just supposed to tell you when I need something? I mean, I really hate not having my own money. I wish I could contribute somehow, but clearly, working is out of the question. I don't really have any savings, but if we kept a tally of what I borrow, then I could pay you all back one day with interest," she offered.

I couldn't help but laugh.

"Lil, seriously. The only reason that you can't work is because you were changed into a shape-shifter. It's not like we just decided to give you a place to stay. You are part of this pack now. Whatever you need, we will supply it. There will be no paying back. We all use the same bank account. All of our money accumulates in there. Most of it was left to all of us. The pack has always been affluent, and we haven't had to bust our balls for it. So please, please don't feel like you are burdening us in any way. It truly is meant for the pack as a whole. We will get you a bank card of your own. Therefore, if you want or need something, you may get it yourself without having to ask. I realize as a female there may be things that you are not comfortable asking for." I looked away, realizing I was taking this conversation to a very weird place. Not a place I really wanted to be. Feminine products and whatever really was not my forte.

"Ha, okay, well, whatever works I guess," she replied, obviously feeling as completely discomfited as I was.

"So what do you say we work on your shifts? I think we should try to get a handle on that as much as possible before we start looking for Mayla, and I guess Tony. It would probably benefit you more if you could shift when needed and refrain from it when not."

"Sure. So where do we start. In here?" she asked gesturing toward my bedroom.

"Uh, nah, why don't we head down to the parlor? We can lock the door so no one interrupts us. Also, there is more room in there." I lied. The real reason was because I wouldn't be able to stay on topic with her sitting on my bed.

I stopped at Duke's room to fill him in on the key that would be waiting for him in the lobby of Lily's apartment before we headed downstairs to the parlor.

I flicked the fireplace on simply for the calming effect. I sat down on the floor next to it and motioned for Lily to follow. She sat a few feet away and looked into my face.

"All right, let's do this," she said seeming completely determined.

"Okay, well, I guess we should first talk about the triggers. What were you feeling the night I left you in the parlor? The night that you changed then bolted out the window? Were you angry? Scared? Both? Do you remember?" I asked.

"Oh, I remember. I was terrified. I remember feeling completely closed in. It was a horrible feeling being in the house the first few days after I was brought here. I guess I was used to being in the alley and then the park but always outside. Then you brought me here, told me outrageous, unbelievable stories, and left me in a room, alone and scared." She looked down at her knees while speaking.

"Lil, I'm so sorry. I didn't realize it would be like that for you. I guess I just thought you were angry. Angry with me, which I fully understood, it was a lot to take in and difficult to accept. If I would have known how terrified you were, I never would have left you there. It was not my intention to hurt you," I apologized.

"Oh, Jack, I'm not blaming you. It was not your fault at all. You were not the one who changed me, and all you have ever done is help me. You have been too kind, Jack."

I didn't know how to respond. I just sat there looking at her. Desperately wanting to take her back to my room but knowing damn well that we couldn't afford to not work on this now. Mayla was out their supposedly running with Tony, posing a threat to anyone and anything she was near. They both needed to be dealt with, and I certainly couldn't take Lily out there without having some sort of control.

"So, um, I guess we know that fear and claustrophobia could be triggers for you. Also, you seem to shift when you get, err . . . um, excited . . . in any way? Or is excited the right term?" I said uncomfortably.

"Uh, I guess you could call it that," she said, blushing uncontrollably. I loved that fact about her. She was so real. Not like Mayla who would never show a weakness such as embarrassment. It was unacceptable for her to show weakness in any way. It made her such a robot. I liked that Lily embarrassed herself and blushed when others embarrassed her. It made her who she was, and I wouldn't change it for the world.

"Good, so we know a few emotions that you should avoid while trying not to shift. In order to be able to control your emotions, you should have a balance thought. Something you can think of that will take away the fear or the excitement. For example, say you choose to think of a plunger. That should not excite you or frighten you as it is simply a plunger. So when you feel threatened, you need to try and clear your mind and picture only the plunger, visualize it as if it was really right in front of you. Pretend you are using the plunger if that helps." Her laugh made me stop.

"Really, Jack? Of all the things you could pick, you chose a plunger?" She continued to laugh.

"Okay, well it doesn't have to be a plunger, that was just an example. It can be whatever you want as long as it is completely nonfrightening and unexciting and something that you can easily picture. You should try working on this. Choose something to use, and then we will try a little test."

"Uh . . . it's hard on the spot. All I can picture now is the stupid plunger. And you were right, by the way. I see it in my mind, and I don't feel the least bit fearful . . . or excited." She laughed.

She sat directly in front of me with her legs crossed. I slowly placed my hand near her knee and moved it up her leg until it squeezed her inner thigh. I only knew of one way to truly excite her. I leaned in toward her and gently nipped her earlobe then moved my mouth to her neck. She inhaled sharply.

"How about now?" I asked in my cockiest voice.

"Uh, well . . . still not fearful . . . but perhaps a little excited," she said breathlessly.

"Lil, you need to concentrate. Picture the plunger. See if it takes it away."

I continued to bite and nibble her neck, slowly dragging my mouth down to her collarbone. I now had both hands on her thighs gripping hard. Her breathing was getting harder by the second, and it was driving me crazy. I was having to practice just as much control here as she was, if not more.

"Are you kidding me? Do you want me to picture a plunger every time you suck on my neck, Jack? Because I think our sex life will go straight down the toilet if that is the case. No pun intended."

"Not every time, just right now. It's the only emotion that I know I can work. Please, will you just try, Lil? Just picture the damn plunger."

She was silent for a few seconds. Face scrunched, clearly trying to picture the plunger. I tried to get control of myself. I didn't want her to picture the plunger either. I wanted to spend the afternoon naked with her. But I knew we needed to do this.

"Okay, I'm picturing the stupid plunger. Now what?" she asked, slightly irritated.

"All right, you need to keep the picture of the plunger in your mind. Keep visualizing it. I'm going to continue trying to excite you. If you start to feel the tingle of the shift, then you aren't picturing the plunger good enough. Got it?"

"Yeah, yeah . . . concentrate on plunger while you try to distract me. Got it."

She was so cute when she was irritated. I laid her out on the ground flat on her back. Slowly climbing on top of her. I lowered my mouth to hers and forced it open with my tongue. She resisted at first then let me in willingly, fully kissing back. I highly doubted she was still picturing the plunger. My suspicions were soon confirmed.

"Crap, the tingle stared," she said sounding quite disappointed with herself.

"Did you stop picturing the plunger?" I asked.

"Yes, Jack, of course I did. You stared kissing me. What was I supposed to do, picture myself kissing a plunger? Unacceptable. I pictured you," she said defensively.

"Lily, the point is to learn to stop the change. Now let it happen. Look at your hands." I pointed out that her fingertips were slightly distorted, telling me once again that she didn't notice the tingle right away. This could be harder than I thought.

"Okay . . . I get it. It just sucks. It is completely unfair. Why don't you let me suck on your earlobe and rub you down and tell me if you picture a plunger the whole time?"

"I already have a 'balance thought', thank you very much. I already know how to control my emotions and concentrate on something to stop a change if necessary. In fact, it is so easy now that I merely have to picture it once and the shift stops dead in its tracks. It will get easier for you as well. You're still just so young," I said.

"Please don't ever refer to me as 'just so young,' you make me feel like a child," she hissed.

"Lily, you know that is not what I meant. I meant young to this life. New if you will." I flashed my charming smile, trying to soften her. It appeared to work a little.

"So, Jack, what do you picture? What's your 'balance thought?'" she asked, clearly trying to change the subject.

"Nothing, it doesn't matter what I picture. We are working on your control right now, Lil, not mine. Stop stalling," I replied, not wanting to reveal my balance thought.

"Fine, let's do it again," she agreed.

CHAPTER 7

LILY

WHAT THE HELL was Jack thinking? Doing this to me? How did he ever expect this to work?

"Lily, try harder. Your hands are still shifting," he said.

Crap. Concentrate, Lily. Okay, wood-handled rubber plunger. Oh my god, his hands running up and down my thighs. Eh, plunger plunger plunger plunger plunger plunger.

Nope, not working, I could feel the change coming on harder now.

"Lily, if the plunger is not working, think of something else. Don't lose it," he whispered in my ear.

He was right. How was I ever going to be able to live if I couldn't control myself? I didn't want to have to go through this every time Jack made a move on me. I refused to let my shifts become our only form of foreplay.

I cleared my mind and fully tried to concentrate on something completely lackluster. Toasters, laminate flooring, toe jam. Anything I could think of to get my mind off the feel of Jack's body against mine.

"Lil, whatever you are doing, keep doing it, it's working. Your hands are shifting back," he encouraged.

So I tried harder, wanting nothing more than to please Jack. Pillowcase, laundry detergent, throw rug.

"Open your eyes, Lil, look at your hands," he said with a wide grin on his face.

"Ha, it stopped. I stopped it, Jack. I did it," I said quite pleased with myself.

"What were you thinking of?" he asked.

"Never you mind. If you can keep yours a secret, then I can mine."

"Oh, come on, Lil," he teased, shoving me lightly in the shoulder. "Don't be like that."

I quickly got up off the floor and started walking toward the door. Realizing it must have been close to lunch time by then and all this hard work was making me hungry.

"You first, Jack," I offered.

"Where do you think you are going?" he asked.

"I don't know about you, but I'm starving. I'm going to grab a sandwich. Would you like one, Jack?"

"Uh, sure. But hey, Lil, we aren't done here. So when the grub is ready, bring that cute butt back in here." He winked at me and my legs turned to Jell-O.

"If you're lucky." I winked back then flung the door open and left.

Wow, Jack and I never acted this way together. It always seemed a little ungainly between us. Not today. I actually felt like he was enjoying our time together. I was also. I would admit it was a little difficult but nonetheless enjoyable.

I threw together a few roast-beef sandwiches and grabbed a box of Oreos from the pantry. Casually, I walked back to the parlor.

When I opened the door, Jack rushed over to help me with the food, taking one of the plates and the box of Oreos from me.

"Thanks, Lil," he said.

"Yeah, no problem," I said not looking at him.

We didn't talk while we ate. Just sat there in silence, glancing at each other every now and again.

The way Jack looked at me did crazy things to my body.

His eyes appraising me in such a way. I wish I knew what he was thinking. I wanted to know how he felt about me. Today it seemed like he really enjoyed my company. But was that merely because he was getting a kick out of teasing me? Did he actually care for me?

The phone interrupted my thoughts. Jack crossed the room to the table the phone sat on.

"Jack here," he answered, eyes remaining on me.

"Oh, hello, Leo."

Leo—he was the person that informed him of Mayla and Tony in the first place. I wanted to know what was happening. Had he seen Mayla again?

"Yes, I understand," Jack replied to something Leo had said. "We will take care of it right away. I will send some out tonight. So don't be startled if there is an increase in wolf activity in your area."

I glanced at him, wondering if he meant to send the pack down there looking for Mayla and Tony. Wasn't this supposed to be my and Jack's problem?

"Absolutely. We will fix it. Where was the trail the strongest?"

Jack was now marking something down on a piece of paper.

"Thanks again, Leo. Take care." He said his good-byes and hung up the phone.

"What's going on?" I asked as soon as the receiver hit its cradle.

"Mayla and Tony are still in their area. I guess there are a few sent trails all leading to the same general area. Tonight me and a few of the guys will go check out the situation," he said gravely.

"What do you mean you and some of the guys? I thought that this was our job? You and I?" I asked feeling completely left out.

"Lily, I'm not taking you right now. I don't want you to get hurt. You are not ready for this," he explained.

"Are you kidding me? I have more of a reason than anyone else to go with you, Jack. They have both done something terrible to me. I want to be there. How can you take this away from me?" I begged.

"Lil, please, this is not a situation that you want to involve yourself with. It could get ugly. As you probably recall, Tony is a huge threat. He is ruthless and wants nothing more than to hurt us. I can't risk you being there. I just can't."

"Not a situation that I want to involve myself in? Are you serious? I'm the main person involved here. Tony changed me into what I am. Mayla stabbed me and took off because of what she saw us doing. How could you involve the others? Is it better to risk them for something that they are hardly involved in? I should be there, Jack."

"No. The guys are trained for this. They know how to fight if they need to. You don't, Lily. It would be irresponsible for me to take you," he said.

"Oh, so it's just your choice is it? What if I don't want to listen to you? Who died and made you king of the frigging universe? You are not the boss, Jack, and if I want to go, I will go, and you can't stop me. We are a pack, and I will be beside my pack where I belong."

"No." was his simple answer.

"There came the tingle. And this time I didn't want to stop it. I quickly pulled the door to the parlor open and ran out before I changed completely. I ran straight into the kitchen and shoved open the backdoor, leaping off the deck just as my body wretched into the shift.

I landed on all fours and kept running. I would go with them tonight. If Jack didn't want me there, then too bad. He would just have to deal with it. I would lie if I had to and follow afterward.

I ran through the trees feeling the wind on my face. I caught the scent of a rabbit; my mouth watered. It seemed like it had been years since I was actually outside during a shift. The last time I was outside during a shift was when I took off and Mayla found me and Jack.

I didn't want to think about that right now. I just wanted to feel free. To just run and let my instincts take over. I toyed with the rabbit for a while before tiring of him. I wasn't overly interested in eating him right now, and I wondered if that was for the fact that I had just eaten in my human form.

It seemed like hours had passed, and I wasn't ready to go back yet. I wondered if I should just remain out here in my wolf form until they left. It would be easiest for me to follow them if I was already shifted, and I wouldn't have to worry about not being able to change once we were there.

It was a big decision. Perhaps I should have tried working on the shifting thing. Try shifting back then see if I could return to my wolf form.

I decided that I should work on it. Lying down on the ground, I focused on the memory of Jack's voice. Calming me down, trying to talk me out of a shift. I could do this. I didn't need anyone else to help me. I would figure this out on my own.

I pictured his beautiful face, his hands scratching between my shoulder blades, his soothing voice.

After only about five minutes, I felt it working. I had really done it. I lay there letting the full change happen. Letting my body fully return to its human form before I moved on to the next step, the more difficult step.

I had always eventually shifted back whether it was in my sleep or Jack helping me. But I had never shifted into wolf because I had wanted to. I never had actually tried to shift to wolf before. I realized this was definitely a lesson I would need to learn right away.

I guess it was luck in the sense that I knew what my main triggers were. The trouble was that I couldn't just frighten myself or excite myself, not in the way Jack did anyway. Another problem with this was the fact that the excitement only seemed to work once. I was fully able to control myself after my shift last night, and the night Mayla stabbed me, I had shifted prior to me and Jack romping.

Maybe my shifts couldn't be too close together. Did I need to wait a certain amount of time between them? There was so much I needed to know, but there was no one to ask.

I resolved to simply try. I would think of everything I possibly could to trigger it. The way I felt in the alley, how terrified I was, all alone and paralyzed. The night I was locked in the parlor. And finally how I felt when I was with jack.

Nothing seemed to be happening, but I refused to give up. I needed to do this. I needed to learn; I wanted to learn.

So I continued, thought harder, imagining exactly how everything felt, every emotion. Finally, after what seemed like close to an hour, I felt something. It started out as a subtle tingling in my fingertips but flared through my whole body within a matter of seconds. I couldn't believe how intense the feeling had become, and then before I knew it, it was over. I struggled to focus on myself, realizing that I shifted in about thirty seconds flat.

I couldn't grasp the meaning of that. Jack said it would get easier, but I never imagined it would be that easy. I never got off the ground, having absolutely no intention of running as a wolf. I had work to do and lots of it. Practice makes perfect. I would do this over and over and over, all evening if I had to, until I could do it with ease.

The shifts came quicker after that. The more I did it, the faster they happened. Within the next three hours, I shifted back and forth for what felt like twenty times. I would have continued if I wasn't so starving. I decided it was time to head back to the house. I would find out the guys' plan for tonight, act like I was going along with the plan for me to stay behind, then I would follow them. Completely unwilling to miss it.

As I broke through the trees heading toward the back deck, I saw him. Jack was standing with his arms crossed looking straight at me. Clearly waiting for me to return. How long had he been standing there?

I climbed up the deck and made eye contact with Jack.

"What?" I snapped.

"Do you know how worried I have been, Lil? You were gone for so long. I know that you are mad at me, but I hate when you take off like that. The guys had to spend their afternoon convincing me not to come after you." He looked terrible.

"Oh, so it's not okay for me to shift and run in the forest for a few hours, but it's okay for your to do it and be gone all day? You're such a hypocrite, Jack." I walked right past him, not wanting to continue this conversation. I was still mad at him.

"That's different, Lily. I know these forests. I know how to take care of myself. I have been a shifter my entire life." He snapped back.

"I can take care of myself, Jack. I don't need you to babysit me anymore." I threw open the door to the kitchen and walked in, noticing the guys standing near the open window clearly listening to our conversation.

"Er, uh, hey, Lily," Reagan greeted.

I just looked at them standing there trying to look so innocent. It irritated me that they were eavesdropping. Eh, just like real brothers. I didn't want to talk to any of them; I just wanted to retreat to my room and ignore the world. But I knew that if I didn't talk to anyone, I would never get the scoop on their plans for the evening.

"Hey, guys," I said in my most pleasant voice.

"We got your stuff today, put everything in your room, everything except for the furniture, which we gave to goodwill," Duke said in a deep, calm voice.

"Thanks," I said. "So I guess you all get to go on the trip with Jack? I asked as casually as I could muster.

"Nope, not all of us. Don't worry, Lily, you're not the only one being left out. You should be happy that Jack didn't include you, it might not be pretty. Not something you would want to see," Flynn offered.

"So how many of you are going?" I asked

"Jack said he is taking me, Johnny, Duke, PJ, and Mike. Luke and Reagan will stay here with you," Flynn offered.

"Jack said, eh? Does he always get to make the rules? Do you have no brains of your own?" I asked a little ruder then I intended.

I noticed them all looking among one another, clearly not saying something.

"What?" I asked

"Lily, we listen to Jack because he is our alpha. He is the boss. As much as he likes to deny it and say that he is nothing more than our brother, nature has branded him our alpha, and we all accept that. He is the best suited for the role, he makes the decisions that benefit us. He is the one inside trying to protect our pack while we are all in the basement acting like a bunch of teenagers. He is the responsible one, and we trust him," Mike said in a serious tone.

"Alpha, eh? Why didn't he ever say anything? Why was I never told of this? Don't you think I should have been informed that he was the boss?" I was getting more irritated by the second. I was mad at Jack for keeping that piece of information from me. I was irritated at myself for sleeping with the boss. I was irritated at everything.

"He doesn't think of himself that way, he won't even refer to himself as the alpha," Mike answered.

"Really, well he sure does a good job of bossing people around."

"Lily, try not to be so hard on him. He has to make a lot of difficult decisions, and it can't be easy for him. I know he never wanted to hurt you. Contrary to what you believe, he really cares about you," Mike said in a low voice as if scared Jack would hear him.

His comment faltered my anger. It set off a weird sequence of flutters in the pit of my stomach. Jack cared about me, and even the guys knew it. Not wanting to look like a lovesick girl, I just nodded one stiff nod.

Finally, Jack came in. He just glanced at us then walked straight past heading out of the kitchen. It maddened me. What was his problem? I was supposed to be the one mad, not him.

I followed him. Making every step I took just a little louder than necessary. He didn't so much as turn around to look at me. He just kept going, heading straight up the stairs to his bedroom.

He closed the door behind him. Leaving me standing in the hallway alone.

That was not going to happen. I grabbed the handle, thankfully finding it unlocked, and pulled it open. He was sitting on the edge of his bed with his face in his hands. The sight broke my heart. I instantly forgot what I was mad about, wanting nothing more than to comfort him.

After a few silent seconds, he lifted his face and looked at me. He looked so tortured. Was this my fault? What could possibly have had him this upset?

"Jack, what is it?" I asked, voice filled with concern.

"It's nothing for you to worry about, Lil. I'm fine, I just need to relax for a little while before we take off. I'll need all the strength I can get tonight," he answered, obviously trying to assuage my concern.

I realized what he must have been upset about. He was heading out to kill the only woman he had ever loved. His mate, his lover—Mayla. That couldn't be easy for him. I was right; I did do this to him. I ruined what he and Mayla had, and now he had to resort to this—to hunting her like an animal and destroying her. I felt so unbelievably guilty.

"Oh, Jack, I'm so sorry. I never meant for any of this to happen. If I could take it back, all of it, I would." My voice broke and I could feel my eyes filling with the traitorous tears.

"Lily, stop. Why are you crying? This is not your fault. I didn't want to fight, Lily. I just really couldn't stomach the thought of you coming tonight. I would not be able to concentrate knowing you were there. I would worry so much. It would kill me if something were to happen to you, Lil." He said it with such emotion, it made my eyes burn—worse, filling up with more tears.

He was upset because I was mad at him. Not because they were going out to hunt his mate. The thought was so overwhelming. There was no way I could stay behind now. Knowing how dangerous he obviously thought this quest would be. I would not survive sitting there worrying about them, worrying about Jack. I would be there, ready to help if I had to. I would not let him do this without me. I couldn't let him risk his life and the lives of our pack over problems that I created. I just couldn't.

"I understand," I lied.

He looked at me with such gratitude; it almost made me change my mind. Almost. He wanted so badly for me to be safe. Well, as far as he had to know, I would be. I would stay far enough behind them that they would never even know I was there. I would only make my presence known if absolutely necessary, if they absolutely needed my help.

Jack and I curled up on his bed, spending as much time with each other as possible before he had to leave. When the time came, we headed downstairs so he and the boys could prepare.

Jack ran them through the plan, explaining what Leo had told him earlier today. He described the spot where their scent was the strongest.

Finally, the time came. Jack surprised me by grabbing my arm and pulling me into his warm embrace. He leaned down and kissed me, right in front of everyone, not caring what they thought. It sent my mind reeling. He eventually let go and turned toward the group, ready to head into the forest to change. They were going to travel in their animal form. Running would be faster than driving and less conspicuous.

I excused myself, saying I was tired and going to go to sleep. Turning back to Jack, I asked him to please wake me when they returned. I had to make sure I made it back before them.

Once in my room, I opened my window. I climbed onto the roof and made the two-foot jump to the elm outside. I carefully lowered myself to the ground and ran into the forest, hoping the guys would be inside for a few minutes longer. I quickly lay on my back and focused all my concentration on the shift.

It came as swiftly as I had hoped. I rose up on all fours and disappeared deeper into the forest, ready to follow my pack.

CHAPTER 8

JACK

I WAS GLAD LILY went to bed before we left. Since we were travelling in our animal form, it made sense for us to leave naked instead of trying to stash our clothes outside. So if she would have stayed down here, she would have gotten quite the eyeful, and that was something I was not sure I would react well to. I didn't want Lily to see any guy's junk but mine.

I took a glance down the hallway to make sure she wasn't heading back down to the kitchen. Coast was clear; it was better to make this quick.

"All right, guys, let's get going. Luke, Reagan, keep Lil company if she comes back downstairs. I don't want her worrying."

"Sure thing, boss. If you think you need backup, just call. We can be there in twenty minutes," Reagan said.

"Yeah, will do."

I glanced at the note that I had written Leo's instructions on one last time then started stripping my clothes off. The guys followed suit. In the buff, we all headed outside and quickly shifted so we could begin.

Once we were in our animal form, it was impossible to communicate with one another any other way than by body language. So I checked behind me to see if everyone was fully shifted and noticed they were patiently waiting for me to take off.

I turned around and bolted into the forest. The best part of being a wolf shifter was the speed. We could clear the fifty miles in approximately twenty minutes, way faster than a real wolf, but not near as fast as the cougar shifters.

I picked up the most delicious scent the first few paces into the forest that I took. Lily. I could smell her all over the forest, evidence of her long run today.

I wanted nothing more than to deal with this Mayla and Tony issue as soon as possible so I could get home to Lily. I had to admit, the fact that Mayla was with Tony had me a little on edge. He had so much hate, so much resentment for us. It wasn't that I was scared we would lose this fight; I was just concerned that perhaps not all of us would make it out unscathed. It was my job to worry, my job to protect. These guys counted on me, and I didn't want to let them down.

Another glance over my shoulder revealed the guys were keeping close pace with me, so I kicked it up a notch.

Finally, we bordered the cougar territory, and I decided I better slow it down a little. I took a minute to grasp my bearings. It was strange; I could still smell Lily. Not near as strong as in the forest surrounding our house but distinct all the same. It must have been coming from me. That kiss we had in the kitchen left me with the sweet gift of her smell. I took a minute to enjoy it before coming to almost a complete stop.

I looked to my right. Leo told me that Mayla and Tony's scent had been strongest on their western border. He specified almost exactly where I should pick up their scent so I could follow it from there. Well, we were pretty close to where Leo directed me. Trying to get Lily's scent out of my nose and focus on Mayla's, I put my nose to the ground and sniffed.

Duke was the best tracker; he had the best nose in the group. I looked him in the eye then motioned my snout toward the ground, telling him to sniff the trail out. He understood and got right to work.

Within minutes Duke caught the trail and we all took off after him. He led us west, which was a good sign that we were on the right trail. I realized I didn't have much of a game plan for when we did find them. I guess the element of surprise had to work; I just wanted the problem eliminated.

I wanted to be the one to kill Mayla. Just remembering the night that she stabbed Lil was making me see red. I never would have guessed I could have hated someone so much in my life, especially someone I thought that I once loved.

We must have been close because Duke came to a grinding halt, Flynn almost slamming into the back of him. I closed the gap between us and stopped at Duke's side sniffing the area.

It was definitely strong here. So strong in fact that it was as if they had been staying here full time. The problem was there was no one here. I motioned for the guys to spread out and try to see what they could find.

The search was futile. They definitely had been here and recently, but they weren't now. The strange thing was we couldn't find any strong trails leading away from the direct area.

After what must have been an hour or so of searching high and low and up and down the cougar's western border, I finally decided to shift back so I could speak to the guys.

It took us less than twenty seconds to completely shift back.

"Jack, I don't understand. Their smell is all over this place, but I can't pick up where they went. It doesn't make any sense," Duke said, completely baffled.

"Yeah, I know what you mean. It's as if they knew we were coming and figured out a way to throw us off," Duke warily said.

"How is that even possible? You can't just stop from leaving a scent. Not unless you disappeared into thin air," Mike offered.

"Sure you could, if you put enough thought into it," I said.

This was not giving me a good feeling. I should have thought this through a little harder. It was stupid of me to underestimate Mayla. She had been a part of our pack her whole life and my mate for many years. If anyone knew how I would proceed in this matter, it would be her. I was beginning to think that their being in Leo's territory had more to it than I thought. I guess I just presumed that Mayla would want to be as far away from us as possible but still within the forest. I never imagined that she would be there simply because she knew that Leo would sniff her out. Of course she would. Of course she would know he would phone me, and of course she knew I would come. But the confusing part, the part that made no sense, was why lure us and then not be here when we arrived?

It was not making sense. I wasn't sure what to do. Should we wait for them? Stay there until they returned? Were they watching us now? Just waiting for their best chance to attack? Perhaps Mayla underestimated me. Maybe she didn't realize so many of us would come. She could have presumed that just I would come, believing I didn't know about her comradeship with Tony.

"I don't like this, guys. I think we should head back. Try to regroup, come up with a better plan. Either she got spooked when she saw how many of us came and took off, or she has something up her sleeve, and if that's the case, I want to be prepared to deal with that. I don't like not feeling in control of this situation, not knowing what to expect," I said knowing they would be disappointed.

"But, boss, we came all this way. It's not like she can take us. Let's just wait it out. What's the worst that can happen?" PJ said.

"That's the problem. I don't know what could happen. It's not something I want to find out. We will deal with her, but clearly, they are not here, and I'm not willing to stand here defenseless waiting for god knows what," I said, angry now.

"Oh, come on, we are hardly defenseless." PJ was struggling to hide the irritation in his voice.

"We're going." It was final.

We promptly shifted back and began the run back to the house. I needed to think; I needed to concentrate. I was less prepared for this than I thought. It was supposed to be simple. Rush in, tear them apart, then get home to Lily. Now I was going to have to spend the night trying to figure out what Mayla was doing. Trying to figure out why she would lead us there.

The run seemed to take less time on the way back. My mind was reeling with questions. Questions I couldn't figure out the answers to. I didn't even know where to start. I realized I didn't know Mayla as well as she clearly knew me. I guess I just never really cared enough.

The house came into view, and once again, I hoped that Lily was in her room. I shifted then jumped up the deck, all five of the guys in tow. We all headed in the backdoor into the kitchen. Luke and Reagan sat at the table playing a game of cards, both snapping their heads toward me as I walked in.

"Jack, how did it go? Find 'em?" Reagan asked

"No. We got problems. Let us get dressed then we will discuss it," I said

I pulled on the jeans and white T-shirt I left in the kitchen. We were going to have to figure this out, and the best way to do that would be talk through it together.

Everyone started taking their usual spots at the table; a few grabbed a beverage from the fridge then sat.

"Better wake Lily up, boss, or she will be pissed that she was left out of this discussion," Johnny said.

Right, I bet he was concerned that she would be mad. He just wanted to see her as bad as I did. As much as it pissed me off that he was the one to point it out, he was right. Lily would kill me if I didn't wake her for this. She would want to know everything. She would want to help.

"Yeah, you're probably right," I said without looking at him.

I got up from the table a little too eagerly and speedily walked out of the kitchen into the hall. I took the stairs two at a time. I couldn't wait to have her in my arms. I wished we didn't have to spend the night with the guys brainstorming. I wanted nothing more than to just crawl into bed beside her.

I stood outside of her door wondering if I should knock. Were we past that? Were people ever past that? I wasn't sure. It was never an issue with me and Mayla because we always shared a room. I resolved to knock lightly, and if she didn't answer, then I would go in and wake her.

"Lil?" I called and knocked at the same time.

No answer. I turned the knob, hoping it wasn't locked. It wasn't, so I pushed it all the way open and started toward her bed. My eyes adjusted to the dark, and I noticed the bed was empty. Automatically, my head turned toward the en suite, but the door hung open, and the light was off. I glanced back at the bed, which was still perfectly made and undisturbed.

A smile spread across my face. She was in my bed. She just didn't stop surprising me. When we first met, I thought she was shy and reserved. That assumption was slowly changing. The thought of her lying in my bed did crazy things to me. I hoped she was not naked, because if she was, we weren't making it downstairs.

I jogged down the hall to my room and threw open the door. I snuck up to the bed.

My heart sank. The bed was empty. She was not there. She wasn't on the main floor, and she wasn't asleep in one of our beds.

Frantically, I started checking every one of the guys' rooms. I threw open Johnny's door first. Pathetic of me, I know, but I couldn't help it. Every bedroom was empty. Every bathroom was empty.

I raced down the stairs to check the parlor; maybe she went in there to watch the movie we never got to last night. But when I threw open the door, I saw it too was empty. The basement was the last place in the house that she could have been. I ran down the stairs so fast, I lost my footing and crashed into the wall at the bottom, putting a two-foot hole right through the wall. Great.

"Lil? Lily, you down here?" I yelled, unable to control my worry.

Fuck. I ran back up the stairs and into the kitchen.

"Where is she?" I yelled at Reagan and Luke.

My booming voice made everyone at the table jump.

"Who?" Reagan asked, looking honestly confused.

"What do you mean *who*? Lily! Where the hell is she?"

"What are you talking about, Jack? She is in her bedroom. She went to bed before you left. Haven't seen her since," Reagan answered

"She never came out at all?" I said, still yelling.

"No, Jack, we presumed she went to bed. Usually, when someone goes to bed, they don't come out till morning. I never thought anything of it." He looked as worried as I did.

"Shit, shit, shit. She is nowhere in this house. I checked everywhere. She is gone."

"Maybe she went for a run," PJ offered.

"We have been in the kitchen all night, and I can't imagine her using the front door to go for a run. Well, I guess if she didn't want us to see her," Reagan said.

I couldn't believe this. Where could she have gone? She spent the entire day on a run; I couldn't imagine her needing to get out that bad that she would sneak past the guys.

"I'll check the front door for her scent. We barely use it, so if she left through it, her scent will be prominent," Duke said then jogged toward the front door.

Could she have left? Left me? Would she have wanted to? I thought it was going well. I thought that she was getting along with everyone. I mean sure we have had our little disagreements, but all in all, I thought she was enjoying it here. Besides, she would have nowhere to go. It didn't make sense for her to leave. Her apartment was no longer her apartment, and it was completely empty anyway. Also, she didn't want me to go tonight; obviously, she wanted me around. She was genuinely concerned.

"There is no recent trail of her at the front door," Duke said jogging back into the kitchen.

"Hey, boss, I don't want to freak you out or anything, but Lily's scent was really strong outside when we left today, I just thought it was left over from her run earlier. You don't think she was out there, do you?" Mike asked, worry creasing his forehead.

"I smelled her too. But not just near the house, I smelled her the whole time. I thought it was Jack though, thought he had her scent all over him," Flynn said.

Shit, I had thought the same thing as both of them. Could she have been out there when we left? How would she have gotten out there if she hadn't used the front door? There was no way she could have gotten out the back door we were all in the kitchen.

"I smelled her too. I also thought that it was left over from her run today, and I presumed I had her scent on me as well." I was struggling to keep composure.

"Jack, I don't mean to sound like the downer, but let's look at this realistically. Lily wanted to come tonight, and you forbade it. She was dead set on coming, it didn't matter what you said. Then all of a sudden, she just caves and is willing to stay home and be babysat? Does that sound like Lily to you? I hate to say it, but I got a feeling she was with us all night. She is probably outside right now waiting for us to go to bed so she can sneak back in," Duke put in.

I struggled to remember the last few words that transpired between me and Lily. She told me to wake her up when I got back. Why would she tell me to do that if she knew she wouldn't be in her bed? That wouldn't be very smart of her if she was trying to sneak back in before I realized she was gone.

"I guess she could already be back in her room right now. Just didn't make it up there before you did," PJ offered.

"How would she have gotten back up to her room? We would hear the front door or the stairs at least," I said. I wanted to believe so bad that she would be upstairs in her bed so I could tear her a new one. I couldn't believe she would do this to me. She lied to me, right to my face, and like an idiot I believed her. How stupid was I? Looking back, it was completely obvious that she played me.

"Well, she does have the room beside the tree, Jack. It would be pretty easy to climb out the window," PJ answered.

"Shit." I hadn't even thought about her window. She excused herself to go to bed so she could get out her window before we got outside. She wanted to be hiding before we got out there and saw her. That meant she followed us tonight.

I was going to kill her. She had better have been back in her room because she was gonna hear it from me. I spun on my heels and raced back up the stairs and straight to her bedroom. Not bothering to knock this time, just slamming the door open so hard it bounced off the wall and came back at me. I probably put a hole in the wall where the knob hit, but oh well.

My hand searched the wall for the light switch. The light flared on, evidencing the still empty room. I spun to head toward my bedroom, realizing it would be smart of her to go to my bed. Presuming I would have only checked her room and found her missing. Then she could have said she had been in my room the whole night. Little did she know I checked my room already, when she was not in it.

Once again, I slammed open the door, fully prepared to wake her from her fake slumber. But the room was empty.

Maybe Duke was right. She was probably outside still waiting for me to go to bed. Praying I wouldn't notice that she was gone. Well, wouldn't she be happy to know that wasn't happening. She'd be pretty surprised when I would find her outside hiding in a bush waiting to sneak back into the house like some fourteen-year-old girl.

I walked into the hall with the full intention of heading directly outside and finding her, but Duke was walking out of her room at just the same time and stopped me.

"Hey, Jack, her window definitely has her scent all over it. As far as I can tell, that was the way she exited the house. The scent is fading slightly, so I don't think she has tried to come back in yet." There was a small grin on Duke's face as he said it. Perhaps he saw the anger in my face and thought it was somehow humorous. Whatever. I didn't have time for this. I had to find Lily, haul her ass back into the house, find out what the hell she was thinking by following us, not listening to me, and then after all of that, I still had to figure out what the hell Mayla was doing.

"Yeah, I'm headed out there now. Get everyone back in the kitchen. We still have shit to discuss. After me and Lily have a little discussion about her listening skills," I growled.

I bumped past Duke and raced down the stairs, heading straight for the door in the kitchen. I shoved it open with one hand and stepped outside into the night air. I took a deep breath searching for that alluring scent that I was so fond of. Getting it, I followed it to its strongest path and realized Duke was right. She definitely went out her window. But I wasn't concerned about where she was when she left. I needed to find her now. I followed the scent from the base of the house to a spot behind the first couple of trees lining the forest. She must have hidden waiting for us to pass so she could follow.

I broke off searching the surrounding area for a fresh trail, something that could tell me where she was.

"Lily, I know you are out here. I know that you followed us tonight, so get your ass out here. I'm not fucking playing hide-and-seek all night. We have problems, which I guess you already know because you would have seen. So just do me a favor and come back in the house," I yelled, hoping she was close enough to hear.

There was no answer. She either didn't hear me or was outright ignoring me, the latter seemed most likely.

I continued to search and search, finally deciding that I would have to start from the beginning because that would be the only way I could trace every step she took right to where she would be right now. If I was going to do the twenty-minute hike back to cougarville, I had better let the guys know what I was doing.

I ran back to the house and leapt onto the deck, flung open the door to the kitchen, and prepared myself to run into the basement but realized all the guys were still in the kitchen.

"Hey, I can't find her. She is clearly trying to avoid me, so I'm going to start at square one. I'm gonna follow her whole trail down to wherever she was hiding while watching us tonight right back to wherever she is hiding now," I said while ripping my shirt off my chest and unbuttoning my pants.

"Well, boss, you're not going alone. We will come, just in case Mayla is back in cougarville as you called it," PJ announced.

"No, it's fine, you don't have to come. I'm not sure Mayla will be going back there anytime soon," I said.

"Well, that's not a chance we are willing to take, so we are coming. Let's go, boys," PJ said with finality in his voice.

Before I could even argue, they were stripping off their clothes and heading out the back. I followed, and we met at the ground beneath Lily's window. I really didn't like that they would be with me when I found Lily.

If she was human, she would be stark naked. If she wasn't human, then I wouldn't be able to yell at her, and it would be harder to coax her back into the house.

But I knew they wouldn't let me do this on my own. They cared about me too much to let anything happen to me. They would always have my back just as I would theirs. We truly were a family.

We all shifted in silence and followed Duke into the forest. It wasn't exactly necessary for us to follow Duke as her scent was still pretty prominent. We all could smell it I was sure, but we grew used to following Duke when we were tracking.

It took forever, but we finally made it. I was sniffing around the area and noticed that Lily had been watching us from about fifty feet away. Her scent was all over the shrubs, and it was a clear view to where we had all been standing deliberating.

She was right here the whole time, right below my nose, and I never thought anything of it. Actually, I had thought that I had her scent on me. That I smelled like her because I had kissed her before I left.

I turned to follow where the trail led and noticed that instead of heading back toward the house, it zigzagged all over the place. She must have been trying to dodge us when we were running around looking for Mayla all over the place. I couldn't believe we totally missed it. Strangely, her scent shot off toward the east. It struck me as odd because we stuck to the western border. We followed the trail for about two miles when another scent seemed to punch me in the gut.

Mayla. I didn't understand how I never picked her trail up before. Why could I smell it now? I quickly shifted to human, my heart racing, mind reeling. Mayla found Lily.

The guys shifted as well.

Once we were all standing there, Duke said, "That is not a good sign. I can't pick up Tony, but I definitely smell Mayla. It seems as if Mayla came at her from the south. That would explain why we never had her trail. She was nowhere near where we were searching."

I dropped to my knees, bracing my hands on the ground. My legs were too weak to hold me anymore. I couldn't stop imagining the things that Mayla would do to Lily.

"Boss, the trail stops here. It's as if once Mayla found her, they disappeared. No scent past here for either of them. All I'm getting is Lily's coming from the west and Mayla's coming from the south. They meet here," Reagan said gesturing with his hand toward a spot on the ground. "And that's where they stay. Nothing, absolutely nothing."

This was the worst thing that I could imagine. Mayla had found Lily. This was probably their plan from the beginning. Mayla probably presumed Lily would be with us, and she would sneak up and snatch her. My heart sank. I was helpless. Without a trail, I couldn't find her. I had nothing to go off. I didn't have the faintest clue about where she could be, where Mayla would take her. I didn't have a clue how Mayla could just make her scent disappear. Make both their scents disappear.

I placed my face into my hands and let the anger, fear, and despair rip from my throat in a deafening growl.

CHAPTER 9

LILY

I WAS TOO SCARED to open my eyes. My head was pounding where Mayla hit me, and I could feel the dried blood on my face. This was not at all how I had planned for this evening to go.

I had absolutely no idea where I was. There was a hard, cold surface below me, sort of lumpy, which lead me to believe I was still outside.

That scent that was all Mayla lingered close by. I knew I was not alone, but the most terrifying thought was that Tony was somewhere near too. I hadn't yet picked up his scent and wasn't sure if I would recognize it when I did. The fact that I was human last time we saw each other didn't help.

The patter of footsteps pacing sounded somewhere to the left of me. Should I risk taking a peek? The last thing I wanted was to alert her to the fact that I was awake. I was still holding on to the hope that she thought she had killed me, not rendered me temporarily unconscious. With any luck, she would leave me here thinking she killed me, and soon, Jack would realize I was gone, and surely he would come for me.

Finally, I decided to sneak a quick peek. Opening my eyes just a fraction seemed innocent enough. The first thing I noticed was that I was no longer in the forest; it was somewhere enclosed yet still outside. Perhaps a cave or a hole in the side of a rocky hill. I couldn't be sure. All I knew was she took me somewhere, and that thought scared the shit out of me.

Would Jack be able to find me? Could he pick up on my scent? How long had I been out? There were so many questions running through my mind, and each one just added more fear. I had to try and keep myself in check; I didn't want to begin a shift. A fight with Mayla was not something I was prepared for alone.

Opening my eyes a little bit more revealed that Mayla was in fact pacing to my left. What was she doing? Probably pondering the best way to dispose of me.

I tried to do a quick review of my injuries. More time must have passed than I had thought because I couldn't feel the wound on my head where she hit me with the tire iron. You could leave it to Mayla to fight so dirty.

Jack was going to be so pissed with me. This whole time, it was about luring me out there. I should have stayed put just like he had said. Now look what I had done. I thought it was all going well.

Jack and the guys had been searching, and I did such a great job evading them. They didn't even appear to smell me so near them, and if they had, they never thought about that fact too deep.

Jack had trusted me; why would he worry that I would follow? Would he be so mad at me that he wouldn't try and find me? Resolve to himself that I deserved what I got? I couldn't say as I would blame him if that was his conclusion.

When the guys started searching all over the western border, I got a little freaked. The last thing that I had wanted was for Jack to find me hiding in a bush. They started getting a little too close for comfort, so I decided to run east, thinking that once I got far enough away from them, I could wait it out then find my way home. Planning to use the excuse of a midnight run if they beat me home. But Mayla ruined all those plans.

I believed that I had run far enough east and decided to take a break, wait it out. Give them a little while longer before I decided to head home, when I saw her. She was in her human form running straight at me. I didn't have time to think, let alone react. I saw the tire iron in her steel grip too late. It had connected with my skull in a deafening crack, instantly knocking me out. The last thing I remembered was the feeling of the iron hitting me, cracking my skull wide open. I remembered thinking, *Thank God, I am a shifter, or that blow would have killed me for sure.*

The crunch on the ground pulled me out of my reverie. Instinctively, my eyes darted in the direction the noise came. For a second, I thought for sure Jack had found me and was here to rescue me, like some goddamn fairy tale. Well, I was severely disappointed. Thankfully, the culprit did not look in my direction, as my eyes were wide open staring straight at him. The sight of him made my blood boil. All the built-up anger and hatred I had been storing away raged to get out. I wanted to jump to my feet and hurt him, physically tear him apart. But I remembered how strong he was, remembered how terrible he was, and my resolve faltered.

I automatically closed my eyes, pretending to still be unconscious.

"Mayla, what the hell is this? You were supposed to lure them, the whole pack, here. That was the deal. I would protect you and let you stay with me if you lured the pack to me," Tony said in a clearly pissed voice.

"I know that was the plan, what do you think I'm doing? She is the perfect bait. They will all come for her, and when they do, you can do what you wish with them. But she is mine," Mayla hissed.

"No. I don't like her being here, Mayla. You know it bothers me to see her," Tony said in a sort of broken voice.

"Look, Tony, I know you may not have a problem with her, but I do. I hate her. She ruined my life, she stole everything from me. My home, my life, my spot in the pack, and worst of all, my mate. Can't you understand? You of all people should understand how important this is to me," she pleaded.

"Mayla, of course I understand, the fact is that she may have ruined your life, but it is only because I made her what she is. I never meant for this to happen. She was supposed to die. All the rest died, I don't understand how she could possibly have survived what I did to her in that alley."

My mouth filled with vomit, and I tried to choke it back. I really did not want to hear about that night, especially from him.

"Oh, seriously, Tony, is that any better? Killing her? If anything, you should feel better that she is alive. I will never understand your twisted thought process behind that," she said, clearly baffled.

"I've explained this to you numerous times, Mayla. I don't kill these people because I enjoy it. I rip them apart to put a target on your heads. If enough people get attacked by what looks like a wolf, then the authorities will have no choice but to eliminate the problem. The last thing I ever wanted was to curse someone to the fate that your pack cursed me to," he spat.

"Well, no offense, but your plan isn't working so well. No one is out hunting them. No one cares. People get attacked by animals all the time. The city is surrounded by forests and hills. They know damn well they will never eliminate the problem, so why even bother. Jesus, Tony, can't you just admit that you're twisted and kill people because it makes you feel better about yourself?" The condemnation in her voice was thick.

"Yeah, well, I realized now that that plan isn't going to work, hence why I agreed to you coming with me. I will get the pack, I will kill every last one of them by myself if I have to. They will pay for what they did to my wife and for what they did to me. You're lucky I let you live, so I would quit irritating me if I was you," he growled.

"Whatever, I agreed to bring you the pack. What do you care if I get what I want out of it too? Those people were my family, my friends, and they turned on me for this little tramp. I will kill her, but not after I teach her a lesson or two. And I would appreciate if you would stay out of my way. I promise they will come for her, you will get your revenge just as I will get mine." I could hear the smile in her voice.

My stomach sank. She was going to kill me. How could I have been so stupid? There was no way I could take both of them, so my chance for escape was slim to none.

"Well, she is your responsibility then. I don't want to be part of whatever sick game you are planning for her. Just remember that. My beef is with the pack, not her," he said.

"Tony, she is as part of the pack as the rest of them. How can you not have a beef with her? You don't make any sense."

"She is not one of them! I screwed up, she should have died that night, but she didn't, and the pack was there to help her. Therefore, they were her only choice. She never had the option, she wasn't born into that pack. She did not have a hand in what happened to me and my wife so long ago. In my mind, she is as innocent as me and my wife were," he said with finality in his voice.

"Fine, whatever you say. I will deal with her, and you can have the rest of them," she agreed.

It got quiet after that. Everything was starting to fall together for me. It seemed that somehow Mayla had come across Tony sometime after she took off. He was probably going to kill her when she made a bargain. A bargain he couldn't refuse. She could deliver the pack to him. Give him the chance to kill them all, and in return, she could live. What he hadn't bargained for was she would also get something else she wanted—me.

I was beginning to wonder how long they would let this charade of me faking unconsciousness go on when Mayla started toward me. I felt the hair rise on the back of my neck. I didn't want her anywhere near me.

She stopped about a foot from me and stood there. I didn't know what to expect. Was she waiting for me to open my eyes? If she was, she was going to be thoroughly disappointed.

All of a sudden, my face whipped back and exploded with pain. Automatically, I reached up to try and soothe the pain, giving myself away. I was awake and she knew it. The bitch had kicked me right in the face. I spit the blood out that was filling my mouth and noticed my front tooth was no longer where it should be. It was embedded into my lip, completely disconnected from my gums. I spat that out too.

"Rise and shine, whore. We are gonna play a little game. It's called 'I ask questions and you answer them.' Sounds fun, eh?" she said.

"Fuck you," I said through the blood still flowing out of my mouth.

I realized my eyes were still closed and forced them open to look at her. She looked as beautiful as the last time I saw her. Glancing down at myself, I realized she was not thinking the same about me. I was naked and covered in blood. It must have been from my head wound when she hit me with the tire iron. Thank God for fast healing.

I tried to sit up, fearing if I didn't, I was going to choke on the blood that refused to stop pouring out of my gums.

Bad idea, Mayla pulled her leg back, and before I could dodge it, she connected again, with my shoulder this time. The pain was worse than when she kicked me in the face. It felt as if every bone in my shoulder shattered. I risked a glance at it; my arm hung limply at my side, and my shoulder was clearly not where it belonged. Shit. I wasn't sure if that would heal right without being put back in place. Should I risk moving and trying to reset it? Or would that bring on another blow from her?

"I guess you have realized by now that I don't want you to move. I want you to stay right where you are and answer my fucking questions. That sound good to you?" she asked sarcastically.

I hope she didn't expect me to answer. I was in too much agony to even think about speaking. I wished she would just kill me already. I didn't know how much of this I could take.

"All right, first question. Does that pack know I'm with Tony?" she asked.

I tried to open my mouth to respond but then thought better of it. Would any of the other pack members answer her questions? I felt like I would be betraying them if I did. Jack was right when he said I wasn't ready for this. I didn't know the first thing about fighting or even being a captive.

"Lily, you had better answer my questions, or you will regret it. I promise you that," she hissed.

I couldn't bring myself to answer her. She planned on killing me anyway. Whether I answered her stupid questions or not. I heard her say that to Tony. She was going to kill me and make me suffer first. There would be no quick and easy death for me. I was smart enough to not drag the pack down with me. I would leave her questions unanswered and pray it would give the pack the fighting edge I never had.

"Fine, you asked for it," she said right before kicking out my kneecap.

So the game went until she finally decided I had had enough for one night. She picked me up and threw me into the back corner of what I believed was a cave. I landed hard on my broken shoulder that was just beginning to heal. I waited for her to head toward the front of the cave before I reached my good arm around and yanked my shoulder back into place.

My injuries were worse than I had thought. The loss of blood had me beyond light-headed, and I just prayed I could stay conscious long enough to finish setting all of my broken bones.

I had retreated into myself, hiding in my mind from her attacks. I realized that if I thought of Jack, imagined I was at home with him lying in his bed, her blows didn't seem as bad. I learned to block it out somewhat.

Once all the bones felt as if they were where they were supposed to be, and I felt like there was nothing left for me to do, I curled into a ball, wincing at every pain that motion caused, and began to sob quietly.

Everyone has always wondered how they would die. I never once thought it would end for me like this. Not even after I knew about this world. I never thought someone could do such terrible things to someone. It was different than when Tony attacked me. He never tortured me; he simply tried to kill me and failed. Killing me was the last thing on Mayla's mind. I knew that now. I knew how much she enjoyed hurting me.

I could feel my body trying to put itself back together, but I knew this would not be as easy as the stab wound. My right shoulder was busted, along with my left knee and thigh bone. My jaw had been kicked out of place, and my tooth was still gone. A large amount of my hair had been pulled out, three of the fingers on my left hand were broken, and so were numerous ribs. My naked body was covered in my own blood from the numerous places she broke my skin.

I was sure it looked even worse than it felt. I closed my eyes and tried to lose myself in sleep. If I had to deal with this for the next however long it took until she got bored and killed me, then I would try to spend most of it unconscious. The less I had to feel, the better.

Sleep was not coming. I couldn't seem to drift off. Could be the fact that I was in a cave with a man that beat me in an alleyway and then left me for dead, not realizing instead he had turned me into a shifter, and a woman who wanted nothing more than to spend all her free time torturing me.

My left side was beginning to feel tender due to me lying on that side trying to avoid making my injuries worse. Instead I rolled onto my back and winced as my right shoulder seared with pain.

I reached up to feel my face. My lip was swollen and had to be sticking a good two inches off my face. My eyes felt puffy, which lead me to believe they were both black. I must have been a gruesome sight.

I strained my ears when I heard light footsteps coming from the front of the cave.

"Tony, I'm heading out for a bit, need to get something to eat, it's been a very long day," Mayla said. "Please keep an eye on her. If I come back and find you did something as crazy as letting her go, our entire deal will be off."

"Yeah, yeah, just hurry up. I don't want to have to deal with her. I told you I didn't want to be a part of this, and somehow now I am stuck babysitting," he bitched.

"Oh god, Tony, stop being so dramatic. I will be back in like an hour," she promised, then I heard her voice and her footsteps recede.

After Mayla was clearly gone from the cave, Tony came back to my area. Crap. I didn't want him near me. Why couldn't he make sure I stayed put while remaining in the front of the cave? Then he startled me by speaking.

"Lily, I just had to come in here and talk to you while she is gone. I wanted to apologize for everything that I have done to you. I never meant for any of this to happen. I know that you probably don't want to be sitting here listening to me, but I really need to get this off my chest." He glanced at me, obviously waiting for me to stop him. Not knowing that I couldn't have said anything if I had wanted to. My head was pounding, and it was using all of my concentration just to hear what he was saying.

"Anyway, I guess what I'm trying to say is there is more to this than you know. I would never have done this to you on purpose, and I want you to know that I don't agree with what Mayla is doing to you. I would stop her if I could, but the truth is we both have our reasons for doing what we do, and I need something from her before I can try and help you. Please know that if you are alive when she brings me what I want, then I will do everything I can to keep you that way."

I wanted to tell him not to do that. If he succeeded in killing the pack, then I hoped Mayla would kill me too. How would I ever survive on my own? Without the pack, without Jack? It was hard to remember my previous life and anything in it being important to me. It all seemed so long ago, like it was someone else's life, not mine. Just as I was beginning to feel like I finally belonged somewhere, like I really had a family, this had to happen.

My body was beginning to feel a little better. My bones were starting to mend themselves, and I could feel my cuts sealing themselves over. I desperately wanted to sleep. I was completely exhausted and broken. I wanted to sleep and not wake up until this nightmare was over. However that might have been.

"Did the pack ever tell you about me? Tell you what happened to me? Well, since we have plenty of time to kill, I will tell you anyway," he began. "I met the love of my life on vacation in Vegas. I never used to get out much. I was an ethologist, and I loved my job. I rarely took time off, but finally, on a whim, I flew to Las Vegas for the weekend. It was fate, I swear it, I met my wife. Her name was Gail, and she was everything I could have imagined in a woman. She had long brown hair and the brownest eyes you could ever see. She was the most beautiful thing I had ever laid eyes on. I approached her in the casino of the Wynn hotel, and she actually let me buy her a drink. Sounds strange, letting a man buy you a drink in Vegas since you drink for free as long as you are gambling. But I wanted to impress her. Then she said the craziest thing. She told me that she was a zoologist. This blew my mind. Zoology, as you probably don't know, is the biological study of animal function, behavior, structure and so on. I had originally studied zoology before branching off to become an ethologist. We talked long into the night and into the early morning. By the end of the weekend, she decided to move here with me. It took off from there. We spent every minute together and eventually began working together. We were married in eight short months and were expecting our first child. It was the most exciting time of my life. Suddenly, work seemed less important to me. The following June, she gave birth to our son. He was beautiful. He had her brown hair and brown eyes and the face of an angel. My life was finally complete. Shortly after his first birthday, Gail decided to come back to work. She wanted to begin our studies as soon as possible. Together we headed out into the field. We studied all sorts of nature's creatures, but one caught our eye the most. It was the strange breed of wolves that lived in the forest, the ones that didn't travel like normal wolfs, the ones that only seemed to be around sometimes. We threw ourselves into our research. We spent years following the pack, and as you can imagine, we found out their secret. They were not a pack of wolves at all but a strange pack of human animal shifters. We watched them. We followed them to their home and researched their interaction together. We wanted to get all the evidence we could before we went public with the disturbing things we found, but collecting evidence was proving difficult. We began taking our video camera with us, hoping to get some good footage, and finally, the time arrived. We stumbled upon one of them midshift. It was just the proof we needed. If we could get this on video, then how could anyone deny our claims? But our plans were thwarted when we were attacked. There was nothing I could do. I opened my eyes to find my wife dead and my life changed forever. At that moment, I vowed to myself I would not rest until every last one of them paid for what they did to me and to my beautiful Gail," he said, his voice breaking on her name.

I basically had heard the same story from Jack, but for some reason, it actually touched me to hear it from Tony himself. Hearing the way he spoke about his wife, the love he felt for her, and the hurt he felt when she died bothered me. I didn't want to pity this man, but I did. All the times I told myself no matter what he went through, I would never forgive him, I would never understand. I wouldn't say I understand why he did this to me, but I did understand his want for revenge. However, I also understood how the pack had no option. It was do or die. They had to kill Tony and Gail before they revealed our secret world to everyone. It was a huge misunderstanding. Both sides were right in their anger toward each other; they just handled it in all the wrong ways.

"Well, I've talked your ear off enough for one night. Mayla should be back soon. I'm gonna run and grab you an energy bar quick, you must be starved. Our little secret though, all right? I don't feel like fighting with Mayla anymore tonight." With that, he stood and sauntered back toward the front of the cave.

He brought me back an energy bar, opened the wrapper for me, and held my head steady while I chocked it down. I was not in the mood to eat, but I knew I would need the energy to help myself heal.

Just as Tony was helping be with the last bite, Mayla walked in.

"What the fuck is going on?" She screeched.

CHAPTER 10

JACK

I F I WAS ever going to find Lily, I had to get a better grip on myself. The trip back to the house was the worst twenty minutes of my life. I hadn't wanted to leave the forest where I found her scent. I felt like I was leaving her, giving up on her, but the guys insisted there was nothing else we could do. Better to head back to the house and figure out a plan.

First thing on my list was to contact Leo, let him know what happened, and request help from him and his family. Typically, we would never work alongside the cougars—the odd telephone conversation or helpful tip, but never full-on working together. We were cats and dogs after all.

While the guys sat at the kitchen table tabulating our next plan of attack, I walked to the parlor to call Leo. The best I could hope for was their cooperation in searching for Lily.

I picked up the receiver and dialed his number. His wife, Cher, answered on the third ring.

"Hello," her beautiful voice rang.

"Hello, Cher, it's Jack. Is Leo around? It's kind of urgent," I said, trying to keep my voice steady.

"Oh hi, Jack, I'll just run and grab Leo for you. Can you hold for a second?" she asked.

"Sure thing."

I waited for Leo to get to the phone. Every second that ticked by felt like a lifetime.

"Jack," he finally greeted me.

"Hey, Leo, listen, we were searching your border tonight and ran into a little problem. We were unable to find Mayla or Tony. I fear we were lead into a trap," I said in a distressed voice.

"Jack, you're going to have to explain a little better than that. What kind of trap?"

"It's a long story, but we have a new addition to the pack, Lily, whom I have been recently . . . uh, dating, and Mayla, as you can imagine, does not quite approve of the fact. I screwed up, and she caught me and Lily in the forest, indisposed, and that is when she took off and, apparently, when she met up with Tony."

"Wait . . . wait, slow down Jack. Tony is the guy with the scar, I take it? And I don't understand what that has to do with what happened tonight."

"Yes, Tony, is the guy with the scar. I'm sure you have heard about the recent murders in the city. The ones that looked like wolf attacks? Well, that was Tony's handiwork. He has a vendetta against our pack. Anyway, that is a story all on its own. Tonight we went to the spot you told me, and you were right, their scent was all over the place. The weird thing was that we couldn't track the scent leaving the area. It was as if it had disappeared."

My mind was going a mile a minute, and I couldn't get everything I wanted to say out. But I had to make Leo understand the urgency of the matter. Therefore, he needed as much information as I could give.

"Yes, that is strange. Tell about the trap, Jack," he prompted.

"Right, uh, well, you see, after Mayla had caught me and Lily together, a fight broke out, and she stabbed Lily. We hadn't seen her since. I carried Lily back to the house and mended her. The problem is, Mayla is vindictive and spiteful, she wanted Lily dead. So when I received the tip from you as to their whereabouts, me and Lily fought over whether she should come or not. I didn't think it was safe for her, she is still so new to this life, and I made the decision for her to stay home. She reluctantly agreed. I should have been more careful, I was stupid. I didn't think she would disobey me. The pack always listens to me. Lily didn't, she followed us. When we finally gave up on our search for Mayla and returned to the house, I realized she was gone. Automatically, I went out searching for her and tracked to the western border, and then she headed due east, where her scent abruptly stopped. We stopped to try and figure out where she could have gone when we picked up Mayla's scent heading at her from the south. The scents collided and never branched off from there. I don't understand how the trails could just stop." I sped through the story, hoping it made a bit of sense to him.

"So you think that your lady friend Lily was taken by Mayla? You think it was set up? That she wanted you to find her on my land so that you would lead Lily there?"

"Yes, that is exactly what I think. I have to find her, Leo, I just have to. I'm asking for your help. God only knows what Mayla will do to her. I can't let her die. She is a member of my pack, and, Leo, I care deeply for her. I care more for her than I ever have anyone else. I'm going fucking crazy."

"Shit. This is bad, Jack. Really, really bad. Of course we will help. I would expect the same from you if it had been Cher in your Lily's shoes. Tell me what we can do, and I will make it happen," he offered.

"Leo, I can't explain how grateful I am. I'm going to sit down with the pack and formulate some sort of plan. So until I get something concrete, just keep your eyes and ears peeled. Will you call me if you catch any trail from them?" I asked.

"No problem, Jack. The boys and I will run a few searches a day. Between all of us, we should be able to find something. I will call you with whatever news we have. Once you come up with a solid plan, just let us know how we can help. Good luck to you, Jack, try to keep your head. You will need to be at your best in the days to come. I know how it can feel to be in charge sometimes, like everyone is counting on you, expecting you to make everything work out. Well, just know that you are not alone. We will help you with this."

"Thank you, Leo. I will call as soon as I have something. Talk to you soon," I said.

"Bye for now, Jack." He hung up.

I placed the receiver back in its cradle and walked toward the kitchen. I had to make sure someone was home at all times to ensure we didn't miss a call from Leo. If he would catch a trail anywhere, I wanted to make sure we could be there in no time flat. I was grasping at straws; any lead I could get I would take.

As I got into the kitchen, the guys grew abruptly silent.

"Hey, boss. How did it go with Leo?" Reagan asked.

"They are going to help. He is going to have his family run a few searches a day and let us know if he finds anything," I answered.

"Great. That's perfect. Is there anyone else we can ask for help? Do you think we should take something of Lily's out to Leo so they can have her scent? It might help if Mayla has her stashed away somewhere or if she gets away from Mayla and is on her own," Duke said.

"That's a great idea. Johnny, can you grab something from Lily's room? Preferably a piece of clothing from her hamper. Her scent will be strongest if it is something she has worn recently. Then can you run it out to Leo?" I asked

"Sure thing, Jack." He got up and beelined for the stairs.

"What can we do?" Flynn asked.

"I want a couple of you to go with Johnny, make a couple laps while you are there. Take your cell phones. I don't exactly know how you are going to carry them being in your animal form, but you will have to find a way. If you find anything, I want a phone call right away," I said.

"I have that little black duffel bag, we can throw a cell phone in there, and I can take it around my neck. Once we get there, I will stash the bag somewhere, and if any of us finds anything, we can head to the phone and call you right away. You'll stay here?" Flynn asked, incredulous. Clearly not thinking I could sit here idle.

"Yeah, I'll be here. I plan on making a sketch of the forest, a grid of sorts. Once it is done, we will split it with the cougars and search every inch of this forest if we have to. I will find her," I said in my serious alpha voice. Leaving no doubt for the pack.

"Sounds good, do you need help here? Or would you prefer if we all went with Johnny?" Reagan asked.

"Uh, how about one of you stay here, I don't care who. Someone needs to take care of the mundane tasks. These boys are going to be hungry when they get back. I want everyone to be at their strongest. We will sleep in shifts and take turns searching for their scents. For now, one of you can stay here and make something to eat. When the guys get back, we will discuss the sleeping order," I said.

"I'll stay. I am the smallest after all, it would make most sense if the muscle went, you know, just in case there is trouble," Luke said.

"You chickenshit. Are you scared of the big bad wolf, Luke?" PJ teased.

The boys were always picking on Luke because he was so small. I knew it bothered him, but he would never say anything, fearing he would make himself seem weaker.

"I'm not a chickenshit, nor am I scared of the big bad wolf, asshole. I just figured it would be smartest to send the big guys into the den," Luke said in a calm voice.

"Give it up. We don't have time for this bickering bullshit," I snapped.

"Sorry," they said in unison.

Johnny came back into the kitchen then with a pair of Lily's jeans. I filled him in on the plan while Flynn ran upstairs to find his duffel bag. When the boys had everything they needed we dropped it into the duffel bag and I followed the guys outside. They had taken their clothes off in the kitchen again so they could shift easier. I planned to hook the duffel bag over Flynn's head once he was in his wolf form. They shifted quickly, and I looped the bag over his head and watched as they took off, Johnny in the lead.

I headed back into the house and glanced at Luke, who was sitting at the table still.

"Maybe you should get a quick catnap in before you start cooking. The guys should be a couple hours, you could probably get at least an hour's rest in if you would like. I'm not sure how much sleep we are going to be getting in the next little while. You should probably take it when you can," I offered.

"Yeah, that might be a good plan. I am beat. Will you wake me in an hour or so, Jack? Then I'll get started on the food," he said.

"Yeah, sure," I replied.

He stood up from the table and headed toward the stair case. I calmly walked to the parlor and closed the door behind me. I needed to be alone for a while. I was struggling trying to stay calm in front of the guys. I wanted to smash everything in this room. I wanted to find Mayla and rip her apart, limb from fucking limb. My hands were shaking, and I felt a growl growing in my throat. I needed to calm down, or there was going to be one angry wolf ripping apart this parlor. I took two deep breaths and concentrated on my balance thought. My mind filled with the image of Mr. Potato Head. It may seem weird, but to me, it was my happiest thought. When I was a kid, my parents had bought me a Mr. Potato head for my birthday. It was the last birthday I had with both of my parents alive. When I thought about that toy and the way that I had felt the day I received it, I forgot about everything else. It had always worked for me, my happy thought. They way my mother smiled at me when I thanked her for it and the way my father mussed my hair. I could feel my heart rate slow down and my hands stabilize a little.

Finally, I opened my eyes, took a deep breath, and walked to the desk in the corner. I needed to sketch out this forest, every single section. I figured it should be an easy enough task; I had been running these forests my entire life and knew them like the back of my hand. I would separate it into four sections, the typical north, east, south, and west. Within those sections, I would break down the square footage. I Google searched the acreage of forest surrounding the city. It would be easiest if I could specify border lines. Leave it to Google to already have a grid of the forest. I printed it so I could redraw it on my own paper and add a few key points.

It took me around forty-five minutes to complete the drawing and decided I had a few minutes before I would wake Luke to start the meal. I should just let him sleep and start cooking myself, but I wasn't sure if I could concentrate on such a task when I was such a mess.

I needed a shower, and I needed it bad. I ran up the stairs and into my room. I went to grab some clothes out of the closet and noticed all of Mayla's shit was still in there. Without thinking, I started ripping her clothes off their hangers, pulling them off the shelves. I tore open the dresser drawers and flung them across the room. I destroyed it all. Every shirt, every pair of pants, every skirt, dress, pair of socks was shredded. I grabbed her jewelry box that was sitting on top of the dresser and whipped it at the wall, smashing yet another hole. Even the TV that she had bought me two Christmases ago never made it unscathed. I didn't want anything in this room to remind me of her; I wanted everything gone, now.

"Jack, are you all right?" I spun when I heard the sound of Luke's voice coming from my doorway.

"Luke, I . . . uh . . ." I spun around, looking at the disaster behind me. Shit was everywhere and most of it destroyed. "Uh, I just needed this shit out of here. I couldn't help it. I'm sorry if I woke you," I apologized.

"No problem. I had to get up now anyway. Why don't you let me take care of this? You look like you could use a shower. Maybe some downtime? Why don't you head into your bathroom, and I'll make sure all this is gone when you get out," he offered.

Luke was such a great guy. Always trying to please everyone, and I didn't want to admit it, but I needed help right now. I needed someone else to get her shit out of my room because clearly, I couldn't do it myself, not without destroying my room in the process.

"Thanks, Luke, I'd really appreciate that. I'll be in the shower," I said then turned and headed for the en suite.

I could hear Luke in my room trying to clean the mess as quickly as he could. I decided to take extra long so he would have plenty of time.

I let the hot water stream down my body while I tried to force the picture of Lily out of my mind. I felt so helpless, like there was nothing I could do. Mayla had her, and Mayla was going to kill her, and I just had to sit here and let it happen.

When it seemed like enough time had passed for Luke to clean the shit out of my room, I shut the faucet off and reached for my towel that I had placed on the toilet. I dried off my face and body then slipped out of the stall and peeked my head into my room. It was all clean. Every trace of Mayla gone, not so much as a tube of lipstick of hers remained. I silently thanked Luke, who was nowhere to be seen. Must have finished and went downstairs to start preparing the meal for the guys who would be home sometime in the next hour or so.

Shit. I forgot about the phone. I hoped that Luke would have heard it if it rang. I pulled on a clean pair of sweats and a white cotton shirt then ran downstairs to check if anyone had called.

"Hey, Luke, you didn't hear the phone at all, did ya?" I asked, clearly concerned.

"Nope, I was listening for it though, don't worry, no one tried to call," he said.

That wasn't exactly good news. I wanted someone to phone and say they found a trail. Something to get me out of this house, doing something productive. I couldn't stand the thought of having nothing to go off.

I glanced around the kitchen and realized that Luke was browning what had to be four pounds of ground beef in a frying pan. I noticed beside the frying pan was a large spaghetti pot. My initial thought was spaghetti until I saw the unopened box of lasagna noodles sitting on the counter. Good, the guys would be pleased with this meal. I wanted them to be well fed and as well rested as possible because tomorrow we were starting the grid. Speaking of tomorrow, I glanced at the clock and realized it was only 3:30 a.m. I thought it was way closer to morning than that. It seemed like hours had passed since we realized Lily was missing, but I guess it was only around 11:30 p.m. when we returned home the first time.

"Nothing like lasagna for breakfast, eh," I said, trying to sound as in control as possible.

"Try to think of it as a late supper," Luke said back.

I just smiled at him and headed toward the coffee pot. I would need the brown stuff to keep me going. I knew I wasn't going to get much sleep until I found Lily. How could I sleep knowing she was out there?

The phone rang. I shot a quick glance at Luke then dashed for the parlor, picking it up on the fourth ring.

"Hello, Jack speaking," I said in a rush.

"Hey, Jack, it's Johnny," said the familiar voice.

"What is it? Did you find a trail?" I asked all too eager.

"No, sorry, Jack. We have nothing. We can't find a recent trail anywhere. It's as if they aren't even in the area anymore. Anyways, we dropped the pants off with Leo, and he sent a team out to search for a few hours. Told me to call you and tell you he will let you know if they find anything. Figured they would run tonight and let us get some rest. We can take over in the morning. I just wanted to make sure it was all right if we headed back now," he said.

"Yeah, come on home, Luke's whipping up a big batch of lasagna. I guess if Leo is going to search tonight, it would be best for us all to sleep, be fresh for tomorrow," I agreed.

"Sounds good, we will be there shortly. Sorry we couldn't find anything, boss, but don't worry, everything will work out." He tried to sounds as convincing as possible.

"I sure hope you are right, Johnny. I sure hope you are right. I'll see ya in a bit."

"Yeah, see ya soon, boss," he said then hung up.

It struck me as strange that he was calling me boss. Normally, Reagan was the only one to actually call me that. I hoped that it wasn't rubbing off on all of them.

I went back into the kitchen intending to help Luke, anything to keep busy.

"Hey, can I do something? The guys are on their way back, should be here in twenty minutes or so."

"Sure, why don't you set the table then?" he said.

I busied myself with setting the table then walked toward the stove to check the progress of the two large pans of lasagna that were now cooking. There was twenty-seven minutes left on the timer.

"Hey, shut that door, you're letting all the heat out," Luke chastised me, sounding too much like a scolding mother who just caught her kid with his hand in the cookie jar.

"Sorry," I said then turned and headed toward the sanctuary of the parlor. There was something that I wanted to do. I knew it was a long shot, but I needed to try.

I picked up the receiver and dialed the number I had dialed a million times in the past. Her voice mail picked up instantly, not even ringing.

"You've reached Mayla, leave a message and I'll call you back," the voice said.

Obviously, she wouldn't have her phone. And if she did, she obviously wouldn't have it on, realizing I would try to call. I knew it was a long shot, but I decided to leave a message anyway.

"Hey, it's me . . . You had better not hurt her, or I swear on everything that is holy, I will fucking kill you Mayla. I will find you, don't ever doubt that." I hung up the phone then.

Terrible pictures started running through my mind. Pictures of Lily lying there defenseless while Mayla punished her for my mistakes. Everything I did lead us to this. It was all my fault. Had I told Lily I was mated and kept my distance, Mayla never would have left. She never would have turned on the pack, and Lily would have been fine right now. Everything would have been fine. If I had just let Lily come with us to find Mayla, she never would have gotten taken because I never would have let her out of my sight. So many things that I could have done differently to avoid this.

I hung my head, feeling like a complete piece of shit. If Lily was hurt—or worse, if she was killed—I would never forgive myself. I didn't know how I would deal with that fact. She had not been a part of my life for a long time, but she had been a very big part of my life. I fell for her and I fell hard. I needed her to be safe and come back to me.

I felt a tear trickle down my cheek and instantly wiped it away. I was not going to sit here and cry like a baby. I needed to stay positive. I needed to concentrate on finding her. She was counting on me.

I heard some commotion coming from the kitchen; the guys must have gotten home. I glanced in the mirror that hung on the wall, checking my eyes to make sure they were dry. Composing my face, I headed back into the kitchen.

The guys were gathering around the table. Clearly starving and exhausted. I would let them eat then get some sleep. We would start again tomorrow. I would have one of them run sections of the grid out to Leo, have them search every inch of the forest in their section, and we would do the same with ours. I couldn't imagine Mayla taking her out of the forest; she would be completely out of her element being in the city. And what would be the point? She was doing this to torture me. To taunt me, she knew it would hurt me, knew I wouldn't stop until I found her. I just didn't understand how she didn't realize I would kill her if I found her. I would destroy every last piece of her, and Tony too.

It dawned on me then. Tony had been doing everything he could to hurt our pack. Trying to frame us for the murders he had been committing in the city. Was this all his plan? Had Mayla agreed to help him lure us? Were they using Lily as bait so Tony could finally get his revenge on our pack for what we did to him and his wife?

It made sense. Mayla probably felt completely safe with him. He was massive, and he knew how to fight, how to do damage. One on one, no member of our pack would win against him, but as a whole, he wouldn't stand a chance. And as far as we knew, there were only two of them, so how did he expect to best us? Unless they had a plan to pick us off one by one. I would have to make sure we travelled in groups. I wouldn't let the numbers get too close. There were eight of us, so we would travel in two groups of four.

I needed to think this through more; I didn't want to walk into another trap, and now that I had a pretty good speculation as to the grand scheme of things, I wanted to make sure we did everything right.

We would get some rest, then in the morning, I would call Leo, warn him to make sure they were never searching alone, just in case. I would then fill everyone in on my presumption, then we would set out and begin the search for the woman I loved.

CHAPTER 11

LILY

TWO WEEKS HAD passed since Mayla took me. Each second felt like an hour; each hour felt like a decade.

It was all I could do to get through it a minute at a time. Mayla was serious when she said I would pay for what I did. I would wake up every morning and the pain would be less, just in time for her to come to me. Quick healing was pointless if you were being beaten every day.

I could only imagine what I looked like. Naked and terrified lying in a corner of a cave, covered in the same blood and dirt for two weeks. I was lucky when Tony would sneak me something to eat. Mayla was good with giving me water. She didn't want me to die right away; she was enjoying this torture too much.

Mayla had already been over to visit me this morning, which resulted in another broken leg, and I was pretty sure my pelvic bone was shattered. She had taken a recent joy in throwing large stones at my face, and I could feel my right eye swelling at an alarming rate. I was getting good at coping with the pain, concentrating on the healing. Knowing it would get better with every second that passed. I would look forward to the few minutes in the mornings where my body would feel only like I got hit by a bus rather than fell off of a mountain, the few minutes before Mayla came back and sent me into a whirlwind of pain.

My left side was throbbing so badly, and I wanted more than anything to roll over, but my pelvic bone was not allowing that. I had to lie there until it healed enough for me to move on my own.

Jack's face graced my mind, and I lost myself in thought. His beautiful lips, warm against mine. His strong hands holding me in the last embrace we had, the night I so stupidly followed him. I would never forgive myself for what I did that night. Jack told me it wasn't safe, told me he didn't know what to expect from Mayla, but I didn't listen. I thought I knew better, that I could handle Mayla. Boy, was I wrong. She was in a class of her own. I couldn't understand how Jack could ever be with her. She was the most hateful person I had ever encountered, and Jack was the kindest person I had ever known; they definitely did not fit.

I didn't want to give up hope that the pack would find me, but I couldn't help it. I mean, I had only been a member of the pack for like a week when I was taken. The second night I had been there, Mayla had stabbed me and excommunicated herself. I had to wonder just how much effort they would actually put into finding me. And if they were trying, how come they hadn't found me yet? Duke was an amazing tracker; he should have been able to track my scent right to me. Maybe they knew where I was, but they couldn't figure out a way to get me. That didn't sound too likely; I mean, there were eight of them.

It was better for me if I stopped counting on them, stopped counting on Jack. I would just be let down in the long run. Would I have been any different if I was in Jack's shoes? If he had gone missing and I had only known him about a week? Would I search forever? The answer was simple for me. Of course I would. I would never stop, but I had feelings for Jack, and considering how short of a time I had known him, it was strange to think of how strong those feelings were.

There was a time I had thought Jack felt the same, but now, now that I had plenty of time to think about it, I wasn't so sure. I mean of course he enjoyed sleeping with me, but at the end of the day, Jack was a male, and I was the only female around.

That thought stirred up numerous other questions in me. Why were there barely any other female wolf shifters? Was it more common for male children? Another question was where were all of their parents? The guys and Mayla had all been around the same age, between twenty and thirty-odd years old. It was useless thinking of these questions; I would never know the answers.

A strange pain took me out of my thoughts. A pain not like the rest. A more familiar pain. I took me a minute to place it, but I eventually did. Shit. A menstrual cramp. Why hadn't I thought about this before? Oh right, because I was too busy getting my shit kicked in. I mentally tried to count back the days till my last period. Yup, I was about due any day now. Perfect, now to add to the pain, I had to be absolutely mortified as well. It may have seemed that I was being petty thinking about getting my period while I was naked in a cave with two people that wished nothing more than to make me suffer when I should only care about my survival, but I couldn't help it. I wanted to keep my dignity. It was all I had left.

How had this happened to me? Three weeks ago, I had a completely normal life. A boring job, a boring apartment, and a boring social life. It all has changed so fast, so drastically, it was hard to believe any of it had been real. I wished I could turn back the clock, back to the night Tony had attacked me. If only I had left work on time, none of this ever would have happened. As soon as I thought it, I knew it wasn't true. If I could turn back the clock, I simply would have stayed home and not followed him. I had enjoyed my new life. I wouldn't trade the time I spent with Jack and the guys for anything. It had been the best week of my life. Pretty pathetic, but I had never really felt like I belonged anywhere before, and I truly did with the pack. They were my family now, and I would never blame them for not coming for me. I would always think of them as family no matter what, even when I was long gone from this world.

I heard footsteps entering the cave, and automatically, I tried to shrink farther into the corner, remembering the broken pelvis and instantly regretting the action. It was Tony; he walked over to me with clear pity in his eyes.

"Hey, Lily, I brought you some water, looks like you could use it," he said.

I heard Mayla not far behind him.

"Tony, what did I tell you about calling her by her name? She is nothing," she hissed.

He spun on her, dropping the water bottle to the floor.

"Mayla, you are not running this goddamn show, so quit spitting demands at me or you will find your mouth smacked right off that face of yours. Got it?"

She actually looked a little frightened for a second but quickly wiped the look off her face before Tony could notice.

"I told you that she was my deal. I won't interfere with your plans for the pack, so please let me deal with Lily on my own." She tried to sound polite, but it just sounded strange coming from her.

"Ha, how I deal with the pack? What pack, Mayla? They are not here. They have no way to find us because you made sure there was no scent. You know as well as I do they will never find us without a trail. I don't even know why I'm still here," he spat.

The words rang through my mind: "You made sure there was no scent," he had said. My heart fluttered. Maybe they were still looking for me. Maybe that was why they hadn't found me yet, because they truly couldn't find me. Without a trail, even Duke couldn't find me. The thought made me choke on my emotion. I felt my eyes fill with tears, and I tried to hide them. I wouldn't let them see me cry. I wouldn't give them that gratification. Plus, I didn't want them to stop talking, I wanted to hear more.

"Tony, you know I will bring them here. They will come for her when they find out she is here. I saw the way Jack looked at her, a way he never looked at me. They will come, don't worry about that. Just try to be patient," she said.

"Patient? It's been two fucking weeks, Mayla, and all you have done is beat this poor girl senseless, what the fuck is the point? They won't find us on their own. They won't, so this is all for you," he said.

"For me? Tony, you can't be serious. You know I will deliver, we made a deal. I just need more time to pass. I want them to hurt before they die. I want them to feel her loss, feel the stress of her disappearance, let them wonder about what I have done with her. Then I will let them find us. I promise. Just think how much better it will be, Tony. They will come, relief will fill their faces at the sight of her, right before you rip them to pieces. Then once you have killed them, I will kill her," she said with clear victory in her voice.

"How much time, Mayla? I'm sick of waiting, I'm sick of sitting here watching what you do to her. It makes me sick. I wanna know how much longer this is going to go on," he said.

"Why don't you just try and think of it as the buildup to the climax. Embrace the wait, enjoy it. The time will come sooner than you think, and both our lives will be perfect again," she said.

"Perfect? My life will never be perfect again, Mayla. I don't know what you're so excited for. Everyone you know will be dead, and you will be all alone, without a mate, without a pack, and without me."

"I will figure it out. I will find my place, and when I do, it will be a much better place than the pack ever was."

"Yeah, well I guess we will see," he replied.

Another wave of menstrual cramps raged in my abdomen. It was strange; I never really got bad cramps. It must have been from all the kicks to the stomach I'd taken recently that were making it worse. And no doubt, my terrible diet lately. I hoped that it wouldn't come. Especially now that I knew Mayla had no plans on killing me for a few weeks. She said she would let Jack find me, and when they came, Tony would kill them. I couldn't imagine him taking all of them out, but I supposed he must have had a plan, or he would never rush into it.

I didn't want to think about that. I didn't want to think about Jack and the boys being ripped to shreds. Luke, so small, so innocent; Flynn as sweet as ever; Johnny with his all too cocky attitude; and Reagan, I would miss Reagan—he truly was a good friend. Duke's wise eyes and calm collectiveness. I didn't know PJ or Mike as well as the rest, but it didn't mean I would miss them any less. And Jack, the thought of Tony getting his hands on Jack was too much for me to bear. I quickly threw the thought out of my mind and tried to concentrate on the newest problem.

I searched my brain for any information I knew about wolves. Did they have a menstrual cycle? I wondered, if I shifted into my wolf form, would it stop my period from coming? Could it save my dignity? I realized I didn't really know too much about them, but I was pretty sure they only went into heat twice a year. Even with that information, I had no idea if it applied to our species; I mean, we weren't full wolves. We were only half wolf, and I wasn't sure if it worked that way. It was worth a shot I guessed.

I would have to wait until the morning because there was no way I would be able to shift right now, not with a broken pelvic bone and leg. I couldn't even roll over, let alone shift form.

Tony grabbed a book and flashlight out of a backpack sitting by the left wall of the cave. He sat on the ground, flipped open the book, and shone his flashlight at the pages. I realized it was more of a textbook than a novel and wondered at that. I remembered the guys and Tony telling me he had been some sort of, um, what did they call it? Ethnologist? Something like that. I wondered if he still worked at that.

Mayla paced by the mouth of the cave mumbling softly to herself. I hated her; I had never truly hated anyone in my life until I met Tony that night in the alley, but even that was nothing compared to the hate I had for her. It was strange; the longer I was in the cave, the less I hated Tony. He seemed genuinely concerned about what Mayla was doing to me. And I had to admit, he hadn't so much as laid a hand on me. He had helped me in fact. Had snuck me food every day, brought me water, and last week, he told me how to fix my elbow that Mayla had so graciously pulled out of its socket.

"I'm going hunting, keep an eye on her, will ya?" Mayla asked from across the cave.

"What are you worried about, Mayla? Look at her, she can't even move, let alone plan an escape. Relax," Tony said, not once looking up from his book.

"Yeah, I suppose you are right. I should break the major bones more often," she said with a smile.

Tony ignored her comment and let her leave. After a few minutes passed, he closed his book and walked back over to his backpack, pulling out some sort of square object. He walked toward me and offered the object. It was a lunch box of sorts. My stomach growled and my mouth watered.

"I suppose I'm going to have to help you with this. Would it be all right if I propped your head up on my backpack? I don't want you eating lying down. How bad are you hurt?" he asked, concern thick.

I took a deep breath and concentrated on answering. Talking had been difficult lately because I didn't do it often. I tried to swallow some nonexisting saliva in hopes of wetting my parched throat.

"My pelvis is broken and my leg, other than that, everything seems okay. I should be able to sit a little if you help me," I said in a raspy voice.

"Let me grab my backpack, and I'll prop you up." He walked toward the wall and snatched the bag off the floor, bringing it back over to me. He sat on the cold floor beside me and gently lifted my head off the floor.

He had to maneuver me in a painful way to get me onto my back. I had been lying on my side since Mayla finished with me this morning, and as painful it was to shift me onto my back, I was thankful for the action. My side throbbed, and little pebbles were embedded into my skin. I hated the thought that Tony had to help me do this, especially in the state that I was in.

"That better?" he asked once he got me situated.

"Much better," I said. He reached toward the lunch box that he had left on the floor beside me when he went to get the backpack.

He handed me a sandwich that he had so kindly unwrapped for me. I grabbed it with my shaky hands and raised it to my face. I ate the sandwich so fast and instantly hated that I hadn't savored it. I noticed him reaching into the box for something else; it was a bag of cookies. This was the best day I had had in two weeks, sandwich and cookies. He handed me the bag, and I ate them with a smile on my face.

"Tony?" I said when I'd finished.

"Yeah?"

"Thank you. Thank you for bringing me food."

"No problem, Lily, I've told you before, I don't agree with this, and I wish there was another way. So the least I can do is make sure you don't starve to death. How's the pain doing?" he asked.

"Nothing I can't handle. One day at a time," I answered.

"Well, I should let you rest, it speeds the healing process, so the more you can get, the better you will feel," he offered.

"Yeah, until the she decides my wounds are healed too much and begins again," I said.

With that he got up and walked back to where he left his book and flashlight, picked it up, and settled back onto the floor.

The food in my stomach made me feel a little better, and I thought I might actually be able to get some rest in.

I closed my eyes and tried to drift off, but it was useless. They had given me so much to think about today. I had to endure a few more weeks of this torture, and then the pack would come for me, and Tony would kill them. Well, he would try to kill them; I hoped he wouldn't succeed, but nothing seemed to ever go the way I wished it to.

I had a plan though. In the morning when I woke up, I would focus on a shift. If I could just try to stay in my wolf form for a couple days, at least then my menstrual cycle should have passed, and who knows, maybe it would make it harder for Mayla to hurt me. I would have a mouth full of razor-sharp teeth.

For the first time in two weeks, I felt a little hope. If not for survival, then at least for the fact that tomorrow would be a little different then today, hopefully a little better.

When Mayla came back a few hours later, she looked full and satisfied. I envied her. I had never been as hungry in my entire life as I had been this week. I thought of food all the time. This damn new metabolism that I was still trying to get used to really sucked in my situation.

It was now Tony's turn to head out for a hunt and restock his backpack I was sure. He always seemed to have something new in that thing every day. He had to be getting it all from somewhere, and it made me wonder if he had a home nearby. Nearby what, though? I had no idea where we were.

I didn't even know if we were in the same state or ten minutes from the pack. For all I knew, we could have been in Jamaica.

The cramps came back, and I prayed my period would hold off until morning, just until I could shift into wolf and not have to deal with it.

When morning finally came, I assessed my injuries. I could move my legs again, which told me my bones had mended. My eye felt a lot better too. I figured now would be the best time to shift if I was going to attempt it. Mayla was still sleeping, and I could see Tony sitting toward the front of the cave, eyes closed.

I rolled over onto all fours and repeated the steps I did so many times that day in the forest.

Thankfully, I felt the change start quickly. It was a weird feeling. I hadn't changed once in the last two weeks. I never really thought about that fact too much, more important things on my mind I guess. But now that I stopped to think about it, I wasn't sure how that happened. Prior to being taken from Mayla, I had sporadically changed at least once a day. I hoped it had something to do with my concentration and hard work in the forest, but I couldn't be sure. You would think the fear and pain would have been enough to set it off, but nothing.

It happened quickly and quietly, thank god, and before I knew it, I was standing in the cave in my full wolf form.

My eyes automatically darted to the cave opening, wondering if I could somehow get past Mayla, who was still asleep, or Tony, who was sitting right beside the exit. I wasn't sure if I was willing to chance it; Mayla would probably wake up as soon as I tried, and my beating would be worse than ever for my radical attempt.

I didn't have long to ponder it before I heard her stir. Her eyes flew open and flashed in my direction.

"Oh well, what do we have here?" she asked in a humored voice. Clearly not at all concerned over my shift. I was no threat to her, even in my wolf form.

Tony's eyes shot open, and he glanced at Mayla, following her gaze toward me. He smiled.

"I was starting to think you forgot how to shift. Bet you feel pretty good about yourself right now, don't you? Sick of playing in your helpless human form? Well, let's do this your way then." She smiled and launched herself off the ground so fast my breath caught.

Before I knew, it she was shifting. As wolves went, she was beautiful; her fur was long and red as fire. She was huge, considering she was a female.

I backed up until my hind was flat against the rocky wall; I could feel my knees tremble. This was a terrible idea.

She flew at me, snarling; I felt her teeth sink into my neck, blood instantly pooling in my fur. Whipping her head to the side, she ripped out a large chunk. I yelped in pain as her teeth connected with my front right leg. Snapping and snapping over again. I tried to cower and pull away, surrender, but she didn't care. She wasn't attacking me because she felt threatened; she was attacking me because she wanted to. Because she liked it.

Misery washed over me. I closed myself off as I had done so many times in the last two weeks. Drown out the pain and let her continue until she had her fill and I was a broken mess on the ground.

This had been the worst one yet. Didn't seem as if any bones were broken, but I was missing numerous chunks of flesh. I must have lost a ton of blood because I was struggling to hold on to my consciousness. It was weird; even in my wolf form, I was still missing my tooth. As a human, it had been my front right tooth; in my wolf self, it was my right canine.

My breathing was low and shallow, and it scared me a little. Another beating like that and I wasn't sure I would make it until she lured the pack here. I was concerned over internal bleeding; my lungs felt like they were full of fluid. Not that I knew much about that sort of thing, but I could hear a strange wet rattling in my chest and throat every time I took a breath.

I glanced over at Tony, who had remained by the opening of the cave through the whole ordeal. He looked truly pained. Like he was fighting an internal struggle. Mayla was nowhere in sight. Probably outside cooling off, trying to get control of herself.

Finally, Tony got up from his spot and slowly approached me.

"Lily, can you hear me?" he asked. "Shit, this is bad. Lily, move your tail if you can hear me," he begged.

Shit, did I look that bad. So bad that he needed confirmation that I could hear him. That I was conscious. I realized my eyes were closed, which probably didn't help his suspicions.

I tried to swoosh my tail across the ground but settled for a light twitch when I realized how much effort it took.

He let out a sigh of relief and dropped to his knees beside me.

"What the hell were you thinking Lily? You shouldn't have shifted, it just pissed her off more. I guess you may not have been able to help it. I remember when I was first changed. I shifted all the time, usually at all the wrong times. It took me about six months to get in under control."

I thought about what Jack had told me. That I would probably not be able to control it for around a year. Well, apparently, that wasn't a problem for me, maybe because I was thrust into a situation where I had to control myself. Who knew?

"Look, now that you are in your animal form it would probably be best for you to stay this way. At least until you heal more, you seem to have lost quite a bit of blood, and I'm not even sure if you will be able to shift," he said in a quiet voice.

I lifted my eyes to his face. Trying to communicate that I had no intention of shifting back anytime soon. This may have been the worst beating yet, but I felt more concealed, more private in my healing, and that was worth more to me than anything. I liked that she couldn't read the emotion on my face when I was a wolf as much as she could when I was a human. I knew she got some sort of sick pleasure out of that.

Imagine if every woman on earth who had ever been cheated on acted like her. This world would fall apart. It just blew my mind that she would go to such extremes over something that happened every day to numerous women. Chemical imbalance for sure. Or perhaps it was different with shifters considering the male-to-female ratio. But that wouldn't make sense either because she was a female and could have her choice of almost any male shifter she wanted. I could understand why she picked Jack—hell, I picked him too—but I couldn't imagine ever doing this to another living thing if he had ever cheated on me. I mean, it was a little overkill.

Lost in thought, I hadn't realized that Tony was not next to me anymore. I glanced around the cave as well as I could without moving my head and noticed him riffling through his backpack. He hauled out four bottles of water, and I hoped he would bring one to me. I wasn't overly sure how I was going to drink it. Lack of opposable thumbs made drinking from bottles a little difficult. My extended snout wouldn't help either.

He had other plans for the water. I noticed he had some sort of article of clothing draped over his arm as well; it looked like a long-sleeve cotton shirt. Weird. He was walking toward me with his arms full.

He once again dropped beside me and slowly opened the water bottles. He seemed to do everything in slow motion. Like he was weary of me. It made me think back to the first night I met Jack and he had told me that they couldn't approach me right away in the alley because I was dangerous. I could have reacted like a wounded animal. Seemed so strange to me now, strange that Tony, of all people, would be weary; he was three times my size, and I was completely helpless. I couldn't imagine trying to get up, let alone hurt him in any physical way.

My body jumped as I felt the cold water pour into my neck wound. It stung, which ripped the pain from my throat.

"Sorry, Lily, I gotta get these wounds cleaned, they will get infected. They are really deep. I'm not sure how long it will take for them to start healing, and I don't like the amount of blood that's still pouring out of this one on your neck."

I let him clean it; after all, he was right. If I got an infection or lost too much blood, it could take forever for me to heal. Broken bones were so much easier; just snap them back into place and lie really still until they fuse back together. But pieces of my flesh missing, intense blood loss, internal bleeding, lungs filled with fluid—all those things scared the shit out of me. They were vital, and if my vitals weren't working, my body couldn't heal.

Once the neck wound was as clean as he could get it in a cave, he ripped a sleeve off the cotton shirt and tied it around my neck.

"I know that is probably not comfortable, but I need to apply enough pressure to stop the bleeding. Try to ignore it," he said.

He then moved onto the other spots of my body where I was missing chunks, pouring water over all of them and wrapping the worst ones.

I was beginning to feel a little better, wounds cleaned out, blood supply starting to replace itself, and the warmth. For the first time in two weeks, I actually felt warm. Thank heavens for my thick blond coat. Well, it was more red right now, bloodstained, and dirty.

Mayla eventually came back, completely ignoring me, and braced herself against a wall then closed her eyes.

"Mayla!" Tony screeched at her when he noticed her.

"What?" she said a little shaken; his booming voice must have startled her.

"This is not going on any longer. You almost killed her today. You're lucky she is still breathing," he accused.

"*Lucky* isn't the word I would use," she said with a smile.

"I'm being serious, Mayla. That is not part of the plan. Take it easy, you're going to kill her, and then they will have no fucking reason to come here. I've put up with your shit long enough. I'm done," he hissed.

"Then leave, Tony. I will keep her here, and you can go. Do whatever you want. If you don't want me to lead the pack into your little trap, then there is no reason for you to be here. No skin off my ass."

Shit, I did not want to be left alone with Mayla. Tony was the only person I could count on these days. Mayla wouldn't feed me. I would slowly starve.

"Don't try to kid yourself, Mayla, if I left, you would be dead. Your cooperation is the only reason you are alive right now. So get this show on the road. I want this cooperation to be over."

"I've told you, Tony, I can't do that for another couple weeks. They are not ready yet. And Lily hasn't learned her lesson yet," she replied.

"You're sick, Mayla, fucking sick," he said then spun on his heels and left the cave.

I prayed he hadn't gone too far. Prayed he was just outside getting some fresh air. I felt bad for wanting him here so bad when I knew what he had planned for my pack. I knew if he was here when they came, he would kill them. He would kill Jack. I would have to try and stop that. I needed to try and behave so Mayla would go easy on me. I needed to have as much strength as I could when the guys came. They may need my help. And I refused to let them down again.

CHAPTER 12

JACK

"JACK, CALM DOWN. Please, you need to get a grip on yourself," Johnny yelled at me.

"Get a grip? Are you kidding me? It's been two weeks. Two weeks, Johnny, and do you know how much closer to finding her we are? We're not, not closer at all. I don't even know if she is alive, and you're telling me to calm down," I screamed back.

"Jack, you're alpha, you need to relax. We are useless without you. You haven't slept, you're not eating, you look like complete shit. You need to start taking care of yourself. Working with us. We need you, Jack. So pull your shit together," he said, not trying to spare my feelings.

"You don't understand, Johnny. You'll never know what it's like to have everyone count on you. Everyone waiting for you to give them the answer, give them their orders, protect them. I can't do any of that right lately. I couldn't protect Lily, I can't find Lily, and I don't know what to do. I don't have the fucking answers, and for once I want someone to tell me what to do. I want someone to tell me how I can find Lily because I have run out of ideas."

"Well, unfortunately, that's not how it works. You were born alpha and you will die alpha, and until then, you need to get your shit together and tell us what the hell the next step is. We are all sick of you dragging your ass around here, putting holes in the walls, destroying everything in your path because your temper is out of control. The boys are too fucking scared to even come and talk to you. That's why they sent me in. We need our alpha back," he said.

I just hung my head. I knew he was right. I was cursed with alphahood from birth, and it was something I would always have to deal with. Being born with it meant I had what it took inside me to deal with almost anything. But I had never prepared myself for this, and I was concerned the strength it took to deal with this particular situation was something I would never find.

"All right, I get it. I know I need to get my head on Johnny, but come on. I have nothing. I have no options. I have no idea where she could be. We have scoured every inch of this forest. I can't search the whole world. I don't know what else to do, where to look," I shot at him.

"I know that, Jack. But no one is giving up. There are still the mountains. Maybe she took her there. There are enough of us between us and the cougars to scour the mountain ranges."

"Scour the mountain ranges? That will take weeks, I don't know if we have that much time. She could be dead by now. I hate the thought of leaving her there for weeks. I want a solution, and I want it now." I couldn't help the anger in my voice.

"Well, it's a better plan than you have given us in a while, so I'm going to let the guys know that you have decided we search the mountains. We will search every goddamn mountain in this country if we have to, Jack. We will find her." I knew he was just trying to make me feel better, but it made me feel worse. It seemed hopeless. There was no way we could check every inch of every mountain in the area in any less time than three weeks.

"Whatever you say," I agreed.

"Good. Now I'm going to go downstairs, fill in the guys. How about you catch a shower and meet us downstairs. I'll fix you something to eat, and, Jack?" he asked.

"What?"

"You will eat every damn piece, got it?" he said.

"Yeah, yeah, Johnny," I said. I couldn't remember the last meal I actually had. I wasn't actually hungry; I was too far past hungry. The thought of food actually turned my stomach. I snuck a glance at myself in the mirror; I did not like what I saw. My eyes were black underneath and somewhat sunken into my sockets. I looked tired, eyes bloodshot and hair a mess. I had definitely lost weight, and it was not attractive on my frame. I looked like shit. I didn't care though. I knew I should, knew I should pull myself together, put on my alpha face and figure out this mess. But the fact was I didn't know how. I couldn't go around acting like everything was okay, like it wasn't ripping me apart from the inside out having her missing.

I turned on the shower and quickly scrubbed clean. I don't actually remember getting dressed or walking down the stairs. I only realized I was in the kitchen because Johnny told me to sit down.

"Johnny, let's not forget who is in charge around here. Quit throwing orders at me," I snapped.

"Then don't let us forget, Jack. If you're not going to act like an alpha, then someone has to. So eat your breakfast, then I'll leave you alone." Sometimes I wanted nothing more than to punch Johnny right in the mouth.

"Yeah, I'm fine. I got it," I said with finality in my voice.

We ate in silence; the guys spent a lot of time avoiding me lately. They knew I didn't do well with loss. They learned this lesson when I lost my parents. Well, I wasn't the only one to lose my parents—we all did—but I didn't take well to it. They adjusted; they went on. I struggled.

The accident happened about eighteen years ago, shortly after my tenth birthday. Our parents had received a tip that a pack of black bear shifters were migrating into our area. We got the call from a pack of wolf shifters that lived on the Canada–United States border, who we often communicated with.

Black bears are typically not dangerous, especially if they are not in their animal form. Our parents headed out to have a discussion with this new pack of black bears. They wanted to give them the warning that this was our territory and the cougar's territory and they had no right moving into it.

Everyone's parents went, and only one returned. Duke's father was the only survivor, and he crawled home to break the news to us. Turned out they weren't black bear shifters after all. It was a congregation of grizzly bears, just regular old grizzly bears. Our parents went in as humans, believing the bears to be in their human form. It was quite a shock to them to find out they just approached a gathering of grizzly bears.

A grizzly bear, when threatened, is a very aggressive animal. Our parents barely had time to shift before the bears were on them. It was strange; normally, grizzly bears are solitary animals, which was why the border pack had presumed them to be shifters because they were traveling in a large pack. But apparently, it was just a congregation of grizzlies gathering for the salmon spawn alongside a large pond.

It was unfortunate, terrible, and heartbreaking. Most of us were so young, and the only one to return was Duke's father. He didn't live long after the attack; we believed it was a combination of heartbreak over the loss of his wife and friends, not just the injuries he had received.

Duke was eighteen when our parents died, and he took full responsibility for all of us. Raised us, fed us, and took care of us using all the resources our parents left.

He especially spent a lot of time with me; I struggled because I was born with two different-color eyes. One male is born in every generation of a wolf pack with this phenomenon, and its significance is alphahood. My parents knew that I would one day be alpha, just as my father had been before me. So when I lost them, I felt like the world was resting on my shoulders; I was terrified that I would never be half the alpha my father was. Also, I was terrified of hitting puberty and Duke handing over the reins to me. He was the oldest, and in my eyes, he was much better suited to be alpha, but it is not a choice.

When puberty finally hit, I accepted my role as head of the pack, and Duke graciously accepted my leadership. I strongly believed Duke's calm disposition came from all those years trying to raise us kids. He was only eighteen years old, trying to take care of us, eight little boys and one girl.

"Jack, Jack!" I heard Johnny try and break through to me.

"Sorry, I was lost in thought there," I apologized.

"Yeah, we could see that, you've only had one bite of your food. Better get eating, we got lots to do today," he said.

In a way, I was thankful Johnny was taking over a little, relieving me of a small bit of my burden.

"Yeah. Someone should call Leo, see if they wanna help search the mountain range. But I don't want him to think that we expect it. They have helped so much in the last while, I feel terrible to keep asking them to put their selves out," I said.

"I'm sure he doesn't mind, Jack, he knows we would do the same for him. I will call him when we finish eating. Do you have a plan for the mountain search?" Johnny asked.

"Not really, I will finish eating and head to the parlor to grid it out I guess. I'm not as familiar with the mountains as I am with the forest, it may take a bit longer. Hopefully, we can get out of here early this afternoon, right after we eat lunch," I said, feeling good about finally having some sort of plan again. I desperately wanted to get back out there and start the search, but I was so unfamiliar with the mountains. I just hoped we found some sort of trail, anything to let me know there was hope.

"Why don't we try to get an aerial view of the area, see if there are any on the computer, and try to go from there. Seems easier than trying to map it out and draw diagrams." It was Duke's voice this time.

"Thanks, Duke, I'll try that," I said. It actually was a really good idea. I was thankfully that my pack was still thinking clearly at least.

I got as much food into me as my stomach would allow and quietly excused myself. I wanted to see if I could find an aerial printout like Duke had suggested and get started as soon as possible.

My computer seemed to take forever to boot up; I went back into the kitchen to grab another cup of coffee while I was waiting for it. Coffee had become my main sustenance lately, and I feared it was turning into a very unhealthy addiction. I needed to try and get some sleep tonight. My ten- to fifteen-minute catnaps were doing nothing. I was too scared to sleep in case the phone rang and we missed a tip. I would make a point tonight to set up a bed in the parlor so I could sleep next to the phone. It concerned me that once I fell asleep, I would be out forever. I would have to have one of the guys wake me up as soon as they got up in the morning. Because Johnny was right, I looked terrible, and it was freaking the guys out. I needed to pull myself together for them and for Lily.

Finally, the computer was booted and ready to go. I took a sip of my coffee and typed "aerial view of the Three Sisters mountain range and surrounding area" into the Google search engine.

"Hmm," I said out loud to myself when the search turned up fruitful.

I glanced through the top matches until I found a perfect view of the entire area. This would work perfect. I hit Print and snatched the paper off the printer as soon as it came out.

"Hey, guys?" I said poking my head into the kitchen; no one was there, so I opened up the door to the basement and shouted down there.

"Yeah, boss, we're down here," Reagan yelled back.

I walked down the stairs to join them; they were apparently having an early afternoon beer. Sounded good to me. I needed something to take this edge off. One beer then we'll grab some quick sandwiches before we hit the road. I was about a thirty-five-minute run just to the mountain range from our den, and it would take forever to search every inch once we got there.

"Hey, Johnny, did you get a hold of Leo? I asked grabbing a Coors Light from the fridge and dropping myself down onto one of the bar stools.

"You bet, he said they would love to help with the mountains. They spend a lot of time up there anyway. I told him we would call back once we had a solid plan," Johnny answered.

I would have to remember how much I owed Leo and his family after this whole mess was over. He had done more than I ever would have expected from them.

I cracked my beer and ran over the printout with the guys. We decided to run in two groups of three. Two people would stay home at all times in case Leo or anyone else called with information we would need.

Today Luke and Flynn would stay back. We would leave at 12:00 p.m. sharp and try to be back for about 10:00 p.m. tonight. It would be a long run but we had to put as many hours in a day as we could if we had a hope in hell of searching the mountain range this month.

Once our beers were done and our back pack was loaded Luke followed us outside to loop the duffel bag with our cell phone in it over one of our necks. I figured I should carry it because I was the leader I should have to carry the burden but Duke shifted first and walked over toward Luke and dipped his head. Luke hooked it over his neck and backed up waiting for me to change and lead the way.

We raced through the forest toward the mountains as fast as we could. It felt great to be doing something again. The wind in my face, earth under my paws.

We made great time to the range; I realized we had forgotten to call Leo before we left. I was going to have him meet us here. Oh well, I would call him tomorrow morning before we left. That would give us today to get a feel for the area.

The mountains were covered in snow, making it difficult to pick up a scent of any kind. We started by looking for footprints in the snow. Rabbits, deer, elk, the usually mountainous animals, and a few wolf prints. But upon closer inspection, we realized they were just from a regular old wolf, not a shifter.

Up and down the mountain range for hours. Every piece of ground had to be inspected, every bush, every tree, just as we had done in the forest.

By 9:30 p.m., we had found nothing. I had to keep reminding myself it was day one. It was only the first day; had I really expected to find anything the first day? But my disappointment proved that I did. I needed to get the guys home; they were hungry and exhausted. We would head home, eat a late supper, and get some sleep. I quickly raced to the spot that Duke had deposited the duffel bag, swiftly changed back to my human form, and phoned the house.

"Hello," Flynn's voice answered.

"Hey, Flynn, it's Jack. We haven't found anything yet, so I'm bringing the guys home. Can one of you make sure there's some grub ready? These boys are starving," I said.

"Sure thing, Jack," he said.

"Thanks, Flynn, see you soon."

"Bye."

I dropped the phone into the bag and hung it around Duke's neck again as he was standing near me already in his wolf form, waiting. Turning in the direction of home, I took my wolf form once again and took off running. It was the first time in a while that I actually felt hungry.

It was strange how I could still remember exactly the way Lily had looked the day she was taken and the way she smelled and the way she would smile at me. I could picture every curve of her face and every curve of her body. I wanted her back in my arms. I wanted to know she was all right; I wanted to give her a life with me, a good life, better than her upbringing. I wanted to give her everything that she had never had. I felt the rage start to boil up in my throat again, which just seemed to fuel my legs. I was running faster than I ever had before.

I reached the house a few minutes before the rest of the pack and raced inside to check the progress of the meal. There was a large plate full of barbecued steaks and baked potatoes. I could see a large pot on the stove filled with corn on the cob. My mouth watered.

"Hey, Jack," Luke said, seeming oddly shy. He was never shy with me. It must have been my recent mood that had made him timid. I needed to make sure I kept the temper under check; I hadn't realized I was affecting the guys this bad.

"Hey, Luke, Flynn," I tried to say in my bubbliest voice. It came out sounding fake though, which made Flynn giggle lightly to himself.

"Where is everyone?" Flynn asked.

"They are coming. I was a little ahead of them," I was beginning to explain as the backdoor opened and five naked guys strolled in.

"Mmm, smells good in here," PJ said as he passed by the guys, quickly grabbing his seat at the table. The guys followed suit, and I grabbed the platters of food off the counter and carried them to the table. Flynn grabbed the plates and cutlery, quickly setting the table around guys.

"Anyone want a bottle of water while I'm up?" I offered

A few of the guys raised their hands, unable to speak because their mouths were already filled with food. I grabbed an armful of bottles and put them in the middle of the table, turning it into a free-for-all just like the rest of the meal.

It actually tasted delicious, and I scarfed mine down in record time. I decided that after dinner, I would head out to the garage where we kept all the house supplies and find what I needed to repair all the holes I had put in the walls recently. I knew there was a large vat of spackling from when Lily destroyed the parlor her second night at the house; Flynn had to repair three small holes that night. We usually stocked up on that sort of stuff. I would check, and if we had everything I needed, then I would repair the walls. Try to show the guys that I was feeling better, that I was in control.

I deposited my dishes in the sink, not caring if the dishes got done or not, then headed for the garage. Luckily, the box with the wall repair stuff was right beside the door. Hadn't gotten too far since Flynn used it. Perfect plenty of mesh paper, spackling, and sandpaper. I knew we had leftover paint to from when we had the house painted, but I think that was in the basement. I could find that another day as I wouldn't be painting tonight anyway.

I started with the parlor and worked my way through the house. The holes were easy enough to fix. Sand down the edges, stick on the mesh paper, paste on the spackling, then move to the next hole. Once they were all dry, I would go back to the beginning and sand them all down.

It went surprisingly fast; the largest hole to fix was the one at the bottom of the stairs leading to the basement. The boys stared at me while I tried to jimmy rig the mesh paper to fit over the hole I put my body through the night I was searching for Mayla. Flynn offered to help, but I waved him off, telling him I was fine.

Once the spackling was setting on all of them, I returned to the first hole to see if it was dry. Just as I was rooting through the box to find the sandpaper, the phone rang.

I stood up as fast as I could and tripped over the box trying to get to the phone.

"Hello, Jack here," I said finally, hoping it was Leo calling with good news.

"Jack," said a familiar female voice.

My blood boiled. Mayla.

"Where is she, Mayla?" I growled.

"Wouldn't you like to know? But for right now, Jack, that's for me to know and you . . . uh, not to." She laughed.

"Mayla, if you hurt her, I swear to god I will hunt you down and I will kill you," I spat.

"Yes, because clearly you're the best hunter. You can't track me down, Jack, you've been trying and trying, and I bet you're still not one step closer to knowing where I am, are you?" She thought it was all so humorous.

"Mayla, what do you want? Obviously, you want something. If it's money, we will pay whatever you want for her. Is that it? Are you holding her at ransom?" I asked, trying to keep my composure, scared that if I got to angry with her, she would hang up.

"No, Jack, I don't want the pack's money. I'm simply phoning to make sure you haven't given up searching for your precious Lily," she spat.

"Of course we haven't given up. I will never give up," I said.

"That's a good thing because let me tell you, Jack, she ain't looking so good," She said, and my heart sank.

"What have you done to her?" I asked in a whisper.

"Oh, Jack, I guess that's something you're just going to have to find out for yourself. But I will tell you this, she is counting on you, and every day you don't find her, the worse it gets for her," she said, then I heard the click telling me she disconnected the call.

I instantly dialed her phone back, but it was shut off. So she had her phone, but she was choosing when to use it.

My guts were turning. Lily was alive and Mayla was hurting her, and she would continue to hurt her until I found her. If she died, it would be because I never found her in time. How was I supposed to sit here? How was I supposed to rest? Every minute counted.

I headed back downstairs to tell the guys about the phone call I just received.

"Jack, it's crazy, we can't go back out there tonight. It's late, we need rest," Johnny protested.

He was really starting to irritate me. I mean, one minute he is on my case because I wasn't not doing enough, now he was pissed that I wanted to do too much?

"I'm not asking you to come with me. I'm simply telling you that I'm going back. I won't be coming home at night. I will stay up there. Sleep there if I have to, but I will not stop until I find her. Mayla said she is not in good shape. I could hear it in her voice how much she was enjoying this. I need you to understand how I can't just sit around here. I'll expect you guys to meet me up there daily. We will run together as long as we can, and at night you can come back and rest."

"No." It came from Duke, and my head whipped toward him in astonishment.

"Pardon me?" I said, baffled at the thought of him telling me no.

"No. You will not go alone. I will go with you. If you have to search nonstop, the I will be right beside you. I can't let you alone," he said in his usual calm voice.

"That's not necessary, Duke. You guys need rest and food, I can't ask you to stay away from home for god knows how long," I said.

"You're not asking me. I made the decision all by myself. And it doesn't matter what you say, I'm coming," he said simply.

I knew there was no arguing with him. Once he made up his mind, he wouldn't change it. I didn't want to admit it, but I was thankful.

"All right," I said in agreement.

"We can send two shifts out a day, each shift will fill the duffel bag full of food, you won't have time to be hunting if you're searching for Lily, so we will bring food," Reagan said.

"Good, that's great. I will leave it up to you guys what shifts you want to be in. I'm sure you will find us easy enough, we will leave a clear trail. Also, we will have the cell phone with us. You guys will have to pack us a new charged one every couple of days. And don't forget, someone always has to be here in case the phone rings."

"Don't worry, boss, we will take care of everything," said Reagan.

"That reminds me, one of you will need to call Leo in the morning because I won't be here. Fill him in on everything, tell him where he can meet me," I said.

They all nodded in agreement. I trusted they would do everything I asked of them. I planned on letting Duke catch a nap once we got out to the mountains while I searched a new section. I would try to get a few winks in during the day when I knew there were others looking for her. I wouldn't feel as if I was wasting as much time if there were people still looking.

"All right, well, let's get out of here. We got a long night ahead of us," Duke said and spun for the stairs.

"See you later, guys, take care, get some sleep, and we will see you in the morning," I called over my shoulder as I followed Duke to the stairs.

"Be careful," came Luke's voice.

We stripped in the kitchen, and I grabbed a grocery bag from the pantry. We needed to take a cell phone, but I couldn't take the duffel bag; the boys would need it in the morning to bring us food. I figured I would drop the phone into a coffee thermos and then drop the thermos into a grocery bag and hang that over my neck until we got there. The thermos should keep the cell phone from freezing in the snow when we stashed it.

As soon as we were outside, I shifted, and Duke hooked the bag with the thermos over my head then shifted, and we headed into the night.

CHAPTER 13

LILY

ANOTHER WEEK HAD passed, and things were getting strange. I was concerned that I had some permanent damage. Or the internal bleeding was not healing the way it should be.

I was still in my wolf form. I hadn't been able to shift back when I tried a few days ago. I think it had something to do with the low amount of blood that my body held at all times.

My stomach had been bothering me lately, bloating in a terrible way, and I couldn't seem to find any strength. The most I could do through my days were lift my head to slurp water out of a bowl that Tony had brought for me or when he brought me a raw steak or dead rabbit to eat.

I spent most of my time counting minutes as they passed by, until they turned into hours, which turned into days. I was living in some sort of parallel universe. Most of the time, I didn't know if I was awake or asleep anymore.

Today was different. It was an exceptionally bad day for me. I needed to move; I wanted to be in a different corner. This one I was in just wasn't right. The other corner was deeper set into the cave and seemed cozier; why I was concerned about finding a cozy spot to curl up, I had no idea. It seemed irrational to me as well, but I just had to be there.

When Tony came to feed me that evening, and when he knelt on the floor next to me, I struggled to get up, hoping he would help me.

"Do you need to stretch your legs, Lily?" he asked.

I tried to bob my head up and down. Thankfully, Mayla was out on her nightly hunting ritual, so Tony would let me get up if I wanted to. He gently helped me to my feet and stayed by my side all the way to the cozy corner. I slowly did three circles around the area and curled myself into a ball.

"Wow, you must really have wanted to lie in this corner to go through such pain to get here," he said.

He was right. I mean, the other corner had worked just fine for three weeks now, but I just had a strange need to be over here. Simple things like this were all I had to look forward to these days. The coziest patch of dirt to lie in or what color rabbit Tony brought me to eat today.

The nights were starting to get colder, so Tony started lighting a fire in the cave. It kept it nice and toasty, but the smoke sometimes got too thick, and it was hard to breath. I didn't know if it was such a problem for them, but my sense of smell had been so strong lately that it really bugged me. I chalked it up to the fact that my eyes were closed most of the time, so my other senses were working overtime.

Like clockwork, Mayla came every morning with a new wave of pain for me. It was simply to disable me through the days so she wouldn't have to worry about me trying to escape. I mean, the fun of it had to wear off by now. I was so used to the pain by now that I barely even yelped when she kicked me or beat my head off the rock wall. I just took it, knowing that there was nothing I could do to stop it, and if I tried, she would just make it worse.

Mayla was irritated last night when she came back to find I had been moved. She shrieked at Tony for moving me, and he explained that I had to move my legs. He told her to relax; what difference did it make where I wanted to lie? But she had been keeping a weird eye on me ever since.

My Stomach started out awful again today. I was really begginging to worry that I has some sort of nasty infection. Why else would the bloating seemed to keep getting worse, never any better. I was so skinny everywhere else except for in my stomach region. It reminded me of those commercials that World Vision used to play on the television, the little children that were so thin but their stomachs so bloated because they were so sick and malnourished.

I had to pay more attention to protecting my stomach perhaps in the beatings. Try to take the blows elsewhere, just until my stomach started to get better. I was worried that maybe something was ruptured and I was pooling with blood.

That afternoon, I tried again to shift back. Wanting to be in my human form to survey the damage to my stomach. Then if it was something serious, it would be easier for me to guess what it was when I was in the shape I was most used to, but I couldn't do it. I was too weak, and my body completely refused.

"Tony, have you noticed the way she looks lately?" I heard Mayla ask.

"Yeah, Mayla, of course I have. She looks half-dead. What did you expect?" he asked incredulously.

"I was specifically referring to her stomach, asshole," she said.

My eyes shot open. So it really did look that bad. Crap. I was hoping it was just paranoia, but I guess not. I glanced at Tony, who was now looking directly at me. Surveying the condition of my stomach.

"Well, yeah, I noticed it, but I presumed it was just bloating from the disgusting living conditions you are keeping her in. I mean seriously, Mayla, she stays in the same spot, the same spot where she eats and uses the bathroom and bleeds, did you really expect her not to get some sort or nasty infection? That's probably why she insisted on moving to the other corner. Trying to get away from her own filth," he spat.

I felt the blood rush to my face in embarrassment. Thank god my face was covered in fur to hide my heated cheeks. I had barely been able to get up; I supposed I had made quite the mess. And he was right; it was completely unsanitary conditions. I was filthy, and every day I had open wounds that were coming in contact with it.

"You don't think she's . . . ?" She left the rest unsaid.

Dying. I presumed that was the end of her sentence. It made my heart rate accelerate. I didn't want to die. I wasn't ready to give up yet. I glanced at Tony to see his reaction to her question.

"Think she's what?" he asked, clearly not jumping to the same conclusion as me.

"Pregnant?" she asked.

Whoa, not what I was expecting. And totally impossible, thank God.

"Oh shit. I fucking hope not," Tony said, his face clouding over with despair.

Shit, why wasn't he telling her how ridiculous she sounded? How impossible that was.

"Well, when was that last time you were in your wolf form near her?" she asked.

"I haven't been, I shift once I'm outside," he said.

"Well, what are you waiting for? You are a male wolf, you'll smell it if she is pregnant. Shift and find out," she said with urgency in her voice.

What the hell was happening? There was no way I could be pregnant. The only person I had been within the last eighteen months was Jack, and that was only three weeks ago. Well, I guess four weeks ago if you count from the first time. So even if I was pregnant from him, I wouldn't be showing at four weeks pregnant. That barely even classified as pregnant.

I watched as Tony shifted and walked toward me. It didn't take long for him to shift back.

"Shit. Fuck. Shit" was all he said.

"You've got to be kidding me. She's fucking pregnant, isn't she?" Mayla said.

"Yup, she's definitely pregnant. Who knows for how long, look at the condition she is in, Mayla. It stops now. Right now. You won't lay one more hand on her," he ordered.

"The bitch is pregnant with my mate's baby? Wow, this is going to be more fun than I thought. I wonder if Jack knows. Probably not, considering they only started screwing four weeks ago," she said mainly talking to herself.

"Four weeks ago, eh? So how many days would that make her? Twenty–eight, right?"

"Yup, twenty-eight days. Not long left. I have so many things to think over. There are so many options." She began laughing.

"Mayla, what are you talking about options? This game is over now. She is carrying a fucking child."

"A child that was conceived with a mated man. It's as disgusting as she is. And just imagine how crazy Jack will go when he finds out. This is going to be insane. He will go ape shit." She stopped, lost in her thoughts.

This was not good; I instantly tried to curl around my belly to cradle my baby. My god, it was weird to think. My baby, my and Jack's baby. Jack would go crazy. He was going to be pissed. I never thought to use protection because we were shifters. I guess I didn't think everything worked the same. And what was it they meant about twenty-eight days? Why did that matter? Not like they gave a shit about my due date. It made me curious though.

"Mayla, calm down, this is not a good thing. You are not going to lay your hands on her now that we know she is carrying a child."

"Yes, I am, Tony. I mean, what does it matter, I'm killing her in the end. You're killing the pack, so what the fuck does it matter if she loses her baby? It will die without its parents anyway."

I wanted Tony to protest for me, to tell her she was insane, but he just nodded, clearly agreeing with her logic.

Fuck, I was truly on my own now.

"I will have to call the proud father soon and let him know. But not yet. I guess it's time to go set some trails, better if they find us soon. Honestly, I would rather kill her when she is still pregnant rather than after she has the baby," Mayla revealed.

"Well, let's hope they gave up with the forest because they are never going to find us in there. Do you think they will come to the mountains?" he asked.

The mountains? Hmm, strange, I didn't realize we were in the mountains.

"I'm not sure, but we will lay some trails, then I will phone and give him a little tip," she said.

"Well, we have no more than thirty-four days, unless you want to deliver a pup in this cave."

I choked on my breath. Thirty-four days? Were they still talking about me? Thirty-four plus twenty-eight was sixty-two days; that's like two months. What the hell were they talking about delivering a pup in thirty-four days?

Then it hit me like a brick wall. I was a goddamn wolf. They weren't pregnant for nine months. I wasn't sure how long they were pregnant, but if Mayla and Tony said sixty-two days, well, then that must be right. I had a cat that had kittens once and remembered she was not pregnant for very long. Not that I was trying to compare myself to a cat.

Thirty-four days, the number was taunting me. I couldn't stop thinking about it. I was almost halfway done being pregnant. I was terrified for the poor thing; I was in absolutely no shape to be carrying a child.

Mayla was going to go and lay her trail first. She figured she would run some trails all over the place so that no matter what direction they came from, they would be able to find our cave.

Mayla insisted in taking some traces of my blood along to drive them crazy when they found my scent. She busied herself with that while I watched from my new corner. Thank god she was using my old blood.

As soon as she was gone, Tony made his way over to me. He dropped to my side and put his hand on my back.

"Lily, I'm so sorry about this. I'm sure that you heard everything, and I'm sorry. I'm sorry about everything. But I want you to know, I'm not going to let her kill you. I will get you away from here, I promise you that. I just need to make it seem like I'm agreeing with her to appease her. I mean, I'm still going to kill the pack, I have to. It is my whole life's purpose now, and I realize that is something you feel strongly against, and I apologize again, but there is nothing I can do to save you from that pain. Their death is inevitable. The only life I can spare is yours and your unborn child's."

My heart was broken. I just found out that I was pregnant with Jack's child and I could never share that with him. I would have to watch him die along with my pack members. It left me even more broken than I already was. I no longer could wish that Mayla would kill me too; I had to be strong for this child that I was carrying.

Tony got up and walked away from me, clearly needing to prepare himself for the war that was coming. I prayed that Jack wouldn't find out, that he would be oblivious to the fact that I was pregnant. It would mess him up if he knew; he would be too focused on saving me and not focused enough on saving himself.

I still couldn't understand how Tony planned to kill the pack. I mean, Tony was big, but he was drastically outnumbered, even with Mayla at his side. I had to pay close attention to him, try to figure out what he had planned. If there was anything I could do to stop him, I would.

The time passed, and finally, Mayla returned. She threw a disgusted look at me and walked over to Tony.

"All right, I stunk up numerous areas of the mountain side. It should lead them to us if they find themselves on the right mountain. I'm not sure how long it will take for them to make their way here though. I'm thinking tomorrow I will put in a call to Jack. Give him a bit of a hint," she said.

"Yeah. I doubt they are even in the mountain range searching. You'd think they would be concentrating mainly on the forest, that is the most likely place that we would be," he said.

"Yeah, well you don't know the pack. Jack will search this entire country for her if he has to. I know it. You should have heard the desperation in his voice when I called him the other night."

Called him? What was she talking about? She called Jack? And he sounded desperate? My heart fluttered.

"When the hell did you do that?" Tony asked, mirroring my curiosity.

"I don't know, couple days ago, maybe a week. I phoned him to make sure he was still searching. I was checking for you, Tony, you were concerned that they had given up. Well, don't be because he sounded like a complete basket case, a determined basket case. He hasn't stopped looking for her, and he assured me he never will," she reassured him.

"Hmm, well, that's a good thing."

"So do you have a plan yet? How are you gonna do it now? Clearly they won't come separated. They will all be together, and you know as well as I do that you won't stand a chance in a hands-on fight against them all," she said, clearly interested in his plan.

"I've been thinking about that, and I guess the easiest way would be to peg them off as they are heading to the cave. I checked out a spot up the mountain a little, and I could get a clear shot at them, no matter which direction they came from. Figure I will just put a bullet in each one of their heads and be done with it," he said nonchalantly.

This was horrible; the pack wouldn't stand a chance if he just planned to shoot them as they approached. They would never know. They would be too focused on my scent coming from the cave, they would never think to check the mountain for Tony and his gun. I found myself praying that Tony was a terrible shot. That maybe he would miss and the sound of the gun would alert the guys to Tony. Give them time to take cover and come up with a plan of their own.

"So how much time do you need? When I call him, should I lead them to this mountain then let them sniff us out? Or do you need a few days to get your shit together? It won't be long after I make that call. If I know that pack, they will be here within a few hours," she said.

"Yeah, well, I will need time to head to my place. Grab my weapons and make sure that I have enough ammunition."

"You got a silencer on your gun? Don't need someone reporting mass fire on the mountains. Fish and Wildlife will rush up here thinking you're hunting out of season," she said.

"Of course I have a silencer, Mayla. I'm not stupid, and I'm more concerned about the pack hearing the shots and scattering. My hope is that there will be a little bit of distance between them when they come up, enough that I can peg them all off before they notice anything is a miss." I could hear the laughter in his voice.

I felt a growl ripping up my throat. As much as Tony had helped me recently, I wanted to rip him apart for talking about my family like that. I would stop this. I couldn't let this happen, couldn't let him kill the only people that cared about me. They were looking for me because I followed them. Because I disobeyed our alpha, and now they were all going to die. This was not an option. I could not let them die for my mistakes.

Mayla noticed me trying to get to my feet before I even realized I was doing it. Not sure what my plan had been, but I needed to do something. She stared at me and laughed.

"Ooh, don't like what you hear, do you? Don't like hearing how Tony plans to kill your precious Jack. You gonna do something about it? You gonna hobble over here and stop us? Please! Lay back down before you do something you will regret," she spat.

I couldn't; there was so much anger inside of me for this woman. So much hate, and if I didn't release, some of it I would explode. So I gathered all my strength and launched myself right for her throat.

My teeth actually connected, but not for long. She rammed her fist into my throat, forcing me to let go. She was bleeding pretty bad where I bit her, but that didn't stop her from coming at me. I raised my hackles and growled. A fierce growl. For the first time in my life, I felt ready for a fight. I didn't care about anything but killing this woman standing in front of me. I was a wolf, a predator, and she was standing there human, defenseless. Or so I had thought.

When I launched myself again, she was prepared, and from her waistband she pulled a trusty dagger, just like that night so many weeks ago that led to all of this.

The dagger connected with my body, and I instantly collapsed. It went straight into my chest. A nasty snap let me know that it penetrated my ribs and kept going. Frothy blood instantly filled my mouth, and I started choking trying to find air. She hit my lung; I knew it.

Suddenly, I felt another pain, in my back this time. She stabbed me again and threw me back in the corner. The jolt to my body sent me reeling, gasping for air, but every breath I tried to take was like fire in my chest.

"You stupid female. Have you not learned yet that you are no match for me? Stop trying to be a goddamn hero."

What was I thinking? I was thinking about saving my family's life and saving my baby's life. Oh god, my baby! How would these new injuries affect the baby? I was so lost in my anger that I didn't stop to think about the effects on the baby. I wanted Mayla dead, and that had fuelled me. Pushed me to do something stupid yet again.

"Mayla, shit. She's bleeding from her lungs, what the fuck did you do? Fuck off. Get out of here," he hissed.

"Are you kidding me? She fucking attacked me. I had to stab her. She is in her wolf form, that is hardly fair," she tried to defend herself.

"Fair? Really? You have been beating this woman within an inch of her life every day for four weeks, and you are concerned about fair? Give me a break. Go cool off. I'm gonna have to fix her up best I can because you can't control your damn temper," he said.

"I don't need to cool off. I'm fine. Let's just get on with this bullshit. When do you want me to call the pack?"

"Not right now, Mayla, I need to try and stop her bleeding. Then when that is done, we can discuss the plan," he replied then rushed to my side.

He pulled the shirt over his head and began ripping it into strips.

"Shit, throw me my backpack, Mayla," he ordered.

"Why are you even bothering, Tony? She'll be dead soon. It's pointless," she said.

"Just throw me the damn bag."

She walked to the wall where his backpack was propped up and tossed it at him. He caught it with his left hand and hauled out a couple bottles of water.

I couldn't get a handle on my coughing. It didn't work as well in wolf form as it did in human form. It sounded more like mass gagging. Maybe it was; who knew? I just knew that the fluid coming out of my mouth and pooling on the floor did not make me feel very good.

"Shit, Lily, what have you gotten yourself into?" he asked quietly.

Any allegiance I had felt with Tony was over. He was going to kill my family and leave me alone and helpless with no father for my child. I didn't even want the man touching me to bandage my wounds.

I just wanted to wake up from this nightmare. I wanted to wake up in Jack's arms and realize I had a terrible, terrible dream.

I winced as he tied a large strip around my rib cage. The pressure forcing more blood into my mouth, further confirming my fear of a collapsed lung.

Tony spent the next ten minutes cleaning and bandaging my back. When that was finished, he propped my body up slightly so that the blood would stop working its way up to my mouth.

"I'd better head out to my place and grab my shit. Mayla, try to keep your hands off her for a while. She clearly has a blown lung and god knows what other damage done to her insides," he said to Mayla.

"Whatever. So are you planning on doing this soon? You still haven't answered me," she asked.

"Yeah, I'll go get my shit right now. So tomorrow should be good enough. Maybe you could call the pack in the morning. Then they will be here sometime in the afternoon or morning," he offered.

"That sounds good. Leave your scent around when you go. When you get back, I will need to hunt, so try not to be back too late," she said.

"I'll be back when I'm back and not a minute sooner," he said then turned and walked out of the cave. I glanced at Mayla, who was digging in her pocket; she pulled out what looked like a cell phone.

Definitely a cell phone. My nerves flared; what was she doing? She told Tony she would call them in the morning. What the hell was she doing?

I watched as she dialed then held the phone to her ear.

"Where's Jack?" she snapped.

Her face scrunched as she listened to whichever unlucky pack member had answered the phone.

"Well, you tell him that I called and my phone will be on for one hour. No more, no less," she said then snapped the phone shut and rammed it back in her pocket.

She slowly walked to my side and casually snapped my back hind leg. The yelp tore from my throat, forcing me once again into a coughing fit.

"Guess we will need you as debilitated as possible for tomorrow. I won't be able to babysit you nonstop. I'll have work to do, and I don't want to worry about you trying to sneak off," she said then kicked me right in the face, the pain swallowing me in darkness.

CHAPTER 14

JACK

THE LAST WEEK had been a tough one. We had found a good system though. Duke and I camped in the mountains, trading off throughout the night on sleep. Not that I was getting a whole lot even when I tried.

Every morning, four pack members would show up with our breakfast. Two pack members would stay home and prepare the meals for the boys when they returned, and so the cycle went.

We spent at least sixteen hours a day searching the mountain range, and I had to admit I was starting to feel a little better now that we were in action. Leo had been true to his word. At least three of his family members showed up every day to help. We were actually getting a lot of ground covered.

The Three Sisters mountains were precisely as they sounded. A trio of connected peaks. They had originally been named the Three Nuns by a man named Albert Rogers in 1883. The name was later changed in 1886 by a Dr. George Dawson, figuring the name Three Sisters was more appropriate.

I had originally figured it would take us weeks to search the entire range, but it turned out it was going a lot faster than I thought. We had already scoured Big Sister, which was the proper name of the tallest peak belonging to the Three Sisters. Big Sister was approximately 9,634 feet high. There were many parts on the mountain that were impossible for our kind to get to; therefore, it cut out some major square footage. I figured we could scour the two smaller peaks—formally known as Middle Sister and Little Sister—in approximately the same time it took us to do Big Sister.

Today we had started on Middle Sister, and so far, the search was going well. It was a lot easier to maneuver on this portion of the mountain than it had been on the last. Right now we were currently waiting for Luke and Flynn to return with some food for us. It had been a long day even though we were only about one-sixth up the mountain. I planned to eat then keep the boys out for a few more hours.

The second day me and Duke had been out here, I asked the guys to bring out some clothing. We spent most of the time in our animal form, but we always shifted to eat when the boys brought meals, and we learned right quick how unpleasant it was to sit naked on a snowy mountain trying to enjoy a meal.

I sat next to Duke, Reagan, and Mike; we were all now donning our clothing that we had stashed at our campsite, a campsite that was constantly moving, with our search party.

The patter of paws running through the snow drew my attention. It must have been Luke and Flynn with the food. Good, I was absolutely starving today. All this running and constant shifting was hard on the old metabolism. They made really good time today; usually, it took a full hour for them to run back to the house, load up the food that the two remaining at the house prepared, then run back. Today only took about forty minutes. They must have been running like the wind.

A wolf crashed through the trees and sped to a halt in front of me. I quickly pushed to my feet while the wolf in front of me shifted to human.

"Johnny, what the hell are you doing here? Where are Luke and Flynn?" I asked, confused.

"Boss, we got a problem. You wouldn't believe the phone call I got. I ran here as fast as I could. I don't have much time to explain. PJ and I were at the house, and the phone rang, I ran to answer it expecting it to be you or perhaps Leo, but it was Mayla. She wanted to talk to you, but you weren't there. I tried calling the cell phone you have, but no one was answering. She said she wanted you to call her. She said she would leave her phone on for one hour. No more, no less. Those were her exact words," he sped through his speech.

"Shit, someone find me that cell phone," I ordered. "How long ago did she call, Johnny?"

"Maybe thirty-five minutes, forty max, I ran out of the house as soon as she disconnected the call," he said.

"Where's my goddamn phone?" I screamed, getting impatient.

"Here, boss, catch," Reagan said, throwing me the flip phone.

No service, of course.

"Shit, there is no service here," I swore.

"Try heading up the mountain a bit. See if you can get a reading," Duke offered.

I raced up the mountain a few yards, eyes not leaving the phone. Finally, I got some service, only two bars, but it was something.

I punched in Mayla's number as fast as I could but, in my haste, dialed it wrong. I quickly hung up and tried again, getting it right this time.

The phone rang four times before she finally picked up.

"Jack?" she answered.

"Mayla," I said.

"So glad you could find the time in your schedule to call me. I was about to give up on you," she said.

"I called you as soon as I got the message. I was not at the house when you called," I snapped.

"Out searching for me again, Jack?" she asked.

"No. Searching for, Lily, thanks to you. Where is she, Mayla? Just stop this game, and tell me where she is," I barked.

"Oh, don't worry, you will know soon enough. I actually wanted to speak to you for another reason tonight. Give you a kind of update on Lily."

"How is she? Is she all right?" I asked, trying to sound calm.

"Well, I'm not sure if I would use either of those terms. To be completely honest with you, Jack, she looks like shit. For some crazy reason, she has been spending all of her time in her wolf form lately, which makes it hard to communicate with her as you can imagine, but my guess is, if she could tell me exactly how she is doing, she would say 'terrible,'" she said and followed it with a laugh.

My stomach lurched, and my hands trembled. How could Mayla do such a thing? How could she dishonor her family like this and hurt one of her own? I knew I hurt her, but this was so out of hand, so past revenge of a cheating mate.

"What have you done to her?" my voice cracked on the question.

"She tried to get a little frisky with me earlier; forced me to use my dagger again. She took a good stab in the chest, which I'm afraid has collapsed one of her lungs. Well, I'm guessing that is the outcome, seeing how hard it is for her to breathe and the blood frothing from her mouth and all. She took a good deep one to the back as well. But don't worry too much. I gave a swift kick to the head, knocking her out cold. Thought she should sleep it off a little."

I dropped to my knees. My whole body was shaking, and I had to struggle to control myself. The last thing I needed was to shift right now. I needed to keep her on the phone as long as I could. I needed some sort of clue, anything. Lily was in worse danger than I had thought. I knew Mayla would hurt her, but a collapsed lung could kill her. I had no time. I was swallowed by dread.

"You still there, Jack? You got awfully quiet on me," she asked.

"Mayla, how could you? How could you do such a thing? Never in my whole life would I think you capable of something so disgusting. So revolting. She is a living person. Do you have no soul?" I asked.

"Don't start playing the blame game with me, Jack. You know damn well this is your fault. This is all your fault. Everything that happens to Lily and your child is your fault, not mine," she yelled into the phone.

It took me a minute to grasp what I just heard.

"What did you just say?" I asked.

"Oh, that's right, you didn't know. Your precious Lily is pregnant. By you, a disgusting, lying, cheating, sad excuse for an alpha," she said, clearly enjoying every minute of this.

I had no words. I was completely lost in thought. Lily was pregnant?

Was this possible? Well, of course it was possible, we had sex. It only took once. This made everything a million times worse. My child, my woman. I was going to be a father?

"I can tell you are lost in your thoughts, Jack, so I will say good-bye. Keep this phone on you, I will call this number in the morning, and you better answer. Sleep tight, Jack," she said then disconnected the phone.

I dropped the phone and let my face fall into my hands. How could I have been so stupid? How could I have been so fucking stupid? Now, not only did I put Lily's life in danger, but my unborn child's as well. And Lily was somewhere out there clinging to life, waiting for me to come for her, and I was here with absolutely no clue where she was.

I let the sorrow wash over me. Let the tears run down my face. I was the one who deserved to be in her position. I was the one who this should have been happening to. Mayla was right. I was a poor excuse for an alpha. I couldn't even keep the woman I loved safe, or my unborn child. I felt my body vibrate with the change, and I let it happen. I was in no position to stop it.

I lay there in the snow until my nerves calmed enough for me to shift back. I needed to tell the guys what happened. Then I would leave. I would search this entire goddamn mountain tonight if I had to. I grabbed the phone off the ground where I had left it and started back down the mountain to our camp.

Reagan was the first to notice me.

"Boss, you all right?" he asked, clearly taking in my current state. I could feel the redness of my eyes and knew he saw it.

"No. Things are bad," I answered.

I looked around the camp and noticed everyone was there. Not just the current shift. Luke and Flynn were back, and PJ must have followed Johnny when he came to give me the news about Mayla's call.

"Shit, what did she say?" he asked.

"Lily is hurt, and she is hurt really bad. Collapsed lung, stab wound to the back, and a terrible blow to the head. There isn't much time left. Mayla phoned to gloat."

"Fuck. Well, I'll call the cougars, send them out to Little Sister. If we all run through the night, we should be able to get this mountain damn near checked while they search the other," Duke offered.

"It gets worse. Lily is pregnant," I said.

All eyes shot to me. No one said anything, just stared at me in complete disbelief.

"I fucked up, and I know. I never knew she was pregnant. Mayla just filled me in on that fact."

"You don't think she was lying? Trying to hurt you more?" Reagan asked.

"No, I can tell when Mayla is lying, and she wasn't. She was telling the truth. And the fact is me and Lily first had sex four weeks ago. She could be four weeks pregnant."

"That's not so bad, four weeks gives us plenty of time, boss. Don't worry, we will find her. If Mayla wanted her dead, she would be dead by now," Johnny tried to lighten the mood.

"Four weeks is bad. Mayla said that Lily has resorted to her wolf form. She has been like that for a while now. Which means her pregnancy is on wolf terms."

"Shit. That is bad. You're right, there isn't much time," Johnny agreed.

"I'm going to keep searching tonight. I probably won't stop, so feel free to join me until you can't run anymore," I said in a tired voice.

"We all will run through the night as well. Lily is part of our pack too, and if we have to go days without sleep, then that is what we will do. Everybody counts right now, so count us in," Duke said, speaking for everyone.

I looked around at my pack while they all nodded in agreement, and for once, I was not going to argue. As much as I hated making them do this, making them lose sleep, and run themselves into the ground, I had no choice. I needed them right now more than ever.

"Thank you" was all I could manage.

"Just give me a few minutes, I'm going to call Leo, fill him in quickly, and see what they can do," Johnny offered.

He was gone for about ten minutes, but when he returned, he had good news.

"Leo had called in all the male cougars. They are heading to the Little Sister to start there. Leo asked me to pass on his dearest sympathies, and he wants you to know that he fully understands the urgency of this and they will also run through the night and for as long as necessary," Johnny relayed.

I should have known Leo would be eager to do as much possible once he knew Lily was pregnant, after all he struggled with the same problem himself once. It must have brought back terrible memories of when his son Hunter was born. His wife, Cher, had been in her cougar form and, for some reason, was unable to shift back.

I prayed we found Lily soon. I was terrified at the thought of her being out there for one second longer.

We left our camp and began our search. We picked up where we had left off earlier in the evening before we had stopped to wait for the boys to return with our meal. I hoped that the guys had time to get a quick bite in while I was gone. I hated the thought of them being tired and starving, but I wasn't going to stop it. I needed the help.

We ran for hours, smelling out every inch we could reach, but there was still no trace of any of them. I felt so deflated, so completely useless. I knew that this was fruitless; clearly, they had found a way to cover their tracks, so why would I think they would ever stop? If they had a way to erase their scent, they would do just that and continue doing that. But I had to continue, praying we would get lucky and simply stumble across a camp of theirs or anything that would signal they were in the area.

Dawn was approaching when I heard loud thuds heading my way. It didn't sound like wolf paws hitting the ground, so I instantly braced myself for whatever predator it was. With my hackles raised and body braced in a crouch ready to spring, I waited for the perpetrator to come into view. When he finally did, I relaxed. A beautiful golden cougar stood before me. Graceful yet strong and powerful.

In a flash of an eye, the cougar shifted. Leo stood before me, signaling for me to shift as well. Clearly he needed to speak to me. I quickly shifted and stood before him eager to hear what he had to say.

"Jack, I got here as soon as I could. We have been running Little Sister all night, and finally, we caught a trail. It was definitely Mayla's, and, Jack, there were traces of blood. The scent matches that of the jeans you gave to us. Definitely Lily's. I came to bring you and your pack back with me. We will need as many bodies as possible. The trails spread all over the mountain, and they are all fresh. Within the last twenty-four hours."

It was the best news I had heard in weeks. My body shivered with adrenaline; they had found a trail. We would find Lily, and I thought we might be able to save her. I needed to round up the guys ASAP and get them over to Little Sister.

"Thank you, Leo, thank you so much." My voice was thick with emotion.

I quickly shifted and let out a loud howl. Signaling the guys to come. I knew it would be a few minutes before they all made their way to me. They were spread out all over the place, but I didn't doubt they would come. The call of the alpha was a powerful thing, and they would instantly drop whatever they were doing and rush to my side.

I shifted back to my human form to wait with Leo for the others. Johnny and Reagan were the first to find me, and seeing me in my human form, the quickly followed suit.

Within ten minutes, all the guys were at my side, standing on two legs.

"Leo and his pack found Mayla and Lily's scent over on Little Sister. We are going to follow him and help follow the trails. Apparently, there are numerous trails spread out all over the mountain, and they are all fresh. There is no time to waste," I said as quickly as I could.

They all nodded in agreement before we all shifted into animal form including Leo. We took off following him. He was a fair bit faster than us, and I could tell we were holding him back. He had to keep dropping pace to let us catch up, trying not to lose us.

It took about twenty-five minutes for us to join his family. We didn't bother shifting to talk. We all knew the deal and wanted to get started as soon as possible. I could see the sun rising in the east and knew that we had to hurry.

I caught Mayla's scent easily. Leo was right; it was all over the place. This was going to make it difficult. We all were spread out in different directions; if any of us found something, we would howl or snarl—depending on species—to draw everyone to us. The cougars were so fast, they were making great progress compared to us. However, we had the stronger sense of smell.

I was busying myself with a strong trail; it was leading up the mountain, slightly to the west. I prayed that this one would be the one to bring me to Lily. But just like all the promising trails before it, it went so far then curved back down the mountain.

This went on for hours; we were all searching these dead-end trails, sometimes the same ones that we had already searched, when finally a piercing snarl ripped through the sky.

It was one of the cougars. I took off in the direction of the snarl, pushing my feet as fast as they could go. It felt like forever before I came to a clearing where most everyone was already gathered and in the process of shifting. Again, Leo was the one to speak.

"We have found them," he said simply.

"Well, let's go. Why are we standing here? Where are they?" I asked spastically.

"Jack. We need to discuss this. Let me explain to everyone so they aren't rushing in there blind." He snapped at me, clearly of better mind than I was. I instantly felt stupid for being berated by an alpha of a different species.

He continued. "There is a cave set into the hill on a ledge about four hundred feet up from where we are now. My brother did some recon, and it appears both Mayla and Tony are staying in the cave with Lily. Both of their scents are strong outside the cave. Your female Lily's scent was also strong coming from the cave, and Mayla was telling you the truth, Jack, she is definitely with child, her scent was strong."

He looked at me and I nodded, already sure of the fact and not needing it confirmed. I remembered that Mayla was going to call me this morning, and she had warned me to make sure I answered the call. I had left the phone in our camp. I prayed that she wouldn't take it out on Lily when I didn't answer. Prayed that her warning had been empty. Or hopefully, she hadn't called me yet and wouldn't prior to me killing her.

"I think the best plan of attack would be to come in from every angle. There are enough of us that we can spread out. They will never know that we are with you, and there is no way they can fight us. I trust your pack will deal with the threat as it is your kind, we will simply stand by in case we are needed," Leo said.

"Yes, we will deal with Mayla and Tony. I wouldn't expect you to have to. I appreciate you having our backs on this though," I said with gratitude in my voice.

"Well, let's do this then. Let's go get your woman," he said then shifted into his beautiful cougar self.

We climbed the mountain again, four hundred feet seemed to be going by in no time, and the anticipation in my belly grew with each foot. I prayed we weren't too late. Prayed that Lily's lung would hold out. I needed to get her out of there and contact a shifter doctor as soon as possible. I needed her to be okay.

As we got close, we all slowed our pace, creeping toward the cave they held Lily hostage. We all froze as Mayla walked to the mouth of the cave. We stayed in the shadows, praying she wouldn't catch our scent. I could see Tony in the cave not far behind her. No sign of Lily though, which sent a sick feeling washing through me.

Mayla hauled her phone from her pocket and dialed a number. Her voice filled the air for all of us to hear.

"Jack, you didn't answer your phone. I hope you're not still sleeping. Well, take this as a warning, if you don't call me back within the hour, your precious Lily will pay for it." And with that, she hung up the phone.

Tony approached her at the opening of the cave.

"Well?" he asked.

"He didn't answer, I'm sure he will call me back though. I left a message," she answered.

"What kind of message? I hope you didn't give them our location on the fucking message, Mayla. We will have no forewarning of them coming if you did. I need to be prepared," he hissed.

My heart started racing. They were planning on trapping us. Mayla was calling to reveal their location to me, knowing damn well I would race over here. Then Tony had some sort of plan that he needed to be "prepared" for? Well, we definitely weren't going to let that happen.

"Relax, I didn't tell him shit. I just said that if he didn't call me back within the hour, Lily would pay for it," she said, clearly proud of herself.

"As if she hasn't paid for it enough?" he asked.

Mayla never answered him; she simply retreated into the cave, and he reluctantly followed.

Now was our chance. We would barge into the cave and kill Mayla and Tony before they knew what hit them.

I lunged toward the opening, with the sounds of seven sets of paws hot on my trail.

CHAPTER 15

LILY

WHEN I REGAINED consciousness, it was morning. My body was in no better shape than when Mayla knocked me out. It felt as if it hadn't healed at all. I guess I should have expected as much; my injuries were quite severe.

The makeshift bandage was still wrapped securely around my ribs, and my breathing was no better. I thanked God that my lungs kept fighting for breath when I was unconscious.

I looked around the cave and noticed Mayla and Tony were near the opening talking.

I wondered what they could be discussing so heatedly. I couldn't make anything out; they were too far from me, and I was a little out of focus.

I was so sick of the taste of blood, my blood; it hadn't left my mouth since Mayla stabbed me in the chest. It terrified me. The pain was not receding at all, and I feared it wouldn't heal on its own without being operated on. I wish I knew more about our species. Wish I knew exactly how our healing worked.

Glancing back at the mouth of the cave, I noticed they were both heading back in. Tony was shaking his head, heading straight for me.

"Well, Lily, today is the day. Try and rest up because I'm going to try and get you out of here soon. Hide you somewhere when Mayla heads out to take position. You may be on your own from there," he whispered for my ears only.

Before I could acknowledge his words, a piercing growl ripped through the cave. My eyes flew to the opening just in time to see a beautiful black wolf land square on Mayla's back. Jack. He found me. He came for me. My heart filled with relief as the other pack members filed into the cave, each releasing a growl of their own.

I felt such pride watching them. These were my family, and they were here fighting for me. And they didn't fall for Mayla and Tony's trap; they found me on their own.

I was pulled out of my thoughts in time to see Mayla struggle with Jack; she was in the process of shifting, which made getting a hold of her difficult for Jack. Before long, she was fully wolf, and then it was a ball of snapping teeth, razor-sharp claws, and blood. Jack seemed to be handling himself fine, but Mayla was putting up one hell of a fight.

Drawing my eyes toward where Tony had been standing, I realized he was gone. My eyes darted around the cave to find him crouched in the darkness of my old sanctuary.

I snapped my head toward the pack to see what they were doing, clearly puzzled they couldn't find Tony. I wanted to signal them, to tell them Tony was hiding in the corner. *What a coward*, I thought to myself.

A few of the boys were circling Mayla and Jack, ready to jump in if necessary, while the others eyes roamed the cave.

Luke was the first to notice me and instantly started to my side. He was so small even in his wolf form, even if I had never seen him shift, I would know it was him. His fur was just as red as his hair in his human form, and his eyes were as soft as ever. He lurched toward me, taking in my pathetic form.

A strange popping sounded to my left, sort of like someone clucking their tongue against their cheek. Luke had almost been at my side when his eyes clouded over and he crashed to the ground.

Everything got blurry after that. Bodies were moving all over the place. Most of the pack members lunged toward the corner where Tony was crouched. I could see him now, gun in his hand, and my heart sank and I realized what the popping noise had been. His silencer. He had shot Luke, and Luke was lying on the ground motionless.

My eyes darted toward Jack. He was struggling to hold Mayla back while clearly trying to figure out what happened to Luke. It was enough of a distraction that Mayla was able to wriggle from his hold and lunge toward me. Everything was happening so fast.

She reached me with alarming speed and latched onto my neck. In the exact spot she had ripped out a chunk before.

The same pain seared through me while she swung her head back and forth. Realizing this was not a fight she and Tony would win, she at least wanted to ensure my life ended along with hers. Before she could do the damage she wanted, she was yanked from my body. I could feel my fur filling with my blood, and I struggled to hang on. It would be over soon, and Jack would get me help. Slow even breaths, slow even breaths, in and out, in and out.

I looked in the direction of Tony and saw three wolves ripping at his limbs. He never made it to his wolf form, and I couldn't help but feel sympathy for him. He had helped me; he had kept me alive. If it hadn't been for him, I would have been dead weeks ago.

I could see his face; his eyes were open but lifeless, the mask of terror imprinted there forever. The pack slowly moved away from him, assessing the damage, making sure he was dead before they turned to Jack and Mayla.

Jack had Mayla by the throat, and he was slamming her off the cave wall. Sickening crunching sounds were coming from her, and I loved every minute of it. She was getting a taste of her own medicine. The pack could have easily killed her, but they were letting Jack deal with her his way. He would make her suffer before he killed her because she had made me suffer.

I watched as Mayla's head was rammed into the rocky floor, clearly splitting down the back. Jack snapped at her neck and her face, each one drawing a yelp from Mayla.

He kept this up for another few minutes, ripping large chunks of flesh from her battered body before delivering the fatal blow. Mayla lay limp on the ground below his feet. Jack stood over her, panting heavily, saliva dripping from his mouth. So feral and strong.

He raced to Luke's side and checked for a pulse. I wasn't sure if he found one or not because at that moment, he noticed me and crumbled. He shifted quickly to his beautiful naked self and knelt beside me. I could see the tears in his eyes as he stroked the fur on my face.

"Oh, Lily. I'm so sorry. So unbelievably sorry," he apologized.

What the hell was he sorry for? This was all my fault. We were here because I refused to listen to him. And now Luke was dead. As I thought about Luke I noticed the pack was circling him in their human form having now shifted. There were more heads than we had pack members, and it took me a minute to realize there were several of them I didn't recognize.

"Jack, we gotta get them out of here. They both need medical attention now," Reagan said in a worried voice.

"I know. How is Luke? Can he shift? I don't think Lily can, she is losing a lot of blood. How are we going to get them down the mountain?" Jack responded.

I wanted so desperately to shift, to wrap my arms around Jack and never let him go, but I couldn't even lift my head. The pain in my neck was horrible; I feared her bite was even bigger than last time, and I could see the puddle of red forming under my face.

"We will have to carry them in our human form. It is the only option. I don't think Luke can shift, we can't wake him up. His pulse is strong, but we have to get this bullet out of him before he gets any worse," Reagan said.

"I'm scared to lift her. Look at her throat. I don't want to jostle her lungs. Fuck!" Jack said beginning to panic.

"Boss, we don't have any other choice. We gotta get them home."

"All right, Johnny, run back to the house as fast as you can, grab the Cherokee, and meet us as close to the hill as possible. I will carry Lily as carefully as I can, and Duke can take Luke, and we will meet you at the bottom. Flynn, run back to our camp on Middle Sister and gather as much stuff as you can. Find the cell phone and find a shifter medic that can be at the house ASAP, then get there and wait for him or her," Jack spouted orders.

The relief running through me was so overwhelming. I didn't care how painful the trip home was going to be; it would be a hundred times better than the pain Mayla put me through.

I wanted to be in my bed, with my man, getting healthy for my baby. I wanted to be in my human form so I could hold Jack and never let him go.

Jack turned back to me, and I could see the pain in his eyes.

"Lily, I'm going to get you home, but I'm afraid it's not going to be easy. I'm going to have to lift you and carry you. We are on a mountain, and I'm going to have to maneuver down it with you in my arms. I will try my best to make it as smooth as possible. I just need you to be strong for a little while longer, baby," he said.

My heart melted. That was the first time he had called me anything other than Lily or Lil. It made me so happy I wanted to cry; crying was hard, however, in wolf form. I wasn't not sure it was something that was even possible.

"Johnny, get going. We are going to start down the mountain, it's going to take a while. Reagan and PJ, help Duke, he's going to have no arms, so you're going to have to have his back. Mike, can you help me?" Jack asked.

"Sure thing, boss, I'll keep ya vertical, don't worry," Mike replied.

Johnny flew out of the cave.

"Jack, I will come with you. You could use help getting these two down, and I will help Mike with your back. I want to see you all home safely." The voice came from a face I didn't recognize.

"Thank you, Leo, you have been more help than you could ever imagine. I owe you my life, without you we might have been too late," Jack thanked him.

So these were the cougars. This was the Leo I had heard about, and the rest must have been his family. They were here helping my pack search for me. I needed to make a note to personally thank them if I ever made it out of this mess.

"I'm sure there will be a time when we will need your assistance, and I know I can count on you then," Leo said.

"Anything, Leo, we are forever in debt to you," Jack said in almost a whisper.

"No, you are not. This was a favor from our family to yours. If we ever need a favor from you, then we hope it will be returned. Now enough talk about that, let's get these two home," he said and walked to Jack's side by me.

"How should we do this?" Jack asked Leo.

"I suppose the easiest way would be to have her front against your chest with your other hand cradling her, uh, buttocks," Leo offered.

"Yeah, sounds best I suppose. Then she can rest her head against me. Can you help me get her up?" Jack asked.

"Sure" was Leo's reply.

I felt strong hands slide under my front shoulder and lift my upper body slightly from the cold floor while a separate pair of hands lifted my lower half. I winced trying to hide the pain, not wanting Jack to know how uncomfortable this was for me. Finally, they got me settled into the arms of my alpha, and I rested my head against his naked muscled chest.

I heard Jack suck in his breath when we walked out of the mouth of the cave, fully seeing my injuries in the daylight.

"Let's go!" he ordered the pack with sheer urgency in his voice.

Duke walked out of the cave behind us with Luke in his arms, much the same way I was in Jacks. The sight of Luke was depressing, so young, so small and sweet, lying in Duke's arms unconscious. It broke my heart. I wanted to help him, hold him, and tell him everything would be all right, that he was going to be fine, just like his mother would if he had one. But that wasn't possible because I was in not much better shape.

We began the hike down the mountain; Leo and Mike never left Jack's side. There were numerous times when they had to physically support him. Steep slopes that they would otherwise jump off had to be carefully descended, and it took all three of them to do that.

Every now and again, Jack would yell to Duke, checking their status, and Duke would yell back they're okay. It felt like hours had passed, but I wasn't a good judge of time these days.

"We're almost there," Leo said.

I opened my eyes and glanced toward the bottom of the mountain. The rocky part was over; it was just a slope covered in trees now, much like the forest. We would be able to travel a lot faster now.

Being carried through the trees in Jacks arms was unbearable. Every step he took jostled my insides and slammed the air from my lungs. I struggled for every breath. With each passing minute I became more light headed and prayed that our run was almost over. I envied Luke in a way for being unconscious for this part.

I wondered where he got shot; in all the chaos, I never did hear confirmation of that. I wished I had paid better attention; I really wanted to know so I could assess how serious it was. If it was a bullet wound to the shoulder, it wouldn't have been as serious as a bullet wound to the heart and so forth. The thought that he was unconscious wasn't a good sign. Wherever he was shot knocked him right out, so I highly doubted it was as simple as an arm or leg, but I could wish.

Finally, the running stopped, and I heard the idling of a vehicle. It must have been Johnny in the Cherokee. I searched the area, and sure enough, he was close. Jack appeared to be waiting for Duke to catch up, worry creasing his forehead.

"Duke, you all right?" Jack called.

"Yeah, we're good. Well, I'm good, Luke's shaking real bad, and I don't like it. Flynn better have a medic waiting for us when we get back."

"Johnny, flip down all the seats, we are going to need as much room as possible," Jack ordered as I heard doors start opening and the slamming of the seats dropping into the bed of the vehicle.

"All set, boss." Jack walked me to the side of the vehicle and gently climbed inside. It was so warm. He laid me slowly on the carpeted floor of the Cherokee, not caring at all about the blood and dirt I would leave. He curled up beside me and placed his left hand on my belly. It was an extremely intimate moment. Jack was holding my stomach where our child was growing. I hoped and prayed our child was still growing, but I couldn't be too sure until I had confirmation from a doctor. I knew I was barely holding on myself, so how could I expect our baby to make it through this? All I could do was hold on to my hope.

Mike opened the back hatch, and Duke deposited Luke next to me then climbed in beside him. Leo hopped in the front of the vehicle next to Johnny, and all the doors were closed. The others must have decided to shift and run back to the house.

Johnny peeled out of the forest, bouncing over every fucking rock and tree root insite. I had no idea how far from the house we were, but I prayed it wouldn't take long. I needed to get some rest, real rest, so I could heal and shift back. I wanted so badly to talk to Jack and to Luke to apologize to them for everything. I was sure once Jack's relief wore off, he would be furious with me, but for right now, I was going to enjoy his closeness, his happiness to have me in my arms, even if I was in my wolf form.

I heard the sound signaling the garage door opening. We were home; finally, we were home. The last few minutes, Luke hadn't been doing too well; his body was shaking at an alarming rate, and his mouth was filled with blood. I noticed Duke pressing his hands into Luke's right side. That was not good. If that was where the bullet wound was, that meant he got shot in the chest, right where all his vital organs were. He was clearly in shock.

"Duke, get him inside, find the medic, get him stabilized, then send him to Lily in the parlor. I'm going to put her near the fireplace and try to warm her up. I will clean her wounds and bandage them as best I can until the medic is ready for her," Jack said as the vehicle came to a stop.

Duke popped the hatch and scooted out. Jack crawled over me and helped lift Luke into Duke's arms. Leo was at the side of the Cherokee instantly, ready to help Jack lift me out of the side door. Once I was secure in his arms again, Leo followed us inside.

"Jack, do you mind if I stay? I would like to make sure Ms. Lily is all right before I leave. Who knows, I might even be of some help," Leo offered.

"Absolutely, Leo," Jack said.

We entered the house, and the smell was all too familiar, comforting. I was so happy to be home; injured or not, I was home.

Jack walked me to the parlor and asked Leo to stay with me while he ran and got supplies he would need to clean and bandage me. What I really wanted was a long hot shower. Some serious stitches and a respirator, then I could sit back and try to enjoy my first night back with Jack, but I was guessing it wasn't that easy.

When Jack returned, I was finally beginning to warm up. He had a brush, a bucket of warm water, a washcloth, and his first aid bag.

Leo helped him rinse my fur with the bucket of warm water and washcloth, clearly trying to remove as much dried blood and dirt as possible. They had to brush my fur to get the dried knots out, it sucked, but compared to everything I went through in the last few weeks, this was nothing.

"I'm going to have to shave around the stab wounds so we can see what we are dealing with. She seems to be breathing a bit better, but she is still going to need stitches, the only thing stopping the bleeding was the clots in her fur around the areas," Jack said in strangled voice.

"I'll go find some scissors and a razor. I'll be right back," Leo said then got to his feet and left the parlor.

"Lily? How's the pain? Can you nod your head if you're all right?" I bobbed my head as well as I could, trying to reassure him. Truthfully, the pain was still terrible, but I was so used to it by now that it seemed bearable.

"I'm so sorry, baby, so sorry I didn't find you sooner. I'm going to fix you, I promise, and everything will be all right. The doc should be in here soon," he said while stroking the side of my face with the back of his hand.

Leo returned with scissors and a razor a few minutes later and dropped back to my side with Jack.

"Doc said he would be in shortly, I went to check on Luke. They have stabilized him, but he is still unconscious. There was some nasty bleeding internally from the bullet. It entered into his chest but travelled back toward his stomach. Doc had to go in and stitch up the stomach lining to stop the bleeding, but it went smooth, and he is hoping with his quick healing, he should recover swiftly. Duke was able to keep him from losing too much blood, but it's just a waiting game now. He's just sewing Luke up, then the boys will get him up to his bed. They've turned the kitchen into an operating room, and I'm thinking we will have to take Lily in there," Leo said.

"Well, the good news is he is stable. Let's get the stab-wound areas cleaned out so Doc can see what he's looking at." Jack said

They began gently snipping the fur from my wounds, large chunks at first, then trying to get as close to the skin as possible. I was trying to watch, but the angle was hurting my fresh wound in my neck. Once the stab-wound areas were snipped, they moved to my bite marks, clipping all the fur away, exposing the nasty marks. Jack drew in his breath sharply with every new gouge of my skin he saw.

I felt one of them dampening the area with the hot water I presumed. Then I felt the smooth pull of the razor. They were shaving right to my skin around the wounds to make sure no germs or bacteria from my fur would get into them once they were cleaned. I felt completely naked with the numerous shaven patches, and it wasn't pleasant. The air stung the open sores, sores I hadn't even realized I had until they were bared.

A searing pain shot through my neck, and I let out a ferocious snarl.

"I'm sorry, my god, I'm so sorry, Lily, it's alcohol. I have to disinfect this wound on your neck, it's full of dirt and god knows what else. Fuck, I'm so sorry," he apologized.

"Better to just get it done, Jack, don't prolong it. She understands, don't worry. She knows it's necessary," Leo said, trying to soothe him.

"I know, but it doesn't make it any easier," Jack replied.

"Let me disinfect the areas, you distract Lily," Leo offered.

Jack handed the bottle of alcohol to Leo and leaned down to me, whispering sweet reassurances in my ear. I braced myself for the fire I knew would come and focused on not making a noise. I had to be strong for just a little while longer. I had to, for Jack and for my baby.

Leo filled my wounds with alcohol, and my body flamed. It took everything I had to not struggle, to not yelp to do nothing but lie there and take it.

"Almost done now, Lily, just one left, honey," Leo said in a soothing voice.

He cleansed my last wound just as the "doctor" walked into the parlor.

"Jack," he greeted with a nod. "Leo." Another nod.

"Doc. Thank you so much for coming down here," Jack offered.

"No problem, now let's have a look-see. Fill me in on what happened to her so I can properly treat her."

"Doc, to be honest, I don't really know. She was taken from us by a rogue pack member and tortured for weeks now. I received a phone call from the woman who did this to her, saying that she stabbed her in the chest, collapsing a lung, and then stabbed her in the back. That agrees with the wounds that we have found. Every now and again, she will go into a coughing fit, and blood foams out of her mouth," Jack said in a hurry.

"Tell me about the wound on her neck, it looks freshest," the doctor asked.

"Her attacker lunged and ripped a chunk of skin out as you can see. She did it while in her wolf form. We tried to clean all the wounds out best that we could with alcohol. The other wounds I'm not sure. There appears to be numerous cuts across her body, but she was lying in a rocky cave for a long time, so they could be simply cuts from the rocks or worse. I'm not sure if there are any broken bones, but I would presume so."

"She appears to have quite the blood loss, which is why she is barely healing. If a shifter has lost more than 13 percent of their blood supply, the shift becomes impossible and quick healing comes to a halt. Your Lily has clearly lost more than 13 percent. As such, she will remain in this form until we can build her system back up. She will heal as a human would heal until then. The most we can do is stitch her up, clean her up, and make her comfortable. She will need as much rest as she can get," the doctor explained.

"Heal like a human? Doc, that's not an option. She is pregnant." It was the first time I had heard Jack acknowledge it out loud, and it sent a weird sense of pride through me.

"Oh, that makes everything more complicated. How pregnant is she? Do we know what we are dealing with?" the doctor asked.

"No more than four weeks. Well, I hope it's no more than four weeks," Jack said sounding not so sure.

I felt a growl rip from my throat. How dare he say something like that? I saw a grin spread over Jack's face; it was my grin, the one I loved so much.

"I guess that means it's definitely no more than four weeks," he said then placed his hand on my belly.

"All right, so we will say between twenty-eight and thirty days, give or take. That leaves us approximately thirty-two days. Jack, she is not going to be healed enough to shift within the next thirty-two days, let alone be prepared to give birth. Not like this. She has a collapsed lung and a terrible wound in her back," the doctor said.

"What can we do, Doc? How can we speed her healing? What about transfusions? Will that help her blood supply replenish itself?" Jack asked, desperate.

"That may help, Jack, but I will need to run some tests. I will need to know what blood type she is before I can find a wolf-shifter donor. It could take some time if there is no one within your pack that's a match. If we can find a match and administer blood transfusions over the next two weeks, it would help, but it may not be enough. With your permission, I would like to induce sleep. It will help her heal, Jack, and it will allow us to take care of her better."

My heart jumped into my throat. Were they discussing putting me in a drug-induced coma? I did not want that to happen. Being unconscious, not knowing if I would wake up or if Luke woke up or if my baby was okay, terrified me. I prayed Jack wouldn't agree, but I knew he would if he thought it would help the baby and me.

"Let's be straight, Doc, are you talking about putting my woman in a coma? Is that what you mean by induced sleep?"

"Listen, Jack, if you want her to heal enough to change before this baby comes, then we will need to try everything we can. If and only if you let me induce her sleep and we can find a blood match, we might be able to get her healed enough. I can then bring her out of her coma and perform a caesarean section to remove the baby safely without causing further trauma to mommy or baby."

Shit. Jack was going to let him, and now that I heard why the doc felt it was so important, I didn't blame him, but I was terrified. I didn't want to be put to sleep. To be sent into a world of darkness for god knows how long. I felt my body start to tremble, and Jack grabbed my face, looking deep into my eyes.

"Baby, I know you're scared, but it could help. If you don't want to, I won't let him, but you have to understand you can't be in your animal form when you deliver this baby. You will have to be human unless . . ." His words trailed off as both our eyes flashed to Leo, who was sitting silently beside us.

"It's all right, Jack, I realize the urgency of this as much as you do. I trust she knows of my son Hunter?" Leo asked.

"Yes, I explained it to her after she heard me speak of you," Jack admitted.

"Well then, Lily, you can understand. I would listen to the doctor. Not only was my son born different, his birth was hard on him and his mother. We almost lost both of them, and as much as I love my son, I have to watch the torture he goes through every day, knowing he is different from the rest of us. I wouldn't wish that on any parent or any child. Please heed the doctor's warning, and let him treat you as he thinks best," Leo begged.

How could I argue with that? I could see the pain in his eyes when he spoke of his son. I could see how much he didn't want me and Jack to suffer the same fate. I bobbed my head in acceptance, knowing it was the right thing to do.

"Are you telling me to do it?" the doctor asked of me this time, clearly noting my head movement.

"Lily, if you want the doctor to treat you in any way possible, bob your head again," Jack requested.

And so I did.

"It's settled then. I will need to draw some blood and run a few tests to figure out her blood type. If you don't mind, I will take a vial from each of your pack members if they agree to see if any of them are a match. But right now, I'm going to have you carefully transport her to the kitchen, I will need to insert a chest tube to correct the collapsed lung. It's a little bit trickier on an animal than a human, but I will try and do it as swiftly as possible."

Jack gently lifted me with Leo's assistance and deposited me on the kitchen table that had been turned into an operating bed. There were fresh white linens and a pillow on it.

The doctor got out his tools, and I began to feel woozy. I did not want to watch him insert anything into my chest, so I closed my eyes and let the doctor work his magic.

I felt the doctor shave the hair on my right side then rub a cool swab over the area.

"Lily, I'm going to give you a numbing solution via a needle, so please hold very still," the doctor asked.

I felt a tiny prick then the flush as the medicine spread. I didn't feel anything after that until an enormous pressure was released from my chest. The tube had been inserted, and my lung was filling with air again. I could feel it resuscitating itself to my chest cavity.

"There you go, Lily, the blood and air is draining out now, it should feel better in just a few minutes," the docs said.

When he finished with the chest tube, he inserted a needle into my left hind leg and filled two vials with blood.

"Jack, may I use your phone? I would like to call my assistant and have her bring what I will need to administer an IV for Lily," doc asked.

"Absolutely, there is one in the parlor," Jack said.

"Why don't you bring Lily into the parlor, and we can get her situated near the fire to keep her warm. She will be staying there for a while, so let's try to make her as comfortable as possible," he said.

It took about an hour and a half for doc's assistant to show up with the proper equipment. She rolled in a metal IV holder and a box full of goodies for him.

"Here is everything you'll need. I put a healthy supply of pentobarbital in there. Let me know if you need more." With that, she was gone.

"All right, Lily, pentobarbital is the drug I'm going to administer into your system. It will put you into a temporary coma, which will help you heal faster. While you are unconscious over the next two weeks or so, I will attempt to give you blood transfusions if I can find a match. I will pull you out of this coma in two weeks and at which time I will assess your progress."

Jack bent down to my face and held it in his hands.

"I won't leave your side, babe. I promise I won't let anything happen to you," he said then bent to kiss the top of my head, and for the umpteenth time this month, the sleep took over.

CHAPTER 16

JACK

I WATCHED AS LILY'S eyelids closed. She would be out of pain now; she would sleep until we could get her body healing properly.

The doctor was busying himself with Lily's IV, connecting bags and whatnot.

"Doc? Do you really think she is going to be all right?" I asked.

"I will be honest, Jack, I don't know. Her lung will heal now with the chest tube in it, but her blood loss is what worries me, Jack," he said.

"I thought blood replaced itself within hours, shouldn't she already be replenishing?" I asked, knowing I had heard that somewhere.

"It's more complicated, Jack. Blood is made of numerous parts—red blood cells, white blood cells, platelets, plasma, sugars, fats, hormones, vitamins, et cetera. All these components rejuvenate at different rates, and all are vital to her healing in different ways. The red blood cells are vital, they carry the oxygen from the lungs to all the tissues throughout the body. The white blood cells are what defend against disease. Plasma and platelets work together to aid in the clotting of blood and plugging of damaged blood vessels. It can take four to six weeks for a human to fully replace all of those factors from donating a pint of blood. I can assure you she has lost substantially more than a pint of blood. In her wolf form, she is approximately eighty-five pounds I would guess. You can average about one pint of blood per twelve to fifteen pounds, so her body should be comprised of around seven pints. Right now she is carrying maybe four. Being pregnant fluctuates this, but the fact is she needs time to replenish. I will know more when I run the blood tests. Let's just pray the pack members will match," he explained.

"I hope I match. I will willingly give her all of my blood if I have to," I said.

"Jack, I know you really want to do everything you can to help her, but your blood will not match hers. I can pretty much guarantee, we will test it to be sure, but you are alpha, and if I remember correctly, your blood reflects that. Your strange DNA is what causes the distinct eye color trait in all wolf shifter alphas," he said.

"I'd never thought about that before." I was let down.

"Look, we will check just to be sure, but don't count on it. I'm sure we will be able to find a match somewhere. I realize she is new to your pack, which leads me to believe she is wolf because she was bitten, not born this way?" he assumed.

"That is correct, she was changed about five weeks ago now. We found her and have taken care of her since. Well, clearly not exactly taken care of her, but well, you know what I mean," I said feeling like a piece of shit.

"And her creator? I'm inclined to think that her shifter blood will be the same type as the person who changed her? Or is that an impossibility?" he asked.

"Impossible, he had a large hand in her being taken, and we killed him when we rescued her," I said.

"All right, well, let's hope for the best then. I'm going to go ask the pack for a sample if they will, and then I better head out. I will be back in morning to change out her IV if I don't see you before I go. Take care, Jack," he said then headed for the door of the parlor.

"See ya tomorrow, Doc," I said.

I wanted to go and check on Luke, but I didn't want to leave Lily alone, so figured I would wait until someone came to check on us. I looked at Lily, her broken battered body, missing large chunks of hair and skin, her beautiful blond coat covered in bloodstain and dirt. I could see now the protrusion in her stomach. Our child, our poor child.

I heard the door creak open, and Leo popped his head in.

"Hey, Jack. How's she doing?" he asked.

"Well, she's sleeping now, so she is not in any pain anymore. Doc says the chest tube will have to stay in for a few more days. He was gonna take some blood from the guys if they were willing. Hopefully, we can find a match and get some good blood into her. I'm scared to think of what infections she may have," I said.

"Well, let's hope for the best, Jack. I was going to head home, check on the family, but know that if you need anything, we are not far away. And, Jack, Cher would be more than willing to help if there is anything Lily needs that is of the feminine capacity. When she wakes up and all," he offered.

"Thanks, Leo. I will let her know. Hey, can you do me another quick favor on your way out?" I asked.

"Sure."

"Can you send one of the guys in here, I would like to go see Luke, but I don't want to leave her alone," I said.

"You bet, a few of them were just in the kitchen. I'll go grab one of them right away. I'll call you in the morning to check on everyone," he said then disappeared through the door.

A few minutes passed when Flynn waltzed in.

"Shit. How's she doing?" he asked, taking in her appearance.

I gave him a rundown of what the doctor said and what everything was that was connected to her, namely the chest tube.

"Can you stay with her for a little while? Maybe throw a movie in or something? I wanna check on Luke and get myself cleaned up a little. Maybe put some clothes on." I realized I had been naked. Doc knew well enough not to say anything, but it bugged me still.

"Yeah, no problem. I could use some downtime anyway. Do I have to do anything for her? Does she need anything?" he asked a little nervously.

"Nope, she should be content, Doc gave her everything she needs until morning, I just don't like the thought of leaving her alone," I said.

"Understandable. Well, go check on Luke and get yourself together, maybe eat something. You'll need to be strong too," he suggested.

"Yeah" was all I replied. I was getting sick of people telling me I needed to be strong, I should eat. Forgive me for not being overly concerned about my own needs when my woman, child, and pack member were fighting for their lives.

I found Luke upstairs in his bedroom, unconscious on his bed. He looked much the same as Lily, but he had no IV. I guess there was no need for it, considering he was healing as he should have been. I hoped he would wake up soon; I wanted to talk to him, reassure myself that he was okay. Johnny, Reagan, and Duke where spread out around his room, assessing his damage and not wanting to leave him. He was the smallest in the pack, and everyone thought of him as their little brother; it hurt them deeply to see him like this.

"How's he doing?" I asked of no one in particular.

"Definitely getting better. His color is starting to return, and the shaking has stopped. Just didn't want to leave him alone you know, in case he wakes up," Reagan said with pain in his voice.

"Good. I'm sure he will wake up soon," I said as I went to sit on the bed next to him. His side was shaved around his incision where the doctor operated. The incision was long but already healing; the stitches were almost pointless now. I knew that his insides were healing slower than the rest, but still, he was looking better, and I felt relieved that he was healing.

"I ran into Doc downstairs before he was leaving, told me about Lily. Sorry about all this, Jack. We all gave a sample. Hopefully, we will get lucky," Duke said.

"Yeah, let's hope. I don't know much about shifter blood types, but I hope it's easier to find a match than for humans," I replied.

No one said anything else; we sat by Luke's side and watched his shallow breathing for a few minutes before I got up to head to my room in desperate need of a shower.

While I was rooting through my closet, it occurred to me that we were going to need stuff if we had a baby in three weeks' time. Assuming everything went fine, we would need diapers, clothes, and a crib. God knew what else. I didn't know anything about babies.

I racked my brain for any females I knew. Anyone that could figure this all out for me. I was too busy worrying about the lives of my family to even try to concentrate on preparing a nursery.

Only one woman came to mind. One woman who would know everything we needed.

I grabbed a quick shower and raced down to the kitchen to grab something quick to eat before heading into the parlor for the night. It had been an hour or so since Leo left, and I presumed he would be long home by now.

I stopped at the linen closet to grab an extra pillow and blanket so I could make a bed next to Lily and opened the door to the parlor. Flynn was passed out on the couch, and Lily was in the exact same position she had been when I left.

I gently shook Flynn's shoulder and woke him.

"Flynn, I'm back, why don't you head to bed now," I said.

"Ahh, sorry I passed out there, Jack. I'm just wiped. What time is it anyway?" he asked.

"It's just past seven," I answered.

I figured everyone would hit the sack early; this had been a long couple of weeks, and no one had had a good night's sleep since Lily was taken. I hoped they would all begin to catch up now.

"All right, well, have a good night, Jack. If you need anything, just holler," he offered.

"Thanks, Flynn, I'll see ya in the morning," I said and watched as he left for bed.

I walked over to the phone and picked it up, dialing Leo's number.

"Hello," Leo's voice said.

"Hey, Leo, it's Jack."

"Jack, is everything all right?" he asked, obviously concerned I was calling him so soon after he left.

"No, everything is fine, but I was wondering if I could speak to Cher. I was hoping I could get her help, you know, with the stuff for the baby."

"Oh, I'm sure she would be pleased to help, let me run and grab her," he said.

The line went silent while I waited for her to pick up. Finally, her beautiful voice came.

"Hi, Jack," she said.

"Cher, how are you?" I politely asked.

"I'm doing well, Jack, thank you. My deepest sympathies for the recent events your pack has been through."

"Thank you, Cher, your family has been such a help to mine. That is actually the reason I'm calling. I'm sure Leo has filled you in on everything?"

"Yes, Jack, I'm pretty familiar with everything."

"Then you know my Lily is pregnant. And her condition is not good. I will be spending all of my time here with her and Luke, and I'm afraid I won't have much time to prepare as you can imagine. I wouldn't burden you this way if I knew any other females, but Lily is the only one in our pack, and you are our closest friends. In truth, I have no idea what we will require to have a baby. I don't know the first thing about infants, and I could really use your help. Since Lily is in her wolf form, we only have about four weeks until the baby comes. I need your help if you are available."

"Jack, of course I will help. I will take care of everything. Lily will need you now more than ever. I hear she was put into a coma? She will thank you for that later. This is an extremely stressful time, and the pressure on her would not help her healing. I know all too well what she is going through, I'm sure you know about my experience with my son Hunter," she said in a dejected tone.

"I'll be honest, Cher, I don't know that much, just that there were circumstances surrounding his birth that lead to you being in your animal form when he was born, resulting in him being born a cougar and remaining as such," I admitted.

"Well, Jack, I think maybe it is time you learned of the whole story, then perhaps you will have a better knowledge of what to expect with your mate," She offered

"My mate." The words sounded strange. I had never really thought of Lily as my mate, but I supposed she was now. I was alpha, and she was bearing my child, which definitely classified her as my mate. It just seemed strange associating that word with someone new. Wolves usually mated for life. Well, this time I planned to.

"If you wish, Cher, I don't want to pry, but I think it would be beneficial," I said.

"Twenty-five years ago, I got pregnant with my first child. It was a very happy time in my and Leo's life. We were freshly mated and truly in love. Carrying his child was my dream, and it finally came true. Everything was going smooth, I was gaining the proper amount of weight, eating healthy, I never suffered from morning sickness or anything of the such. I knew that it was dangerous for a woman shifter to change while pregnant due to the extreme difference in our gestation periods from human to animal. The gestation period for us in our animal form is eighty to ninety-six days and, as humans, as you probably know, is nine months. So as a rule, we avoid a shift. When I was three months pregnant, Leo went out hunting. He and his brothers were running in the forest, and they had been gone for a very long time. I was stuck home pregnant and bored, missing the feel of the forest under my feet, the wind on my face, so I decided a walk would satisfy my need for adventure. It also couldn't hurt the pregnancy, it was healthy to get as much exercise as possible while pregnant. It was the best walk I had ever had, until I heard gun shots. I instantly panicked. My family was in this forest, and someone was hunting. I had a great need to find them, to get the father of my unborn child home before these hunters caught a prize cougar. I was terrified, and I began running frantically, calling to the boys, praying they would hear me and come running. Trouble was I had walked so far from home I wasn't even sure which direction it was anymore. The fear blinded me and confused me. Before I knew it, I was hit by a stray bullet. It seemed they were flying all over the place. When I crumpled to the ground, I knew I had been hit, but I couldn't tell where. I remember lying there for a long time, screaming for help, but no one came. I was so far from my home, and I knew I would never make it on my own. I finally realized I had been shot in the leg. It was a shotgun, and it had done pretty bad damage. I couldn't hop all the way home on one leg. It was miles to my house, and there was no way I would ever make it. I made the decision that if I shifted, I would have a better chance with three legs. I knew it was risky, but I just prayed I could shift long enough to get myself home then shift back. There was no other way. It was the only option I had. If I didn't take my animal form, I never would have made it out of the forest. I was right in the fact that three legs were better than two, I eventually made it home, but by the time I did, from all the trauma and being approximately ninety days pregnant, I went into full labor. Once the labor begins, Jack, it is impossible to shift. I tried, I tried harder than I had ever tried to do anything in my life. Leo found me on our porch bleeding from my leg while I reeled on the ground from the contractions. Needless to say, it was inevitable. After hours of rigorous labor, he was born. It was a traumatic experience for both of us, but eventually I gave birth to a beautiful 240-gram cougar cub. Don't get me wrong, Jack, I love my son more than anything, but it breaks my heart to see him suffer. Leo isn't sure of his mental capacity. We don't know if he is more cougar or human in the mental sense, and it's hard to say if we will ever fully comprehend that. For me, I wouldn't change him for anything. I love him dearly, but it is not the life you wish for your child."

"Cher, I don't know what to say. I am so sorry. I never knew any of that," I said. Hearing her story gave me a whole new outlook on her and Leo. I understood now why it was so important to Leo to help us. I think it was his way of trying to make up for not being able to help his wife. Not that he could have, but I understood the feeling of your mate being hurt and there not being a damn thing you could do to help her, to save her from the fate that lay in front of her. I would never look at the cougars the same way. Before this whole experience, they were simply neighbors that we had heard stories of here and there. I had spoken to Leo every now and again but had never spent a prolonged time with him or his family. I knew this experience would bring us closer as allies and as friends, and I was glad for it.

"I hope that my story can help you to understand more about her condition. Let's just pray that we can get her out of her animal form in time for her to deliver your baby, Jack. She is strong from what I hear, and I have faith she will pull through this wonderfully."

"Thank you, Cher. Your story has helped, and you are right, it is better she is in a coma. If she was awake, she would be overburdened by the need to get better, the need to shift back. Better to have her simply healing right now."

"Absolutely. So to the reason you called, I would be honored to help you with the baby's requirements."

"Um, I'm not sure how much help I'm going to be, Cher. I was hoping I could give you money and let you go crazy. I need the whole works—paint for a room, uh, diapers, those little blanket thingies, bottles—whatever they need, I want. Clothes, bags, one of them tables to change them on."

Her laughter cut me off.

"All right, Jack, but it's gonna cost ya."

"Well, whenever you are free, I will just give you my bank card. I trust your choice. Just make sure it's all gender neutral, no pink or blue, just greens and yellows, that sort of thing."

"Don't worry, Jack. I know what I'm doing. How about tomorrow? If you want a nursery painted, it is best to do that as soon as possible so that the paint fumes can wear off in time before your baby is born. I will go on a mad shopping spree tomorrow then bring everything to your place and get started. I won't bother you at all, you can devote all your attention to your mate and pack member," she offered.

"That sounds wonderful. Just come over whenever you are ready. I will most likely be in the parlor, I'm sure one of the boys will show you to me. And, Cher?"

"Yes, Jack?"

"Thank you again, for everything. For sharing your story with me, for letting Leo and your family stay by our sides for the last few weeks, and thank you for your help now."

"It's my pleasure, Jack. Take care, and I will talk to you tomorrow. I will keep your Lily and Luke in my thoughts," she said.

"Good–bye, Cher."

"Bye, Jack."

We disconnected the call and sat there for a few minutes reviewing everything that I had learned. I felt terrible for Leo, how bad he must have felt, coming home to find his mate like that on their porch. Knowing if she hadn't been home alone, she never would have gone for a walk. Or if he had been with her, she would have been okay. And the reverse for her, always blaming herself for going out that day, thinking of what it would have been like if she had just stayed home, how different their lives would be now. It was heartbreaking. And she was right; it was not a fate I wished for my family.

I retrieved the blanket and pillow from the couch that I had left there on my way in. I placed the pillow next to Lily. I didn't want to get too close; I was scared to bump her in my sleep or jostle the chest tube. So I got as close as I dared and draped the blanket over me. I reached out to grasp her right front paw, needing to touch her in some way, to prove to myself she was really here.

I was so tired. I had spent so many days on the mountain barely sleeping, running hard all day and most nights, worrying myself sick, and now that I had Lily home and Luke was on the mend, you would think I would have passed out quickly. But I hadn't.

I lay their watching the slow rise and fall of my mate's chest. Watching her eyelids twitch ever so slightly, making me ponder what she was dreaming of or if that was something that even happened when you were in a coma.

By midnight, I couldn't hold my eyes open any longer. I sat up and kissed Lily on the head then lay back down, finally ready to get some well-deserved rest. Tomorrow would be another day.

CHAPTER 17

LILY

S OMETHING MOVED IN my left peripheral vision; I felt my eyes flicker in that direction, but there was nothing. It was so dark, and there was a strange taste in my mouth. I knew Jack was close, but I couldn't see him. I could smell his wonderful scent, but not like it had been the last time I saw him—cleaner, fresher maybe. I struggled to remember when that was. We had been in the parlor, and the doctor was there. They were going to put me into a coma.

The shadow flickered again, and I shot my eyes toward it. There sitting on the ground was a baby cradle, gently rocking back and forth. Where the hell did that come from? It was strange; everything was black except where the baby cradle was, as if there was a spotlight on it.

I struggled to make sense of what I was seeing when a flicker of light snagged my attention in the opposite direction. It was our kitchen table, and it was empty. Not a soul sitting at it. I wanted to scream out to everyone, call them, find out where they were.

I tried to call Jack's name, but it was useless; I couldn't make a sound. It was as if I had become mute. A gust of wind picked up, and I watched as my hair swirl around me. It gusted upward, pulling me away from my body as I slowly drifted toward the ceiling, or sky? My body drifted about five feet then stopped. I looked down to see myself walking around aimlessly.

I shook my head trying to wake up. This was the weirdest thing I had ever experienced. I watched as my human form searched for me, searched high and low looking for the part of me that drifted off. It was like I was playing hide-and-seek with myself, a very detached myself. I tried to lower myself, but my consistency was not human, more of a substance I had no words for. Like air but thicker, not quite mist or smoke but somewhere in between, like a shadow but clear.

My thoughts were fuzzy, like someone took my words and mixed them with clouds. Things were changing all around me; one second I was floating around as a strange haze, the next I was back in my human body.

There was a knocking on a door somewhere, and I tried to find it. I glanced all around my new dark world and couldn't find a door anywhere. It had sounded far away, like it was a door behind a door behind a door. Where could it have been?

That's when the whispering started. I tried to concentrate, to shut off all my other senses so I could hear them, but I had cotton balls in my ears; that or whoever was talking was a mile away. I kept trying harder, and finally, I could make out the words slightly.

"How's she doing this morning, Jack?"

"Same as last night. The draining from the chest tube seems to have slowed down, but other than that, I have no idea."

It was Jack's voice; I could tell. They were talking about me. Why wouldn't they just come and ask me how I was doing? And where were they?

"Did you make any headway on the blood samples from the pack yet, Doc?" his wonderful voice asked.

"Sorry, Jack, haven't got the tests back from the lab yet. I'm afraid it will be a couple days for that. As for Lily, we are going to change out her IV, then I'm going to have to clean her stitches and re-bandage her wounds. Tomorrow we will attempt to give her a bath. I should be able to take the chest tube out by then."

I was starting to get nervous; why were they talking about me when I was so clearly far away? And what was going on with me? I must have been having an allergic reaction of sorts to the drug he gave me; uh, what did he call it? Pentobarbiedoll or something close to that. I heard him say he was going to administer it, and it would put me into the coma, but clearly that didn't work. Or did it? Was this that world? Was this what it was like to be in a coma? I still felt conscious; I could somewhat hear what was going on around me, my sense of smell was still working, but I had absolutely no control over my body, my voice.

It was not a good feeling. It was as if I was trapped inside my own mind.

"Yeah, that sounds good, Doc. Did you check on Luke yet? I haven't been up to see him yet this morning, I didn't want to leave Lily's side," Jack said.

Him saying that confirmed my fear. I wished the doctor had described this chemically induced coma to me a little more; I didn't realize I would be able to hear and comprehend what they were saying around me. It terrified me. What if they couldn't help me? What if I didn't heal? I would be trapped in this dark, lonely, frightening place forever.

Their next words got foggy, as if I was swirling back into an abyss of foam. I struggled to bust through to get back to where I was before when things were beginning to make sense again, but it was gone.

My surroundings began to change drastically; it was no longer dark and daunting but as if I had been kicked into a cartoon. Everything seemed to be 2-D, as if I was walking around as a drawing. Like I was living in a painting. The road stretched out in front of me, and I glanced up at the sky. The sun was a circle with large orange triangles surrounding it, just as I had drawn when I was little. It was strange how this place actually made me feel happy. V-shaped seagulls swerved in and out of the light blue clouds. I lost myself for a while; my mind went completely blank, and I let the feel of this place take over me.

Eventually, the scene changed again, and I felt like I was being yanked from the foam pit. The voices were returning, and I was slowly remembering what was going on. It was like being a kid and trying to watch a movie with your parents—only some parts made sense, and others were way out of your realm of comprehension.

"Jack, I'm back, the guys are unloading the vehicle right now for me. Here's your bank card back." It was a female voice that I didn't recognize. There were no other females. Maybe this was just some dream after all.

"Thanks, Cher, will you be joining us for dinner? Well, I will be eating in here, but you and Leo are welcome to join the guys."

Cher? It took me a minute to place the name, but as soon as he said *Leo*, it clicked. She was the female cougar. Leo's mate. She must have been here with him.

"Thank you, Jack, that would be nice. I was planning to stick around for a few more hours, maybe enlist one or two of the guys to help me paint the nursery."

The nursery. I had forgotten that I was pregnant until right now. Jack must have asked her to help him with the nursery. It upset me in a way; that was something that a mother should get to enjoy, and I was missing it.

"That would be great, Cher, but I don't want to burden you. You have been here all day."

All day? Hadn't it just been morning? My sense of time was lost, and I realized what felt like a few minutes had turned into half a day.

"Jack, please don't worry about me. Just focus on your woman. Talk to her, I hear it helps," she said.

"Do you think she can hear me?" he asked.

"Jack, of course I think she can hear you. A chemically induced coma is much different than an injury-induced coma. If she was in an injury-induced coma, her mind would be completely shut off, but chemically induced comas are different in the sense that she can hear you, sense you, probably even smell you. Her body will fall in an out of sleep in which time she may not hear you, but when her mind is awake, she will know you are there. Or so I have heard anyway, Jack. But it couldn't hurt to try."

"Wow, I never knew any of that. Thank you, Cher."

I heard a door close gently, and I felt warmth spread through my hand. Like someone was holding it but not. I could feel the warmth of a hand but not the hand itself.

"Lily, baby if you can hear me, I want you to know . . ."

I slipped out again. His voice faded out like a stereo being turned down, and I slipped into another new world.

I was in a house, a house that was all too familiar to me. It was one of my foster homes, one of the ones I had tried so hard to forget about. I was walking around the house, which appeared too empty. Obviously, it would be empty; there was no one ever with me in this dream world. No one existed here but me and the shadows.

The house was dark, but I could tell it hadn't changed one ounce since I left it when I was twelve. I walked down the hallway that had led to my bedroom. When I opened the door, I was taken aback to see it was empty except for a picture that hung about where my bed had been. I flicked on the light switch, and thankfully, the light turned on. The picture seemed out of place. It was of an airplane. A small white airplane, and on the bottom of the picture were words. "Feel Me" it read. I didn't understand it, I let my hand drift up to the picture to run my fingers over the words, but when I did, my hand was pulled through. I was falling, falling, falling. It reminded me of the times I would be stuck between sleep and consciousness and my body would have the sensation of falling, but always within seconds I would jolt awake. Well, this felt exactly like that, but without the jolting-awake part.

Eventually, the wind from the fall turned thick, like I was rushing through pudding. It cushioned my landing, which seemed to take forever to come.

I was lying there trying to enjoy my current comfort when it was harshly ripped away from me. Like someone had pulled the rug out from beneath me.

I was zooming back to my awareness again. I knew because I could smell Jack, feel him near me. It was confirmed when I heard him talk.

"Doc, this is terrible. I don't know who else there is." Jack said.

"Do you know none of the other Canadian wolf packs?" the doctor asked.

"Well, we know of a few, but we are certainly not close enough that I can ask them to donate blood to my mate."

"There is one pack member that I haven't received a sample from yet."

"Who's that? I thought you asked everyone?" Jack asked in an angry tone.

"Luke! I couldn't ask Luke before because he was unconscious. But he is awake now and almost completely healed. I could ask him, see if he would give a sample," the doctor offered.

"Yes! Absolutely, ask him. But, Doc, will there be enough time? It's been four days since you took blood from everyone else. What if he turns up not a match, which is very likely, then will have lost eight days."

"Jack, I will get his sample put on an urgent rush. It is different when I send them one at a time to process, not six. If he agrees to give it to me and I get it to the lab today, then I can hope for tomorrow or the next day at the latest."

It seems like the search to find a match to my blood type was not going well. I wondered how bad I was. If I was healing at all.

"All right, it's not like we have much choice," Jack said.

"I'll go see if I can find Luke, he has been up and about all day, against my orders I might add."

"I'm not going to lie, Doc, I'm glad to see him up and moving."

I was so glad to hear that Luke was all right. What was bothering me was the fact that Jack said it had been four days since the doc took their blood. Four days. I didn't like this one bit; how was I supposed to keep track of how long I had left when I had no idea what day it was? What time it was? I was lost in a realm of insanity. It was realism surrounded in a blanket of surrealism.

"Yes, well, it is reassuring, but I don't want him overexerting himself for a few more days, just to make sure that the internal bleeding is fully mended. Anyway, I will talk to you later, Jack. Oh by the way, I did Lily's prenatal check while you were in the shower. The baby appears to be growing healthily, and he or she had a very strong heartbeat. Whatever it is, it's strong like its momma," the doctor said.

My baby was growing, growing properly. I wanted to hug the doctor for saying that when I was conscious. When I could hear it, I needed it. Needed something happy to carry me through my current misery.

"Lily, did you hear that? Our baby is doing well because he is strong like you, wonderful like you. I miss you, baby, I want you to come back to me. I so badly want the time to go faster but at the same time slow down. I just don't know what is going on anymore. Everything has changed so quickly, I just wish I could share it with you. I hope you can hear me. I want you to know . . . I just . . . I'm not sure if I've ever told you how much I care about you. I have never met anyone like you before in all of my life, from the minute you fought for your life in that alley then found your way to the park, I knew you were different. I so desperately wanted to know you, to help you, to keep you as my own. Even when I was mated to Mayla, I couldn't take my mind off you. That fueled the fire with her, I know, and in hindsight, I wish I had handled that situation better, but I do not regret what I shared with you. Every night that I spent with you was one of the best nights of my life. When you were gone, I felt like someone had stabbed me right in the heart. It hurt to move, to eat, to think, to do anything. I don't mean it physically hurt, but it hurt my heart. I felt guilty when I would eat something, knowing you were out there probably starving. It hurt to sleep because I knew you weren't getting much rest. It seemed so selfish to think I even had time to be concerned over those things. The thing is, Lily, this experience shoved me into realizing my feelings for you. They developed so fast, and when you were gone, and I feared the worst, it was a pain I never want to feel again. I will never let anything happen to you again, I will take care of you forever. I love . . ."

Fuck, fuck. I missed it. Missed the end of his sentence again. Had he been about to say what I thought he was? I hoped so. I hoped so badly.

I looked around bracing myself for just about anything. But there was nothing. Absolutely nothing, just white. White everywhere. I couldn't tell if there were walls or if it was sky, white sky? It seemed to stretch on forever. Not even a speck of dirt on the ground. I noticed I was dressed in all black clothing, like I was supposed to stand out. Strange, was this supposed to be some sort of depiction of my life? How I never seemed to fit in? Or perhaps telling me that I always stood out? Was this just a completely random thing that my mind has decided to script? And what in the world was I supposed to do here?

Strangely, walking didn't seem to tire me out in this dream world. Well, I guess that it was not as strange as I originally thought since I wasn't actually walking; I was dreaming I was walking, or something like that anyway. Hours passed, and I began to worry about my real life time. When minutes passed, it was actually days; imagine how long could pass while I spent a couple of hours lost inside myself.

One thing that I would carry with me forever after this experience was how beautiful the human mind truly was. There were things inside of your mind that you didn't even realize you knew about, things you don't ever recall seeing or hearing about. Well, being in this coma introduced me to this fact. I wondered if everyone who had been in a coma experienced this, or was my experience unique due to my shifter blood?

The thought of blood reminded me of the last conversation Jack had with the doctor, and I realized I really wanted to know if Luke had been a match or not. I knew it was a long shot, but I decided to try as hard as possible to suck myself to the surface, just enough to see if any conversation was going on around my body.

It took a while, but I eventually got it. It was equivalent to trying to wake yourself up from a dream. It made me wonder how close to the truth Cher had been in her explanation of a coma, when she said that there were times we were awake and times we were asleep.

"Do you want to see it?" asked a female voice that I now recognized as Cher's.

"If it's all the same to you, Cher, I would rather wait. Seeing the nursery for the first time is something that I want to share with Lily, so I was hoping I could wait until after," Jack said, pleasing me.

"That is very considerate of you, Jack. I am excited for you both to see it. But you are right, it would be best to share it with Lily, then it can be a surprise to both of you."

"Thanks, Cher."

"Well, I better get heading home, told the boys I would make them a big supper tonight. But I'll see ya tomorrow, Jack. Take care of our girl."

"Always," Jack promised.

I heard footsteps receding but felt a different presence getting closer. Was someone else in the room besides Jack?

"Wow, she's looking a lot better, Jack. Her neck wound seems to be healing quite well. That's a good sign, isn't it?"

"Johnny, you scared me. I didn't hear you come in," Jack said, clearly surprised.

"Sorry, I was trying to be quiet. Still seems like she is just sleeping, I guess I feel like I have to be quiet when I'm around her."

"Yeah, it's hard to tell, Cher says she can hear us, I hope she is right, but who knows."

"So how are the transfusions going?"

"Well, so far, so good. She responded well to the first few treatments, as you noticed her throat is starting to heal. Doc said her red blood cell count is getting stronger as well. We got lucky that Luke was a match, really lucky. I feel terrible though, after everything he went through, and now he keeps having to donating blood to help Lily," Jack said in a soft voice.

Luke's blood was a match? I had already been receiving transfusions?

"I wouldn't feel too bad for Luke, Jack. He couldn't be more pleased with himself. Typical hero bullshit," Johnny said in his usually cocky voice.

"Well, he really is. Without him, who knows what we would have done. Doc said that she is healing a lot faster than he had thought she would. That's good because we are getting closer to the due date, and I want to make sure she is in top shape. But I'm starting to feel a whole lot more optimistic about everything."

"What is the count at now anyway?"

"Well, by our calculations, she should go into labor in the next twenty days, give or take."

"So what's the plan then? Continue with the transfusions? Then bring her out of the coma in time for the birth?" Johnny asked sounding slightly awkward.

"I'm not sure how much longer we can do the transfusions. Luke can't keep giving blood, and we are hoping that since she is healing so well, she may only need about one more. We will give Luke a week to replenish his blood supply. As a shifter, it should happen in a few days, but Doc said he would rather wait a week in lieu of his recent injuries. So by the time she gets her next transfusion, her due date will be just under two weeks away. I think Doc plans to pull her out of it at the one-week mark. Give her a few days to prepare herself and for us to make sure she is all right.

"Hmm, well, sounds like a plan then. Listen, I was going to go make some nachos then watch a movie. Would you like to join me? I could bring them in here so you wouldn't have to leave. You've just been in here alone so long, thought you could use some company for a while," Johnny offered.

"That sounds great, Johnny."

It made me so happy to hear Jack and Johnny being friendly; there usually seemed like so much animosity between them.

My mind lost all concentration on the two guys when a gentle nudge came from my abdomen. It was the most amazing thing I had ever felt.

CHAPTER 18

JACK

THE WEEKS WERE passing so fast, and luckily, Lily was healing a lot faster. Her blood supply was almost fully replenished, and for all intents and purposes, she looked well. Asleep but well. Her hair was grown back nicely where we'd had to shave it, and there seemed to be minimal scaring. Her neck was the worst wound. I was also concerned about her front canine that was missing. Not too sure how we would fix that. Clearly, if she got a fake tooth, it wouldn't shift into a wolf canine; I'm pretty sure porcelain didn't work that way. I guess she would always just have to take it out before she shifted, and perhaps we could have the dentist fashion a canine for her. I laughed gently to myself at the thought of my trying to put my mate's denture in for her while she was in her animal form.

I guess this was not something I should have been overly concerned with right now, considering everything else that was going on. But now that she was almost completely healed, I found myself thinking a lot about when she woke up. What she would think of everything. Her missing tooth in particular. I laughed again at the thought. I personally couldn't care less how many teeth she had; I was just glad she was alive and going to stay that way.

I heard the parlor door open, pulling me from my reverie.

"Morning, Jack, how's she doing today?" Doc asked, hauling in some equipment and medical bag."

"She looks pretty good today. I think anyway. You're the doctor, you tell me," I said.

He laughed. "All right, let's have a look-see."

He spent the next few minutes taking her blood pressure—which looked strange—and testing other thingies here and there.

"What's in the bag, Doc?" I asked when he finished fiddling with her.

"Oh, well, just some things I may need in the next couple days," he answered.

"Oh?" I said, hoping I knew what direction this was going.

"Thought we would wean her off the barbiturates today. See what happens."

"The what?" I asked, confused.

"Ha, sorry, uh, that's the stuff that I have been administering to keep her in a coma. Pentobarbital is the medicine, and barbiturates are what that medicine contains. It's what actually keeps her in the deep sleep," he said.

"Right, yes," I said trying to sound like I just temporarily forgot.

"My plan was to do a small test and make sure that she is healing at the rate I want her to be, and if she is, then I would wean her off the pentobarbital. If all goes as planned, she should be awake this evening or tomorrow sometime. At which time we will give her some time to rest before we attempt the shift back," he explained.

"Hey, Doc?" I asked a little nervous.

"Hmm?" he said.

"Is she going to have any long-term effects? I mean, I've heard that after coming out of a coma, people have had to relearn to walk and talk and all that stuff," I said.

"Well, Jack, it's hard to say. I've never put a shifter in their animal form into an induced coma before. It's not something that was ever necessary for me before, and frankly, I hope it never is again. Especially a pregnant one. But I hope that since she was not in it for that long and because of her fast healing, which appears to be back on track, she will be all right. Luckily, we didn't have to administer the breathing tube, so her throat won't be raspy and sore. She will thank us for that I'm sure," he said.

"Well, that's good I guess. So what's this little test you want to do?"

"Well, I thought if you were all right with it, I could make a small cut on one of her legs and see how fast it heals. If it heals within a few hours, then she is where I want her to be."

"Hmm, well, that sounds good. Not a big fan of you having to give her yet another cut, but I guess we need to know. So let's do that then. The sooner we can wake her up, the better. She looks ready to explode."

"Yes, she is definitely growing beautifully. And that baby of yours sure is active, I'll tell you that. I sure would love to get an ultrasound done as soon as we get her back in her human form so I can make sure the baby handled the shift well."

"Yes, that would make me feel a lot better."

Doc walked to his bag and pulled out a small Velcro case. He slowly opened it, spreading it out on the table, then returned to his bag for the disinfectant wipes I'd seen him use a million times in the last few weeks.

"Well, let's hope that she wakes up today then. Tomorrow is a week exactly to her due date, and I hate risking it so close. Already it's too close for my comfort," I said.

"Mine as well, but we need to be sure Jack. I'm sure everything will be fine. She is an amazing healer," Doc said.

"Sure," I replied.

I watched as he spread the hair on left hind leg and disinfected the area with a wipe.

"Is she going to feel this, Doc?" I asked, concerned.

"Hard to say, Jack, but honestly, after what she went through, she probably wouldn't even notice the tiny cut that I'm going to make."

I knew he was right, but I still prayed she couldn't feel it. I hated the thought of putting her in any more pain then she already went through because of me.

Doc made the small incision, and Lily didn't so much as flinch, which was expected since she was in a coma, but it made me feel better all the same.

"Well, that's all we can do now. Sit and wait and see if it heals," Doc said.

"I'll keep my fingers crossed."

"Ha-ha, does that actually work?" he asked.

"Doubt it, but couldn't hurt to try." I laughed with him, feeling great for the first time in weeks. I sure hoped that wound healed and we could wake her up. I felt like a school kid on Christmas morning.

"Well, Jack, I think I'm going to head into the kitchen and root through your fridge, perhaps fix something up for lunch. Would you like to join me?" he asked.

Over the last few weeks, our home had become a sort of second home to Doc and Cher and Leo. They all came and went as they pleased, helping around the house and with Lily. Cher was the most amazing. She took over bathing Lily, saying that she would be more thorough than me or anyone else in the house. I had agreed as I clearly wasn't that good at it. She was so nurturing and wonderful to Lily. She would sit with her when I would shower or take care of other business, and when I would come back, I would hear Cher talking to Lily, telling her stories, and when I would go in, she would be gently stroking her head. I'm sure that after this, they would develop a strong friendship, just as I and Leo had.

I still hadn't seen the nursery that Cher spent days working on. She had it painted in one night, I knew that. Then she spent the next few days filling it with everything we could ever need. I couldn't wait to see it with my mate for the first time.

"Sure, I guess she should be all right for a few minutes alone," I said, hating to leave Lily but knowing I would still be close just in case.

We headed into the kitchen, and I warmed two bowls of leftover chili. Doc busied himself making garlic toast and setting the table for the two of us. The house was quiet today; the boys were out on a run, burning some energy. That was something I hadn't done in a very long time. I wouldn't be able to enjoy it, so it seemed pointless. I would shift when Lily was awake and everything was fine. Until then, I remained human and agitated.

We ate in relative silence, then Doc helped me clean the dishes before retreating to the basement to rest for a few hours until we checked the status of Lily's cut.

I went back into the parlor and sat next to Lily. Clearly, patience was never a strong suit for me; I gently spread the hair on her leg where Doc had made the incision to see how it was doing. Still not healed, but it had stopped bleeding and was beginning to scab. That was a good sign. I felt the anticipation run through my body.

How was I going to get through these next few hours? I decided to head to my computer and search through some baby names. I guess this was usually something the woman would do, but my woman wasn't able to at the moment, and I wasn't sure how much time we would have before the baby came.

Since we didn't know what sex it was, I decided to make two lists. My favorite girl names and my favorite boy names, then when she woke up, she could look through them and see if there were any that she liked.

This was so strange. Three months ago, I never thought about having a child, hadn't really ever considered it seriously. Wasn't sure if I even wanted any. But when I found out Lily was pregnant, it changed my view pretty quick. It was just so hard for it to feel real though. I mean, most men got to pamper their woman, run out late at night and get her strange foods, rub her feet, massage her back, go to her baby classes and whatever else there was. And watch her grow, her belly extend over a nine-month period. Well, not me. I found out my woman was pregnant, and I had to put her into a coma, and she was not even human right now, so when I looked at her, it was hard to really see that she was pregnant. I mean, her stomach was definitely large and full, but she was a wolf; it was different.

I glanced down at my lists and realized I had written about fifteen names on each one. Well, it was a lot of variety but perhaps too overwhelming. I narrowed it down, one name on each side underlined. I hoped Lily liked them because I was becoming strangely fond of them the more I looked, especially the boys' names.

I left the list on the desk and walked back over to Lily, placing my hand on her bulging belly. I hadn't often touched her belly—not because I didn't want to, it just seemed like a weird thing to do when she was an animal. I didn't care though; I wanted to feel it. A little bump against my hand startled me, and I jumped slightly. I quickly put my hand back on the same spot and, sure enough, another light bump. My throat got tight, and I choked back the emotion it sprung on me. That was my baby, my child, nudging me.

I spent the next hour lying beside my mate with my hand on her belly, playing with our unborn baby. A light rap on the door made me pull my hand back right quick, like I had been doing something wrong, how silly.

"Jack, thought we could check out that wound. See how it's doing," Doc said in an optimistic voice.

I felt my gut clench, hoping for the best. I realized I had forgotten about the cut since I felt her belly. "All right, let's do it," I said.

I sat up and moved back so the doctor could get in then glanced over his shoulder to watch. He spread the hair same as I had done then let out a little chuckle.

"Would ya look at that. Nothing but a faint red line," he said.

My heart raced, and my palms got sweaty. I could tell Doc could see the excitement in my face.

I watched as he fiddled with the IV that had been administering her pentobarbital.

"All right, Jack. Over the next few hours, Lily will receive less and less pentobarbital until finally I will remove the medication completely and put in a saline solution. She may wake up faster than a regular human, but I can't be sure. We will just wait and see. I figure I will stay in here with you as long as it takes, just in case," he said.

"Sounds good to me," I said, trying to tone down the giant smile on my face.

"Well, what to do to pass the time then, Jack? Play a game of chess?"

We had just got the chess table set up when the parlor door opened. It was Johnny and Duke. I filled them in on what was going on with Lily, then before we knew it, everyone was in the parlor, not wanting to miss Lily waking up. I wasn't sure how comfortable that would make her, waking up to a room full, but there was no arguing with the guys. She was their family now, and they cared deeply for her.

A few of the guys sat on the couch chatting while Johnny and Flynn took over the chess board. I took up my usual spot next to Lily and watched my family. This was the best any of us had felt in a long time. Luke was fully healed, and Lily would be awake soon. Everything would slowly go back to normal. Well, I guess normal was the wrong word. It would definitely be different around here. Not just for me and Lily but everyone. We would all have to get used to having a baby around.

Johnny stood from the chess table and left the parlor, returning a few minutes later with an armful of beers. I shook my head at his offer, content with the coffee I had beside me. I wasn't going to protest to the guys having a beer though. They could all use one.

I jumped as Lily's claw caught on my left arm, leaving a scratch about two inches long. I quickly glanced at her paw then at Doc.

"Did you see that?" I asked.

"See what?" Doc asked.

"Her paw moved. She caught my arm," I said, excited.

Doc came over and sat next to me. He pointed at her tail, which was slowly moving back and forth.

"Lily, can you hear me?" If you can, I want you to know that everything is all right. We are in the process of bringing you out of the coma we had put you in. Everything is probably really fuzzy and unclear right now, but if you just relax, it will all get clearer soon," Doc explained to her.

"Doc, how is she? What's going on?" Luke asked.

"Looks like she is starting to come out of it," he said.

The boys were starting to crowd around, and I was begging to feel a little claustrophobic. In a way, I wanted to be the only one around when she woke up. Purely selfish of me, I just didn't want to share her. The thought of sharing her attention when she woke up irritated me. I knew it was juvenile, but I couldn't help it. Well, if I couldn't be the only one around, I would damn well be the first one she saw.

"Hey, boss, do you think one of us should call, Cher? She might be hurt if we didn't tell her. She may want to be here to help, you know," Reagan suggested.

He was right. Cher would want to be here. She was the only female around, and Lily may need that.

"That would be a good idea. Can you give her a call, see if she can make it over? I'm not sure how much longer until Lily is awake." I glanced at Doc to see if he had any input, but he just shrugged.

"I'll tell her she better come now just in case."

Reagan departed to the other side of the parlor trying to get some quiet to call Cher. I knew she would speed right over here. There was no way she would want to miss Lily waking up.

"Excuse me, Jack. I'm going to check her reflexes and blood pressure again," Doc said while gently shoving me out of the way. So much for being front and center. Oh well.

"Shouldn't be too long now, guys. Her eyelids are fluttering softly," Doc pointed out.

"Lily? Hon? Can you hear me? Open your eyes, baby," I said.

"Jack, slow down, let her come out at her own pace. Don't rush her, it will only make it harder," Doc said.

I shut my mouth and settled for rubbing her front paw. I wanted this to be as easy for her as possible.

About half an hour after Reagan made the call to Cher, she arrived grinning from ear to ear. She walked right over and lay beside me on the floor. Lily would probably have no idea who she was, but Cher didn't care; she just wanted to be there with her.

The longer that went by, the more Lily started to respond. Her eyes would flutter, and her tail would wag. Finally, her eyes flicked then remained half open without shutting again.

"Lily, can you look over here?" Doc requested as he shone his little flash light.

"Just relax, okay, everything is all right. You have been in an induced coma for approximately twenty-five days, long enough for your body to heal. Please don't try to move right now, we will worry about that later. You are very pregnant, and I don't want you straining yourself," Doc said sort of rushed.

Doc checked a few more things and switched out the empty bag of pentobarbital for a saline solution. Or what I presumed was. Cher had moved around to Lily's face and was stroking the hair behind her ears, whispering gently to her, telling her about the baby and the nursery. Things that she usually told her about. Cher was a wonderful woman; I'd hate to think what I would have done without her in the last few weeks.

"No, Lily. No," I heard Cher say, and I shot my head up in time to see Lily struggling to stand up, IV tearing out of her.

"Lily, no, hun, you need to lie down, okay. Don't stress yourself. You need to stay put for just a little while," I said.

"It's fine, let her try. Just help her a bit so she doesn't hurt herself," Doc said.

We helped her to her feet, and she took a few shaky steps. Doc must have been right; she seemed like she would be able to walk a lot better if she wasn't full term with our baby. Thank God for no permanent damage so far. Touch wood.

She turned toward me and rubbed her muzzle in the hollow of my neck. I brought my arms up to her face and pulled it back, looking deep into her eyes.

CHAPTER 19

LILY

I FELT LIKE A thousand-pound elephant. It was such a disorientating feeling to wake up from a coma and be excessively larger then when you went into it. Strange yet exhilarating. I could feel my baby inside of me moving around like crazy. I needed to be out of this form; I needed to be human and I knew it.

They kept saying to lie down and rest; I didn't want to. My back throbbed and my legs ached. I needed to move around, get my blood circulating properly. I wanted to shift back. Now. But I wasn't sure if that was my decision or the doc's. Was I supposed to wait for his word? Did they want me to wait a few days?

I figured for now I would just try and stick it out. Clear my head and get this walking thing under control. I felt like I was in someone else's body. Especially since I wasn't all that used to my animal form in the first place, let alone being in a coma for twenty-odd days then trying to function. It felt a lot like in the alley, when I tried to walk for the first time as a wolf; the only difference was I was a tank now.

"Lily, I want you to know that you need to be very careful right now. I don't want you stressing out the baby and sending yourself into early labor before we can get you to shift back, which I'm hoping can be in the next day or so. It is only a week from tomorrow that you are due," Doc said.

I froze where I was, his words worrying me. I definitely did not want to send myself into early labor, so I slowly and gently lowered myself to the ground right where I had been standing and glanced over my shoulder.

I heard Jack's giggle and swung my head in his direction. Damn, how

I had missed him. I wanted to rush into his arms and curl up for the night. I really wanted to attempt a shift. Would it hurt the baby? Why in a day or so and not now? Other than the stiff limbs and the obvious pregnancy thing, I felt great. I felt better than I had in weeks.

"Well, I guess that is a good sign that you can understand what we are saying. Happy to rule out any brain damage," Doc said.

I huffed a strange noise that was supposed to be a light laugh, but I was sure they all presumed that it was more of a cough.

Jack came over and sat beside me, just like he had for the last twenty-five days, never leaving me. Well, I presume he never left because every time I was somewhat conscious in my mind, he was there. Then a weird thought dawned on me. What if all of that had been a dream? Had all of that been real or just something that my mind had fabricated while I was unconscious? Had Luke really given me blood? I couldn't wait to ask.

"Lily, I think you should try and get some rest, perhaps in the morning we can try shifting," Doc said.

"She probably wants to kill all of you right now. Keep telling her she needs to rest. She's been asleep for twenty-five days. She has healed just fine, and look at her, clearly she wants to move around, see everyone."

I recognized the voice; it was Cher's. I wanted to hug her. She was right; I didn't want to rest or sleep. Okay, if I had to take it easy because I was pregnant, I got that, but sleep and rest were the last things that I wanted.

"You are probably correct. Ha-ha. I do suppose I am treating her a bit like a human. Do as you wish, Lily, you're not nearly as fragile as I've made it seem. You have proved that in the last while, that's for sure," Doc said.

Jeez, wish he would have told me that before I laid my fat ass down. Now I had to get back up again; that was fun. Jack saw me struggling and gave me a boost. It felt wonderful to have his hands on me, and I wanted so badly for them to be on my human skin. Maybe I could just try to shift. See what happened.

I slowly walked behind the couch trying to get some privacy, hoping they would let me go without following. I didn't want them to see me trying to shift or failing if that was the case.

Jack got up to follow, and Cher stopped him.

"Jack, she clearly needs some privacy. Let her go for a minute. She probably wants to clean herself. She'll be fine."

I silently thanked this woman I didn't know but planned to after this ordeal. If everything that happened when I was in a coma really happened, then I had a lot to thank this woman for. She spoke to me numerous times and did my entire nursery for me. I could really use a female friend, someone to save me from this house of men once in a while.

I glanced around to make sure that no one was looking then lay down and got lost in deep concentration. This was not as easy as I had remembered it. But unlike that last few times I had tried to change, I could feel something. My body wanted to change. I knew I could do it when I felt that all-consuming tingle. It began in my front right paw and spread all the way to my chest. My left paw followed suit. It was taking longer than it used to, probably because I had been out of practice for so long, but I didn't care. Everything was going to be okay. I could do this; I could shift for my child.

I watched as my hands took human shape, but when my face started contorting, I closed my eyes. Much more comfortable that way.

I felt a stabbing pain in my gut and instantly froze. The shift stopped; it didn't recede, it didn't continue, just stopped. I looked down at my deformed self. My arms, face, and most of my chest was human for the most part. My lower half was still wolf, twisted in a way that was all too wrong. I started to panic and closed my eyes, trying to concentrate when the shooting pain happened again. I let out a cry, unable to keep it in.

I heard a ruckus from the other side of the couch.

"Lily?" I heard Jack just as he appeared behind the couch. I could see the terror on his face when he took in my form.

"Fuck! Doc, get over here," he shrieked.

Before I knew it, I was surrounded by people. The doctor, everyone was shouting at once, and I couldn't make out any of it.

"Shut up!" Jack yelled.

Everyone fell silent except for me. I let out another cry as the shooting pain seared through me again.

Jack dropped to my side. "Lily, talk to me. What's going on? What were you doing? Trying to shift alone?"

"I . . . I . . ." My words were not working, the pain was still there, and it was too hard to speak.

The doctor was prodding me with all sorts of things. I glanced at Cher, who was standing off to the side with her hands over her mouth. Clearly tormented by what she saw.

I was terrified. What the hell was I thinking? I shouldn't have done that. Had I hurt the baby? Was that what this pain was? Was I losing the baby?

"Shit, Lily, look at me," Jack said then pulled me toward him. "Talk to me. Please," he begged.

The pain was receding, so I decided to try and say something again. "I . . . I was . . . trying to shift . . . I wanted to get . . . out of that form . . . It was working, I was almost there . . . then . . . then . . . there was a shooting pain in my abdomen, and I lost my concentration. I stopped shifting."

"Jack, get out of the way," the doctor demanded.

Jack let go of my face and reeled back. The doctor shoved something onto my stomach. I didn't pay too much attention; one of the pains was back, and this one took the breath from my lungs.

"Lily, listen to me, you are in labor. The shift brought on labor. I was afraid of this. I should have done this sooner. What was I thinking? A week was too close. Fuck," Doc cursed.

I felt a minute of relief when he said this was labor. I wasn't losing the baby, which had been my fear; I was having it. But the relief faded fast when I remembered I was stuck half-human, half-wolf.

"Do something," someone yelled.

All of a sudden, Cher was right beside me. Holding my face in her hands.

"Honey, you got to concentrate all right. You need to make the shift fully one way or the other. Human preferably, but you need to, and you need to do it now," Cher coached.

"Believe me, I know how hard it is. I wasn't strong enough to do it, Lily, but I know you are. You can do this. Listen to me now, close your eyes and concentrate, as hard as you can."

I closed my eyes and tried, but all I could concentrate on was the pain. The searing, snapping pain. The further along this got, the harder it would be; I knew that, but I just couldn't get a hold of myself.

"Lily, keep trying, try to push the pain away. Ignore it, pretend it doesn't exist," Cher said.

"Cher. Is that what it is? Is that why it was impossible for you to shift when you were in labor? Because the pain was to bad?" I heard the doc ask.

"Yes, the pain is debilitating. You cannot concentrate on anything but the pain, and it doesn't stop for long enough for you to catch your breath, let alone shift. Between the pain and the worry, I couldn't do it. But Lily has to, she is stuck, and we don't know what that could mean for her or the baby if it comes out. Her body is incompatible with itself right now. Two completely different birthing canals. This is not an option."

Her words terrified me even more. I knew that she was saying them so I would grasp the urgency and put more effort in, but it sort of backfired. I felt completely debilitated. I was scared stiff.

"I'm asking because there is enough of her human spine that I think I can administer an epidural. Well, I won't administer it, but I have a colleague who is an anesthesiologist. He is also a shifter. He lives about an hour away, but if I can get him here, then we may be able to administer one and take the pain away. Do you think she could finish the shift then?" he asked Cher.

"I think it would definitely help. As far as I can remember, the pain was the biggest reason I couldn't."

"Jack," I got out.

He shot over and lifted me partly onto his lap.

"Yeah, baby?" he said.

"Stay with me. I'm scared, Jack."

"I'm not going anywhere, I promise. Everything will be okay, all right? We will figure this out."

"Doc, what the hell are you waiting for? Call the anestiosi—whatever, just call him. Get him here ASAP," he demanded.

Doc took off toward the phone, and I could faintly hear him talking in an urgent tone. Everyone was panicking, and it was making it worse for me. I wanted everyone to be calm and tell me to stop panicking.

I heard the phone slam back in its cradle and Doc's harsh footsteps as he ran back to me.

"Said he could be here in about an hour but to try and slow the labor as much as we can until then," Doc said, slightly out of breath.

"How the fuck do we slow down labor?" Jack hissed.

"Warm water sometimes helps. Can we try and get her in the tub?" Doc said.

"She will fit in Jack's tub, he has the biggest one. I just don't like the angle of her hind legs, don't think she would be comfortable in a normal sized-tub, if we could even get her into it," Johnny said.

I really did not want everyone around if they were going to put me into a bathtub. It was bad enough that every male that I lived with could see me half-naked right now, my entire chest bared. Jack kept trying to cover me up with a blanket, but every time I cringed from a contraction, the blanket fell. I noticed the boys were doing their best to avert their eyes from that area.

"I'll take her, with Cher. We will give her a warm bath and hope the contractions slow down. I'm sure she would like some privacy for that, so if you could all stay down here, that would be great," Jack said.

I heard a few of them murmur their agreements as Jack and Cher began lifting me off the floor. My body was so deformed; my legs were going in such a wrong direction compared to the rest of my body.

I could tell that they were struggling with my strange new body as much as I was. It must have been awkward to hold me.

I heard the door to Jack's room creak open and realized that Cher had kicked it with her foot. We made our way to the bathroom, and unfortunately, the first thing I saw was my reflection in the mirror. I was a disaster. My hair was greasy and hung limply by my face; I had a light scar on my neck from where Mayla had bitten me—twice. When I saw my body as a whole in the mirror, I gasped. It was disgusting. My stomach jutting out, half-wolf, half-human, twisted in a sick way. I looked like some sort of fucking science experiment or something off the sci-fi channel. Finally my eyes came back to my face and my open mouth. Exposing my missing tooth. I had totally forgotten about the missing tooth until right now. I quickly snapped my mouth shut and waited for them to run the tub.

The water was hot but not overpowering. It definitely helped the pain of the contractions, not sure if that meant they were slowing down or simply that the water helped balance the pain. To be honest, I didn't care; I was just happy the pain was less.

I had been in the tub for at least half an hour when we heard a light rap at the door. Jack got up and cracked the door and inch.

"Just checking to see how she is doing," I heard the doctor's voice say.

"She is doing well, the hot water seems to be helping, and her breathing is regulating," Jack answered.

"All right, well, I just called Carl, he is the anesthesiologist I just called. He will be here in ten minutes, so whenever you are ready, why don't you get her dried off, and we will get her comfortable wherever you want, but remember, wherever we put her is where she will give birth."

"Well, we will put her in my bed then. It is right here. I will get some sheets and towels and whatever we need," Jack said.

"No, I'll take care of all that, you and Cher just get her out of there and dried off. I will prepare your bedroom," Doc said to Jack.

By the time they got me situated in the bed as comfortable as they could get me in my crazy form, the anesthesiologist was there. He introduced himself as Carl.

It took us a few minutes to figure out how to position me properly for him to administer the epidural. He seemed a little nervous, which scared me, but what could I do? He was my best chance at shifting back and getting my baby born.

Right when he was about to stick the needle in, my body was seized by a powerful contraction. It was so intense, I let out a scream and everyone in the room jumped. Unfortunately, Carl had to wait until I was through the contraction before he could do it.

Fifteen minutes later, the pain was gone. The doctor ran an ice cube down my body, and I lost all feeling just before my wolf self started. I felt the pressure build up, and I realized that I had to do this and I had to do this now. Everyone was counting on me, and I wanted to lie down and sleep. These contractions were kicking my ass, and I didn't have the energy to try and shift, but I knew I had no choice. I had to do this.

"Jack, can you help me? Talk me out of it like you used to?" I begged.

"Of course, baby." He said then turned to everyone and asked them to leave the room. He wanted this to work, and the best chance we had was if I had as little amount of distractions as possible.

He lay beside me and brushed the hair from my face, talking to me in his sexy, smooth voice. That voice I had heard so many times that had talked me out of this so many times. Minutes were going by, and I had to shake my head to remind myself to keep concentrating. His voice was lulling me into sleep.

I clenched my teeth and put all my effort into it. Picturing the change, concentrating on his voice soothing me.

Jack gasped, and I opened my eyes. I was starting; the shift was traveling the rest of the way from my stomach down to my pelvic bone. It was strange, I couldn't feel it happening, none of it. I wouldn't have even known it was working if Jack hadn't gasped. That epidural thing was crazy.

I closed my eyes and kept concentrating. Not opening them until I felt Jack's arms wrap fully around me, lifting me up into a crushing hug. I peeked at myself. I had done it. My body was all mine and fully human. A little different then I had last left it, what with the giant belly, scar on my neck, and missing tooth, but Jack didn't seem to mind any of that. He crushed his lips to mine.

We kissed for so long I forgot I was in labor. Until the doc finally burst in.

"Jack, why didn't you get me?" he asked agitated while he started hooking me up to some strange monitor.

"Well, excuse me for wanting a few minutes alone with my mate."

His words sent butterflies racing through me.

"All right, all right, I have to check her, I also want to give her an ultrasound and see how the baby is doing. Make sure he or she made the shift as well."

His words brought down my high. Of course, my baby made the shift fine. Anything other than being fine was unacceptable. I didn't even want to think about it.

"Ahh," I gasped as the doctor lifted the sheet that was draped over my knees.

I had realized what he had meant when he said he needed to check me; I guess I had just not expected him to be so forward about it. The next step made Jack clearly uncomfortable. That or he wanted to rip the head off the doctor. It made a small giggle rise in my throat, but I tried to keep it to myself.

"Oh boy! Was that ever in time. Lily, we don't have time for an ultrasound. You are nine and a half centimeters, we are gonna start pushing in about fifteen minutes, so get ready," Doctor warned.

Shit, this was going too fast. This was like the fastest labor in the history of labors. Not like I knew, I knew nothing about labor. Fuck. At least the pain was gone. The anesthesiologist had set me up with a drip to my epidural; all I had to do was press this little button to get more meds running through my system. It was perfect.

There was another light knock at the door.

"Yeah?" Jack called.

Cher cracked the door open slightly, eyes filled with tears.

"I was just wondering if there was anything I could do to help?" she asked.

I filled with emotion, this woman who had spent so much time at this house watching over me and helping Jack tend to me really cared, she was tearing up because I was in labor. I choked back my tears and waved her toward the bed. I could tell she just wanted to be in there, and I wasn't going to tell her no. I never had a real mother or a close friend—well, not a good one anyway—and I wanted her here. I wanted someone to be here with me, telling me I was doing well and they were proud of me, just like my mother would have if I'd had one.

She sat down on the side of the bed that Jack wasn't on. "Just kick me out if you want to be alone, please don't feel obligated to have me in here. I am just such a sucker for babies. And I feel close to you, I've watched that belly grow for weeks now, I just can't wait to see if it is a boy or girl," she said through her tears.

"You are welcome to stay for as long as you wish, Cher." That was all I got out before Doc lifted the sheet again and told me it was time.

EPILOGUE

J ACK BROUGHT THE baby, which was now wrapped in a blanket, and laid the bundle on my chest. Cher was gently crying while she peeked over my shoulder. I took one look at my son, and tears welled in my eyes.

"What should we call him?" I asked.

"I thought maybe Cale if you liked it?" Jack said.

"I don't like it, I love it. How about Cale Anthony Cameron?"

Jack shot me a strange look, clearly wanting to ask why I picked Anthony but perhaps not prepared for the answer. So he didn't ask.

It may have seemed strange to someone else, but I wanted to thank Tony. He may have attacked me in an alley, bit me, and changed my life. But he gave me Jack. If he hadn't done what he did, I would have still been all by myself in my lonely apartment. If I could've turned back the clock, I wouldn't change a thing. He was responsible for the family I had now, and he saved my life from Mayla. That was my reason, and I would give it to Jack if he ever asked, although I highly doubted he would.

"I'm going to give you guys some privacy."

I laid in Jacks arms cuddling him and our son for hours. I could't remember a time in my life ever being as happy as I was right now.

Doc finally came in and told me it was time to see if the epidural had worn off yet. Him and Jack helped me to my feet and walked me around the room until they trusted me to do it myself.

A head poked in the door. It was Cher, and she had a smirk building on her face.

"Looks like you're mobile. That's good," she said.

"Yep, pretty tender, but thank God for quick healing. Would you like to hold Cale?" I asked.

"Of course I would." She picked him up from the bed and snuggled him to her chest. "He has your eyes Jack," she said.

Of course he would have his father's eyes; he had alpha blood. My son the alpha.

"Cher, thank you for everything you have done to help me and Jack and our family over the past few weeks. I have a feeling he couldn't have done it without you," I thanked.

"You are more than welcome, honey, it was an absolute pleasure. Now if you're feeling up to it, I have a little surprise for you, Jack, and Cale," she said whisking my baby into the hall, knowing I would follow.

Jack took my elbow and escorted me toward my old bedroom. When she opened the door, my eyes filled with tears. It was the most perfect nursery I had ever seen. The walls were painted a light green, and there was a border around the top with wolves. The crib was oak with a beautiful crib set that matched the border around the room, and dangling above was a charming mobile with little wolves that strangely resembled everyone in our family. I walked up to it and took the black wolf in my hands. It was clearly Jack. A tear rolled down my face as I glanced at Cher.

"I handmade them for you, well, for Cale. Thought that would be a nice thing for him to see before he closed his eyes each night. I also made the quilt that's draped over the rocking chair."

"Cher, it is all so wonderful. Beautiful. Thank you," I said as I crossed the room to hug her.

I glanced at Jack, who hadn't said one word since we came in.

"What do you think?" I asked him.

"I . . . I don't know what to say. This is all more than I ever could have asked for," he said with emotion thick in his voice.

"Well, my work here is done. I will let you and your little family get some rest." She handed me Cale then gently kissed the top of his head. "Good night, sweet boy," she said then kissed my cheek and left the room.

I turned to Jack, who cradled us in his arms.

"I love you, Lily," he said.

"I love you too, Jack."

I placed my sleeping son in his crib, and Jack pulled the blanket over him.

"Good night, my sweet boy," he whispered then pulled me into his arms, where I planned to never leave.

Edwards Brothers Malloy
Thorofare, NJ USA
August 20, 2012